MW00913904

THE SECOND DOOR

Victoria Rachel Clifton

WESTBOW°
PRESS
A DIVISION OF THOMAS NELSON
& ZONDERVAN

Copyright © 2014 Vicki Clifton.

All rights reserved. No part of this book may be used or reproduced by any means,
graphic, electronic, or mechanical, including photocopying, recording, taping or by any
information storage retrieval system without the written permission of the publisher
except in the case of brief quotations embodied in critical articles and reviews.

WestBow Press books may be ordered through booksellers or by contacting:

WestBow Press
A Division of Thomas Nelson & Zondervan
1663 Liberty Drive
Bloomington, IN 47403
www.westbowpress.com
1 (866) 928-1240

Because of the dynamic nature of the Internet, any web addresses or links contained
in this book may have changed since publication and may no longer be valid. The views
expressed in this work are solely those of the author and do not necessarily reflect the
views of the publisher, and the publisher hereby disclaims any responsibility for them.

Any people depicted in stock imagery provided by Thinkstock are models,
and such images are being used for illustrative purposes only.
Certain stock imagery © Thinkstock.

ISBN: 978-1-4908-5644-5 (sc)
ISBN: 978-1-4908-5645-2 (hc)
ISBN: 978-1-4908-5643-8 (e)

Library of Congress Control Number: 2014918399

Printed in the United States of America.

WestBow Press rev. date: 12/5/2014

Look deep into the eyes of a friend,
To see the real person within,
Brown eyes of truth,
Blue eyes of mirth,
But it's the eyes of green that hold a treasure of worth.

Thanks to my Heavenly Father, family and friends. Special thanks to Angela Childers, Pat Kruse, Justin Clifton, Jackie Kruse, and Doug Stitt, photographer.

Contents

CHAPTER 1

They buried the dog on Friday. Local forecasters had warned the townsfolk of the approaching freak snowstorm on the first day of April. The clouds had roared in, dumped their load, and exited in a huff, leaving behind sorrow for one of the town's prominent families. The morning radio announcer awoke the sleepy residents of Wakeegon with the news of the accident. "A local woman suffered injuries when her car hit a dog and skidded out of control on Old Creek Road," he had stated. "She was taken to the hospital and is listed in critical condition. The accident included two other citizens of our town who were also taken to the hospital, their conditions unknown. Their names are being withheld until relatives are notified."

"Get back!" Sheriff O'Connell had shouted to the small gathering crowd of sightseers. He muttered a few things under his breath when the young volunteer firefighter bent over the crumpled car to show him the severed brake line. Sara Reynolds Jacobs, wrapped tightly in blankets, had motioned him to bend down. Her eyes looked as if they held a thousand questions, he thought, as he placed his ear close to her lips. She whispered only three words, "Please help me."

Sara had silently stared at the sheriff, a long time friend, as he closed the door to the aging ambulance. Stepping back from the vehicle, Sheriff O'Connell sighed, glanced at the rooftops that were visible between the immense pines, and shivered. Only yesterday, he had disclosed to his deputy the gloomy premonition he had felt about the little town under his protection. He waited until the ambulance was out of sight before he sat down on the frost-coated rock at the edge of the road and wiped away the tears that had started to freeze on his face.

Three days later, the afternoon edition of the *Wakeegon News* arrived on the doorsteps of the local townspeople. Centered on the front page was an enlarged photo of a curly-haired girl accepting a wiggly puppy from an animal shelter volunteer. The picture was placed underneath the article describing the accident involving Sara. The reporter had stated that the town was still recovering from disbelief when they were told of the death of the oldest member of the Reynolds family the week before. Now, the news of the unfortunate incident that had hospitalized the deceased woman's granddaughter left them with a feeling of doom on this April Fool's Day.

Later that week, Peg Reynolds walked silently from the gravesite to her car. A group of friends from church had given her their support, but now, as she drove home, she wished for the comfort of family. Except for Sara, there was no one left. Stopping for a red light, she shed her gloves and hat, and rolled down the window. The musty, earthy smell of the wafting breeze reminded her of the day her husband died. "Why did he have to die, and leave me all alone?" she whispered.

Her mouth tightened as she squeezed the steering wheel, trying to keep the car on the rough gravel road. Pulling over to the side, she put her foot on the brake and wiped her eyes on the sleeve of her shirt. How would she and her daughter survive this latest sorrow? Peg reached for a tissue in the glove box, her thoughts on the errands she needed to finish before driving to the hospital. Sara would be waiting for her in the tiny room on the fifth floor . . . the one reserved for the emotionally disturbed.

Hyattsville stood on the west edge of the town of Wakeegon. The two locations were so close together that they seemed to blend into one. The hospital occupied the area between the two and no one really knew for sure which boundary it was located in, Hyattsville or Wakeegon.

"Why am I here?" inquired Sara, as her mother walked into the room. "On this floor of all places?" she added, pointing toward the doorway.

"So you don't go mad," replied Peg. Sara's mother walked over to peer out the darkened hospital window. The early spring fog swirled in the moonlight and gave the lawn an eerie appearance. Her heart pounded through the thin, pink material of her favorite sweater. She reached up to grasp the cords of the blind and closed it with a jerk. The swishing sound broke the silence of the ward.

Sara licked her lips and pushed back the soft tendril of dark hair that had escaped her hair band. "Go mad?" she asked. "I thought that was a term from the past.

Peg rubbed her forehead and sat down on the old metal chair that was drawn close to her daughter's bed. "It means the same today as it did years ago. There's just a lot of fancy names for it nowadays," she answered, staring at the white wall.

Sara giggled. "I'm sure there were doctors back then like the great Doctor Thorton."

Peg turned to face her only child and let out a big sigh. "In the past, society felt it was a sickness that brought shame to the family. Instead of dealing with the problem, they tried to hide it from outsiders. Just like your father's parents did with Uncle James."

Sara sat up and adjusted her night clothes, her face rigid and pale. "Mother, why are you scaring me? Do you think I'm crazy like dad's brother? That I imagined the things that I told Doc about?"

"Honey, you know this is entirely different."

"Okay. Then why is everyone treating me like it isn't? I've been here for almost a week! I want to go home! Why don't you take me home?" She grew silent for a while then asked softly, "Tell me. Did Uncle James ever get well?"

Peg shrugged her shoulders. "I don't know if he is still alive. I haven't seen him for a long time," she added, as she mentally drifted away. She remembered her husband's chilly tales of his mother, and quivered as she pictured the two young boys locked in the upper attic bedroom.

"What do you mean?" asked Sara.

"No one was ever allowed past the second door of the butler's pantry! The stairway to the attic was there, you know?" she blurted out, still alone in her thoughts. "They said the key was always kept in Gramma's apron. That evil woman! At least the authorities rescued one of them. That's why your father ended up being raised by the McAllister's from church. Right nice people they were," she added, drifting off again.

Peg leaned back into the chair and closed her eyes. She thought about the yellowed photograph of a little boy with a mischievous grin that stood on her fireplace mantle. That same grin was also apparent years later in the face of the man who became her husband. What would have happened to him if the minister and his wife hadn't requested his removal from the old woman's house, she wondered? Peg jumped as a loud creak from the rusty hinge on the chair forced her to return to the conversation in Sara's room.

"Gramma insisted that there was a curse on the family. I don't know how your father survived all the gossip, God rest his soul," said Peg, as she jumped up and grabbed the handles of her black leather purse. "By the way, did I ever tell you that your father and uncle were identical twins? Meeting him was kind of creepy, you know?" Her voice trailed off as she hurried out the door.

"Mother? Where are you going? You just got here! Where are you going?" Sara repeated, as she stared at the door and listened to her mother's disappearing footsteps.

The stillness of the hospital was interrupted by the soft whispers of two sleepy nurses who were discussing the daily trials of raising teenage girls. "I tell you Mavis," said the younger one to the matronly woman, "I don't understand why girls want to wear their skirts so short. Only causes problems I told my oldest. She just stared at me and left the room."

Sara listened to the conversation for a while, rolled over, and furrowed her eyebrows. She remembered bits and pieces of her childhood, but unfortunately, her marriage to Luke was another matter. Her doctor called it selective memory loss. "Memories too painful to be recalled would be shoved into the deepest recesses of her mind," he had said to her mother. What had transpired between Sara and her husband wasn't clear, but Luke's visits brought with them a wave of fear and apprehension. Within the past few days, thoughts of the accident that had brought her to the hospital were starting to emerge.

The icy breeze from the air conditioning vent surrounded Sara, causing a rash of goose bumps to form on her arm. She shivered and let out a small cry as she crawled deeper under the safety of her covers. Maybe she was going mad.

The five-story hospital looked out of place for a city the size of Hyattsville. The brick surfaces, stained black from the smoke of a recently vacated manufacturing plant, made the building look more like an eyesore than a piece of historic architecture. Doc Thorton, tall and thin, wire glasses dangling on the end of his pointed nose, had heard his share of menacing remarks. When visitors asked for directions to the hospital, locals would respond with, "Oh, you mean the nut house?"

Doc groaned, rubbed his shoulder, and reached for his worn tweed jacket. He placed two tablets in his mouth, grabbed his coffee mug and poured the brown liquid down his throat in one big gulp. Convulsing on the cold drink he absentmindedly sat the mug on top of a stack of yellowed, wrinkled papers. Doc wiped his mouth with the back of his hand and glanced around the room. He knew his office didn't fit the image that the hospital's top administration wanted for its doctors, and lately his disorganization wasn't winning any approval either. He reached into his pocket, but instead of pulling out his keys, he found a book of matches from Willie's Restaurant. Doc took a deep breath to calm his rapidly beating heart as he remembered last Saturday's encounter with Luke Jacobs, Sara's husband. Every week, there had been some kind of confrontation between the rugged-looking man and himself.

"Where are those stupid keys?" Doc asked out loud. This week he had misplaced two important items. He could deal with the loss of his checkbook, but the loss of the Sara Jacobs' file was no minor mistake. He glanced around the disheveled room he had torn apart that morning. Could the file have been stolen or was he losing his mind? He was usually good at locking up at night. Doc reached for his phone and hesitated. He had already called security this morning about his missing checkbook. "This should give them a good laugh and something to talk about among themselves," he mumbled. Perhaps they will suggest he be given a bed and the same treatment he handed out to all of his mental patients. How ironic, he had thought, a taste of his own medicine! Doc could hear their laughter in his mind as he dialed the familiar number. He wiped the sweat that dripped from his thinning hair line with the back of his hand. "Security!" he shouted into the phone, his voice cracking. "I need you in my office . . . now!"

The Reynolds family had lived in the "land of the lakes" area for more than 85 years. Long ago they had been among the failing potato farmers that had arrived in the states during the mid 1850's. When they switched to the more profitable business of logging, they had become one of the wealthiest families in the area surrounding the Great Lakes.

The old family homestead was quietly nestled in the area known as Six Pines. The gothic-styled timber-sided house had retained much of its original exterior, although the paint had long ago chipped away and disappeared. Part of the decorative trim had disintegrated and had fallen from the top peaks of the twin turrets. During the warmer months, flower beds still overflowed with the past efforts of the former gardener and had distracted sightseers from the dismal appearance of the old house. The faded, green velvet curtains that covered the upper story windows appeared as watchful eyes awaiting unwanted intruders. Approaching tourists would quietly gasp and "ooh and ah" at their first glimpse of the formally regal home, as they rounded the bend. They would soon learn from the town's gossipers that their initial, admirable appraisal of the unusual house would sharply contrast with the dark reputation of the former occupants.

Sara pounded her pillow and winced as she attempted to sit up. Sleep had escaped her again. She couldn't seem to stop the constant trickle of information flowing through her mind. It was during these episodes that she would reach for the pen placed on the bedside table and record each memory in the small journal notebook with the pink-flowered cover. She turned to the page she had written earlier and squinted at the scrawling words in the dim light of the bedside lamp.

"I'm not crazy like everybody thinks I am. I can feel it. I really do believe someone is trying to kill me. If so, what do they want? Could it be the Reynolds family treasure? Everyone in town has heard the rumor of the heirloom emerald that came into the family from the uniting of the two successful logging families. There's a so-called picture of it at the local library, but its existence and value has never been officially verified. I've never seen it. My parents haven't seen it. I don't know if it really exists. What I do know is that I have inherited the Reynolds family mansion, belonging to a grandmother who was practically nonexistent in my life. Who would want an old house filled with bad memories and an attic full of bats? Could it be that someone hates Luke enough to kill me? He's certainly caused a few problems for some people in this town. Whoever reads this, please help me." Sara's hand shook as she placed the book under her pillow and fumbled for the light switch.

"Nurse Daly?" she inquired, noticing a faint shadow outside her door. No response followed. Only a slight shuffling of feet was heard in the distance. Confined to her bed, she felt a new fear she hadn't experience before now. Besides her mother, who could she trust when she didn't know the truth? Sara dove further under the rough faded covers.

Peg Reynolds turned into the driveway of the house she had lived in for over three decades. Two of the three windows that faced the road had been replaced and trimmed in white. The materials for the third window were packed tightly in the dust-covered unopened boxes that lined the back of the garage, along with a new kitchen sink and a slightly-used, dented water heater. Her chest tightened as she recalled the diminishing savings account they had shared. Her husband had been generous. Too generous, she thought.

Peg leaned back into the seat. Two years had passed since the day she discovered the body of her husband, Jedidiah Reynolds, Jr., lying at the bottom of the ladder. "Sorry, Mrs. Reynolds," was all the young paramedic said as he bundled the lifeless form onto the metal gurney. Married thirty-five years, she had been totally dependent on her husband's strength. Sara, in shock over her father's death and deeply engrossed in her own problems with Luke, was of little help in the following months. Peg turned to the senior group at church for advice and sought comfort from Roger, a long time family friend, to eventually get her through the dismal days following her husband's funeral. Conquering her fears, she had begun to feel human again. Now, she thought, her daughter's accident and the struggles it brought along with it, could easily send her back to the days following her husband's death.

Sara had taken the passing of her father harder than Peg had imagined. Peg's recent decision to date Roger had unearthed a deep hidden pain, producing a harsh response from her child. She felt guilt once again as she remembered the events preceding Sara's accident. Her daughter's curiosity of Peg's "traitor relationship", as Sara referred to it, had contributed to a turn of events no one could have ever imagined.

Yesterday morning, Peg had arrived earlier at the hospital than usual and had found Sara sitting up in bed, her arms crossed as tightly as her lips. "Why do you hate Luke so much, Mother?"

"I don't hate him." Peg turned her face toward the window.

"Mother! Turn this way and look at me! You do hate him! I know I didn't fulfill the plans you had for me. I don't mind being a housewife and mother. I never would have fit in the business world. Don't be mad at my husband. It was my decision to marry young. I'm happy. That's all that matters, right?"

"Really, Sara?" asked Peg walking over to the bed. "Is that why you and Luke argue so much? You've forgotten that most of your life has been miserable with him! He is a liar and a conniver! Why do you continue to defend him?" Peg paused, "He treats you like last year's worn out boots." Sara had made a huffing sound and rolled over in her bed, pretending to sleep.

Peg's attempts to answer Sara's questions about Luke had been especially hard. Both parents had been against the marriage from the beginning. Peg couldn't exactly find kind words to describe Luke, so, she usually said nothing, which made Sara more angry and distant.

Doc Thorton grabbed Sara's evening report from the nurses' station and walked slowly to her room. He closed his eyes, and was mentally adding up the total of debts owed to Luke, when he collided head on with a stout man wearing a frayed straw gardener's hat. "Excuse me, sir," he said, gasping for breath.

"Hmmff!" replied the ruddy-faced gentleman, shuffling off toward the elevator.

"Sir, indeed!" said the doctor aloud, straightening his tie and retrieving the papers scattered on the hall floor. Bright lights streamed from under Sara's door. Doc shoved the door with his shoulder harder than he intended. The action produced a loud bang as it skimmed over the stopper and hit the wall. Sara, and the two nurses attending her, jumped.

"I heard that you remembered a few details about your accident, Sara. We should contact the sheriff's department," said Doc.

"No! Not yet!" begged Sara, sitting up in her bed.

"Sorry, Sara. I'm required to follow the hospital's agenda. I'm already in trouble with the security here, and I don't want to put my career at risk," he said thinking of Luke and his threats. "Besides, something doesn't feel right. Your mother is counting on me to take good care of you. Listen, I know this is hard. I personally know the sheriff, and I know he's a friend of yours. I'll make sure they send someone decent to watch over you." He paused, "Sara, there is another problem." Sara's eyes widened. "I think someone may have taken your file. I want to tape your recollections of the accident from now on. The tape will stay in my pocket. Give me your writing pad." Sara turned her pillow over and meekly handed him the notebook containing her nighttime memories. "I'll leave it with the sheriff. He can document it for me and lock it away. There will be no more written report here at the hospital. Nurse, please contact Sheriff O'Connell in the morning. Just relax, Sara," he added, holding out his hand. "Now, how about taking this pill for a nice, restful sleep?"

CHAPTER 2

Sheriff O'Connell swallowed the last drop of the strongly brewed office coffee, leftover from his early arrival. He glanced around the room and decided he preferred the smelly, dank room over the silence at the house, at least since the divorce. Cautiously, he leaned back into the patched, brown leather chair reeking of soy sauce and artificial sweetener, and pulled out last week's newspaper containing the article describing Sara's accident. O'Connell sighed and closed his eyes. Sara. Sweet. Pretty. Caring. His mind wandered back to the day of the accident and the fireman's discovery of the cut brake line. O'Connell had written it on the report, but had not discussed it with anyone, yet. Who would want to harm her? Surely, he thought, clinching his teeth, it had to be Sara's low down scum of a husband.

O'Connell slowly scanned the article, his vision straying from the black and white print. His eyes became fixed on the picture of himself and his now ex-wife Susan, taken on a vacation in Maui last year. He had thought she seemed happy. Her smile was focused on her husband, who was dressed in the gaudy, flamboyant Hawaiian shirt she had talked him into buying that morning at the hotel gift shop. She had seemed happy until the new guy at work began telling her how beautiful she looked and how well she did her job. Now, a year later, the new guy had left to take a better position and had taken Susan with him.

The sheriff stood up and removed the picture from the wall. Grumbling, he placed it back on the nail, carefully lining it up with the frame beside it. He sighed, took the picture down again, removed the photo from the frame, and tossed it in the waste basket. No need to throw away a perfectly good frame he thought, placing it on his desk. He stared at the crumbled picture lying on top of the heap of garbage. Had he forgotten to tell her how much he loved her and how pretty she always looked with her raven hair? His large black shoe connected with the green wire-mesh basket under his desk, tipping it on its side. O'Connell watched as it rolled out the door into the concrete hallway, and stopped with a loud clang against the wall.

He rose slowly, and walked over to retrieve the basket and the dispersed trash. Standing in the doorway, he surveyed his desk. A combination of soiled napkins, a half-eaten box of blueberry donuts, and a few empty Chinese takeout cartons was strewn across the top. "Too much sugar just magnifies your depression, Sheriff," Doc had said to him after his last check-up.

O'Connell began to understand why his mother had gained fifty pounds after his father was found drunk in the alley behind the family store. The next day, the school superintendent arrived on their doorstep to inform his mother that her position as a second grade teacher had been revoked. "Parents consider you a bad influence," she had said, as she squinted through the oval eyeglasses that sat at the end of her enormous crooked nose. A year later his mother had shed the fifty pounds. And, with the help of a lawyer, she was invited back to the same school system as a replacement for the former superintendent. O'Connell shoved the donut box close to the edge of the desk and let it fall on top of the trash.

He knew Doc Thorton would question him when they met next time. Although he was glad for Doc's friendship, he did get a little tired of his continual disapproval of his weight. Doc had no trouble with his own girth, and he probably never would, thought O'Connell. The man never sat still! "Maybe I should return the constant nagging with the new reports linking stress to heart attacks. That would shut him up," the sheriff stated aloud, as he adjusted the button that had come undone halfway down the front of his shirt. The ring of the phone outside his door brought O'Connell's thoughts back to the office.

"Well, I'll be," responded the sheriff to the receptionist. "Speak of the devil! Hey, Doc! What can I do for you?" he asked speaking loudly into the phone. O'Connell's eyes widened as he listened. "What kind of reoccurring dreams?" Sheriff O'Connell asked as he grabbed his car keys. "You feel she could be in danger? Listen. We're both professionals, right? Keep this under wraps, will you? The brake line to her car was severed. No, not by the accident. It was cut. Yep. I'm worried about her, too. I've got just the man for you. His name is Jack Wilder. He's a private detective from Chicago. Why is he here? Well, he's had a few rough months so he's decided to give me a hand this summer. Sara couldn't possibly be frightened of him," he added, remembering the haunting words Sara had whispered the morning of the accident.

"Churchgoers say he has the voice of an angel," laughed O'Connell, "though I've seen behavior that contradicts that description. I can just imagine what the church members say about me. Anyway, I think he's your man. I'll send him around this afternoon."

The sheriff hung up the phone solemnly, picked it up again, and dialed Jack's number. What would Jack say when he told him about the cut brake line? Jack. Sheriff O'Connell's frown turned to a smile. He let out a belly laugh that could be heard down the hall. Jack Wilder was the best of detectives, but he had a problem that clashed with his field of expertise. He hated the smell of hospitals, and particularly hated the smell of blood.

The pale green Depression glass shattered on the floor. Jack groaned, picked up the large fragments, and quickly swept up the rest of the tumbler now reduced to bits of green sand. "Not another of Beth's favorites," mumbled Jack. He had already broken three of the twelve-piece set given to her by her favorite uncle for their wedding gift.

Why did he always get so nervous when he was given a new case? When O'Connell, an old friend of his father, suggested moving to a small town with little or no crime, it didn't seem like it was such a bad idea. "Help you get over your father's death and make a great honeymoon spot for you and Beth," O'Connell had said. Six months later, Beth was dead. Jack had barely left the little house they had shared and repeatedly turned down requests from O'Connell to return to the workforce. His father's inheritance money provided him with the few necessities he needed.

One day O'Connell showed up at the house holding the leash of an unkempt, dirty, beige-colored dog with big brown eyes. "Come on. You're getting out today," he said to Jack placing him in the back seat with the mangy animal, who immediately laid his head on the young man's lap. Soon, Jack began volunteering at the animal shelter, which led to meeting Pastor Mike who also volunteered, and the pastor's offer for Jack to join the church choir.

Jack paused at the hall table by the front door. He grabbed the cinnamon-scented handkerchief the doctor had prescribed to fight off the waves of nausea that followed him from job to job. A new case would be good for him, he thought. A smile stretched across his face, as he grabbed his set of keys and his father's old briefcase.

A call from the sheriff wasn't what Sara wanted right now. O'Connell had asked if he could stop by to discuss the accident with her and introduce a private detective working with the town's police department. Did the sheriff suspect that someone wanted to hurt her? Surely, he knows something he's not telling me? Why on earth does he want to bring a detective along?

Jack Wilder. What was wrong with him? Who would want to leave Chicago, the city of crime, and come to a dull place like Wakeegon? Sara struggled to replace the phone back on the cradle. What time was it again? she wondered, glancing at the alarm clock. It seemed each day was longer than the standard twenty-four hours. Sara cautiously glanced at the door and looked over the edge of the bed. Carefully, she hooked her arm under her left leg first and swung it over the side. "Easy enough," she spoke outloud. When she placed her arm under the right leg, it proved to be more difficult. Bandages covered the large area of stitches and made her leg stiff and cumbersome. Could the medication have made it so numb and cold?

She took a deep breath, pulled hard, and lifted her leg so high that she almost tumbled to the floor. Thank goodness the blanket was securely tucked under the mattress, she thought. Sara held tightly to the corner of the faded material, and quickly righted herself. Stretching her left leg to its full length, she instantly felt the tile's coolness with her big toe. She pinched her lips together as the nausea swept over her. Paralyzed? What if Doc was right? Hesitantly, she grabbed her other leg with both hands and lowered her right foot toward the floor. Suddenly, she stopped, and pulled herself slowly back into bed.

"Maybe I don't want to find out right now," she whispered. "What will I do with my life? How will I chase after the children . . . the children?" She unconsciously ran her fingers over her tightly clenched throat, stretched out the leg that was normal, and yawned. The coldness of the drenched sheets had jarred her awake again the night before. She wished the small bits and pieces of her past would stop floating in and out of her head.

Why hadn't anyone mentioned the children? She pushed the red button that would send the floor nurse scurrying to her bedside, and then, reached for the phone to call her mother. Beep. Beep. "She's probably pouring her heart out to you know who!" said Sara, slamming the phone back on the cradle. Mother must have been caring for the kids for the past few days, she thought. Why hasn't she talked about them? Maybe she was just testing my memory. Yeah, that's it. It was just a test. Sara buzzed again for the nurse.

Jack arrived at the sheriff's office and stopped just short of the double doors. He glanced at his reflection in the window and whispered, "Not bad, not bad at all," while straightening his tie. Jack ran his fingers through his unruly red hair and sucked in a giant breath of air. Coughing and choking, he ran into the building right past O'Connell's office, to the rust-coated water fountain at the end of the hallway.

"Wilder, where do you think you're goin? Have you totally lost your mind?" yelled the sheriff.

The water felt cool sliding down Jack's irritated throat. What a great way to make an impressive entry, he thought. Wiping his mouth with the back of his hand, he slowly straightened up and looked around. Three pairs of eyes, frozen in position, stared at him in disbelief.

"Whippersnapper, are you quite finished? It's probably all that cinnamon, you know? Dries out your nose and throat." Jack grinned as he remembered the sheriff's pet name for him. Although O'Connell sounded rough, a smile consumed his entire face. Slapping Jack on the back, he boomed, "How's my favorite private detective?" The words bounced off the cold cement walls, and reverberated throughout the building. The young man sighed and relaxed his shoulders. Onlookers, satisfied with the sheriff's reaction, returned to the work on their desks.

"Great, Sheriff," he responded. O'Connell grinned and pointed to a chair where it looked like last night's supper had taken up permanent residence. Grease and bits of onion clung to the right arm and gave the office its own aroma.

"Just scoop it on the floor, Son," suggested O'Connell. "The cleaning shift begins soon. They expect that kind of thing. Actually, I leave a gift on my desk occasionally for the ladies. You know a box of chocolate or something sweet," he bragged. "It makes up for my disgusting hygiene habits. At least I hope so."

O'Connell shifted his large girth in the tiny chair. The bulges that stuck out the side between the wooden slats reminded Jack of the feeling he had yesterday morning while trying on an old suit. He made a mental check to watch his diet in the future. Spinning his chair around toward Jack, the sheriff suddenly wore a sullen face. "Jack, my boy, I'm not sure if this is a case you care to tackle."

"Oh? Why?"

"Well. There are a lot of unknowns and a lot of suspicious doin's goin' on."

Jack smiled at his friend's Midwest use of words. "Well then, tell me a few."

"This girl, Sara, happens to be married to a member of the most unlikeable family in this whole dang region. Not only that, but she comes from a background that even the *Twilight Zone* wouldn't touch. Why, I've heard stories that would make your hair stand on end," he added as Jack leaned forward in his chair.

Sara struggled to sit up, flung her arm wildly in the air and accidentally bumped the nurse service light by her bedside. The sound of soft-soled shoes could be heard in the distant corridor.

"Sara?" Nurse Daly ran into the room, looked at Sara, then leaned over from her thick waist to catch her breath. "Sara, you will surely be the death of me yet. What's wrong?" She peered into the young woman's eyes. Sara felt her face redden. She grabbed the thin blanket to cover her bare skin.

"Sorry, I must have bumped the controls again," Sara responded in a tired voice. She glanced at the red blinking light while waiting for Nurse Daly to chide her again, but the gaunt look on Sara's face brought silence instead. Nurse Daly knew that Sara's condition had not improved in the last few days. Tiny bits of Sara's past had begun emerging from her mind and had left her with little or no rest, night after night. Doc had said no sleeping aids unless Sara specifically asked for them. "She must remember what happened that evening on her own," he had said. Friends and family knew the touchiness of the situation. Nurse Daly shivered as she remembered the stories she had heard about the family's past. Surely, they could not be possible. Not in a small town like Wakeegon.

"My children . . . help me?" asked Sara, as she sleepily opened her eyes.

"Now, now," replied Daly, tucking in the thin cover around the slim form. The poor thing, thought Daly, wiping a tear from her eye. The sleeping pill she had requested earlier must be making her delusional. "Try to get some rest, darling," added the nurse. "I'll check on you later."

The ticking of her mother's old windup alarm clock made Sara aware of her throbbing head. Three a.m.! Moaning softly, she pulled the blanket tighter around her frail body. Under the soft fold, her still form resembled a young child wrapped in a fetal position.

Dreaming, the distant sound of Doc Thorton's voice burst through the fog and overshadowed her mind. "Sara . . . Sara. You must find a reason to keep going," echoed over and over again. Sara could see herself lying in her own bed back at the cottage that stood on the Jacobs' family property. One night, awakening from a troubled sleep, she had turned her face to see her husband resting quietly, softly snoring. He definitely was handsome, she had thought. His dark head of hair, along with his intense eyes, had often turned the heads of the town's more colorful women. With his face relaxed, he actually had a look of innocence.

She remembered back to the time when he had pulled her behind a large tree after school and said he wanted to marry her. Despite his family's reputation, there was once a gentleness about him that attracted her. But, his violent response to her questions before the accident not only frightened her but made her wonder why he had changed so drastically the past few months. She knew that Luke and his father were always arguing about the family business. What had happened between the two? Was that the reason for the shift in Luke's personality?

Her face fell slowly as she searched her mind for answers. She remembered her mother bending over her bedside during the worst of her depression, coaxing her to get up and care for the children. Why were her thoughts about them so blurred?

She thought about the breakdown and the loneliness she had felt. Luke had called her an embarrassment to the family. He began to work longer hours, refusing to speak to her. Sara stayed, hoping that eventually the children would love their father the same way she had loved hers.

That was the funny thing about Luke, she reflected. In spite of all his hatefulness to her, he acted as if he truly loved the kids. Fortunately, still protected by their youth, they never heard the gossip about their father's affairs with the women around town.

In her dream, Sara rose from the bed to check on their tiny sleeping forms and felt again the anger at his betrayal, not just of her, but of them as a family. Fully awake, she turned over in the hospital bed and cried until she fell into a deep sleep.

CHAPTER 3

Peg rose early, made a cup of weak tea, and paced back and forth in the tiny hallway of the house she had shared with her late husband. Suddenly, she stopped, backed up, and stood in front of the long, antique mirror. Leaning close to her reflection, she gasped at the gaunt, hallowed look of her face. Peg turned left then right, then, faced the opposite wall, glancing over her shoulder to get a rear view of her body. She had lost a few pounds when her husband had passed away and now the stress of Sara's accident had emphasized her sunken cheeks, and the sadness of her eyes. Her visit with Sara didn't go quite as well as she liked, she thought, still staring at her reflection. Would Sara ever regain her memory?

Peg's stomach growled. The sound sent her scurrying to the kitchen to find something to stop the irritating noise. Grabbing a banana she glanced out the window. It could turn into a beautiful day, she thought. Maybe a drive around the countryside would clear her bad mood. Peg slipped onto the cool seat of the car and drove through the middle of town. She watched the eager young businessmen hurrying down the sidewalks, weaving through the bored, stuffy-looking, older men with gray hair who were taking their time to reach their destinations.

Peg thought about the news article that had appeared in the local paper yesterday, describing the town, the businesses that stood within its limits, and the people that owned them. The reporter had stated that tourism produced seventy-five percent of the annual income of the town of Wakeegon. Only a few businesses remained to cater to the local townspeople. The town's eateries included the old renovated bus depot owned by Lolita Gomez. It housed Lolita's Mexican and American Cuisine on the west side of the lake.

Dan's Donut's, located at the end of Center Street, was close to the lake and the police station. The article stated that the owner featured holiday donut favorites, such as pumpkin spice and sweet cranberry apple.

The menu from Willie's Restaurant listed mostly diner foods. The Friday special consisting of fried fish and chips, included a side dish of Grannie's Freezer Slaw, made locally. Willard Conner owned the old white-washed clapboard-sided building that housed the restaurant that stood on the hill of the north curve. Willie's large back room was the local meeting place for the Monday night Cub Scouts and the Thursday afternoon Helping Ladies Knitting Society.

The Barbecue Pit on Pier 6 captured the business from hungry boaters during the summer months. Other than that, the article stated, you could grab a hot dog at the local gas station or an ice cream cone at the seasonal huts along the lakeshore.

The reporter went on to say the townsfolk mainly shopped at the grocery that carried locally-grown meats and vegetables, fresh bakery bread, and milk from the nearby dairy. Anyone wanting to fulfill gourmet tastes would have to travel to Hyattsville, the nearest city. Small businesses lined the main road, Center Street, which dissected the town. This road eventually ran into Lake Drive, a curvy graveled road that ran all the way around the oval-shaped body of water. Ray's Bait Shop stood on the ground at the end of Center Street and Lake Drive. Ray served the community and vacationers with boats for rent and fresh worms for fishing.

The lakeside community consisted of thirty-five residences including the old Reynolds mansion at Six Pines Drive. When the town was in its infancy, Joseph Reynolds purchased six spindly pine trees from a local farmer and planted them on the edge of his property. The trees grew into thirty-five feet giants that later became a landmark for travelers. Residents would say to lost motorists, "Just go two miles past Six Pines, and you'll be there," or, they would say, "Once you see the six pines rising above the rooftops, you've gone too far." Close to the lakefront, an unpretentious looking sheriff's office with the manpower of three watched over the citizens and patrolled the body of water during the busy summer months.

Peg slowed down, pulled over into the public parking lot alongside the lake, and rolled down her window. A rush of warm moist air rushed in and blew her hair in her eyes. Grumbling, she rolled the window up, pushed back her hair and sighed. She knew that a few of the town's businesses, handed down from generation to generation, were greatly indebted to two of the wealthiest men in the area, the very elderly Samuel Jacobs, Sara's father-in-law and Sara's great-grandfather, the late Jedidiah Reynolds, Sr. What had happened between Jedidiah and his strong-willed son Joseph, Sara's grandfather, still remained a mystery. Some said it was Joseph's refusal to follow in the family business, but most people felt that the son's choice of a wife, the former Melissa Sedgwich, sealed the rift already growing between them. Constantly evoking conflict between father and son, Jedidiah Sr. referred to Melissa as the spitfire from Hades.

From the marriage of Joseph, and Melissa, the recently deceased old-lady Reynolds, twin sons were born. The first came into the world robust and wailing loudly. He would later become Sara's father. The second twin emerged blue and frail gasping for air. Faint whimpers and a distorted body left no doubt that something had gone wrong with the pregnancy. Melissa blamed her husband for her misfortune and refused to care for the infants. Joseph named the first child Jedidiah, Jr. to spite her and simply called the second twin, James. Overwhelmed with shame, Melissa confined herself to the giant house on the hill.

The following week while Joseph was repairing the roof of one of the mansion's high turrets, he slipped and lay dead on the grassy lawn below. The roll of caretaker of the twins fell to their mother who was said to have gone "mad." Jedidiah, Sr., died a month later, some said of a broken heart. After nearby neighbors observed Melissa pacing up and down the front yard in her nightgown in the middle of winter, the town's sheriff removed the first twin from the home and placed him with a childless family. Melissa, screaming and kicking, would not part with the second twin. Time had consumed whatever interest the townsfolk had shown over the incident, so the remaining twin, James, was eventually forgotten.

The dusty black pickup belonging to Luke Jacobs was parked beside the loading dock of Fetter's Supply Store. Although the Jacobs family construction business had just celebrated its fiftieth year, there had been rumors that the business was in financial trouble. Ironically, most of their customers came from outside the immediate area. Wakeegon residents were too aware of the family's shady business practices.

Mr. Fetters, the owner, didn't care about Luke's background. His business was suffering like everyone else. Every month he would meet with other business owners from the neighborhood, in the back room of Willie's, to discuss topics such as the slow economy and the lack of early tourists. At the close of last season, the final financial report revealed a drastic decline in profits for the community. Some businesses had dropped out of the race immediately following the report, afraid of ruining the lives of their families any further. "Money was money," said Mr. Fetters. "I don't care who it comes from."

Waving his employee aside, he personally helped Luke load his purchases. "Hey, Luke, how's the Chris Craft restoration coming? Out of anything?"

"No, not yet. It's pretty slow going, but the boat is starting to take shape. I'll probably need to place an order soon." He paused, "I still get a discount, right? By the way," he added, "when are you going to catch up with your payments?"

Flushed, Mr. Fetters stammered, "Soon, soon. I'll . . . I'll get a catalog for you to take home. Boating season will be in full gear before you know it," he added as he rushed off.

"Okay, Mr. Fetters. I'll finish loading." Luke picked up the last two rolls of pink insulation and threw them on top of the lumber stacked in the bed of his truck.

"So, Luke, how's the little woman doing?" asked a raspy voice. Clinching his jaw, Luke turned to face one of his father's longtime business partners. Questioning eyes looked for a response, "Can I help with anything, son?" asked the small hunched-over man. "I know you've been through a lot. Heard the wife is a little crazy."

"I'm doing fine," responded Luke, putting on a smile that could fool even the closest of acquaintances. "Sara's better. Thanks for asking."

The old man nodded as he walked to his car. "Tell your dad that I'm looking forward to seeing him tomorrow night."

"Sure thing!" replied Luke. "Tomorrow night," he whispered, staring at the old man as he drove away. "At least, finally, everything will come out in the open." He slammed the door shut, pressed the gas pedal all the way down, and sent a shower of gravel sailing into the air. Not only would the meeting and the work that followed be a welcome distraction from the grief he continued to push inside of him, it would at least ensure that for once, the young Mr. Jacobs would be noted in this town. "It's about time!" he said to an invisible audience.

The seclusion of the narrow road made it almost impossible to drive at a decent speed. As he neared the Reynolds mansion, Luke made a mental note to discuss the entryway to the property with the developer that afternoon. In a last minute decision, he had arranged a second meeting with Alistair Goodman to go over the plans for the casino once more. His hands shook as he reached for the pack of gum in the glove department. "No drinks before the meeting," he told himself. "Everything must be perfect."

Sara's mother stepped on the carpet and wiped the dampness from her shoes. She cringed at the squeaky sound they made on the newly polished floor. Area storms had unleashed their fury as she ran from her car into the lobby. Peg took a deep breath, wishing again for the comfort of her late husband. He would have known exactly what to do with Sara. Not only did she look like him, but she even thought like him. What could Sara want when she called a few minutes ago?

Sara's room appeared dark and quiet as Peg emerged from the elevator. She paused before entering to collect her thoughts. Only last week, the doctor tried to reinforce the need for consistency when answering Sara's questions about the accident. "One wrong word," he said, "could bring the young woman back to a reality she is not yet prepared to face." She was, how did the doctor say it? "One strand away from a broken rope. Good health and perfect timing would be the key," he had said.

"Timing?" Peg had muttered at Doc's seemingly cold reply. "There will never be a 'perfect time' for Sara to face the life she has now!" She had practiced over and over again the reply to the question that would eventually be asked by her daughter. Peg took a tissue from her purse and wiped the sweat starting to bead on her brow. "Well, at least she still has me," she sighed. With heavy sadness, her sigh sounded more like a deep groan.

"Mom? Is that you?" asked Sara from her room.

"Yes."

"Why are you standing out in the hallway?"

Peg unbuttoned her sweater as she entered and walked over to the window. She wore a forced smile as she pulled the curtains back all the way, exposing the midday sun that was just starting to emerge from behind the stormy clouds. Glancing at her squinting daughter, she took a long breath and nonchalantly asked, "Now dear, what was so important that you needed me right away?"

Downstairs in the lobby, two men entered the elevator at the exact same moment. Deep in thought, Jack almost collided head on with a dark-haired man whose lips were curled in a snarl.

"Sorry," mumbled Jack.

"Stupid idiot," shot back the stranger.

Jack shrugged, held up both hands, and retreated to the opposite corner to survey his oppressor. Unshaven and dressed in rugged work clothes labeled, "Jacobs Construction," the man had a tight look to his chapped lips and an icy coldness in his blue eyes. This must be the infamous husband of Sara Jacobs, Jack concluded under his breath. Jack had spent last evening combing the town for information regarding the Jacobs and Reynolds families, to add to the file of information collected since Sara's accident. Well, he thought, this guy sure fit the image he had of him.

Jack had found that most community members were quite open about their view of Luke, when questioned. "The Jacobs family you say?" asked one old man with a head of sparsely placed gray hair. "Like a tornado, they rip through people's lives, then, exit as quickly as they came. Leave bits and pieces until they appear again, that's what they do," he added testily. The ones that concerned Jack the most were the handful of residents that appeared nervous and fidgety when the younger Jacobs man's name was mentioned. Of those, a few appeared to be either connected with the family business or owed a great deal of money to the old man. "Anyway you looked at it," Jack thought, "Luke was not the most popular guy in town."

Reaching the fifth floor, the rattling elevator strained to open. "What kind of rotting place is this?" muttered Luke, kicking the metal doors. When they finally opened, he quickly exited as if he felt the whole thing would crash to the bottom. Composing himself, he strolled down the corridor with an air of importance.

"You big creep," whispered Jack, following a conservative distance behind him. Jack rounded the corner and heard the voice of an older woman coming from room 504. "Must be Sara's mother," he thought. "They say she comes in about this time." He ducked behind a cart loaded with bottles of medications and looked up just in time to see the questioning look from the floor nurse.

"Can I help you sir?" asked the middle-aged woman, gruffly.

Flustered, Jack stammered, "Oh, I'm just waiting out here until room 504 is not so crowded. I know that too much company is hard on the patient."

"I wish everyone followed the rules and cared about the patients as much as you do," she replied, with a deadpan smile. Jack stared at her disappearing figure, walked cautiously toward the door, and stopped when he saw Luke enter Sara's room. Warily, he leaned his body against the wall closest to the room's door and listened. He pressed his ear to the cold surface and grew quiet as his heart pounded laboriously, pushing his body out from the wall at each beat. A confrontation had already begun in the fifth floor room.

"Luke, what are you doing here this time of day?" demanded Sara's mother.

"Can't I come and see my beautiful wife?" he asked, with a half-smile.

"I thought you were working on the railroad station in Hyattsville?"

"That was finished over a week ago."

"So, it took you a whole week to come and see," she paused and stared at him, "your beautiful wife?"

"Mother, please!" pleaded Sara.

"Listen! What business is it of yours, Mrs. R.?" Luke interjected.

"Luke, if you fight again, I'll call Doc Thorton," said Sara who continued to smooth invisible hairs loosely caught in her ponytail.

"Great, just stick with mommy, little girl. Your family always took precedence over our relationship," said Luke.

"Luke, I don't even know what our relationship is," voiced Sara sadly.

"Well, let's just say that your family was a big part of the reason our marriage stunk."

"Stunk? Last time you were here you said you wished I could remember the great marriage we had!"

Luke darted over to her bedside and reached for her hand. "I . . . I . . . didn't mean what I just said," replied Luke. "I guess I'm tired."

"It's all right," added Sara softly, smitten with his sudden attention.

"I'll leave you now so you can rest," said Luke.

"Goodbye, Luke," said Sara, giving a meek wave to her husband. Luke backed from the room and made sure Peg saw the smug look on his face. Peg shivered beneath the cover of her sweater. Like a foreboding frost, the younger Jacobs' careless attitude wrecked havoc upon the unsuspecting.

"Good riddance," whispered Peg under her breath.

"What did you say, Mother?"

"Nothing, dear. Now try to rest." Peg covered her daughter with the worn blanket and walked over to the window. One thing she knew for sure. Luke's arrogance only convinced her more than ever that he had something to do with Sara's accident.

CHAPTER 4

Jack leaned against the wall and watched as Luke kicked the door open to the stairwell and disappeared. Jack still wanted to question Sara and her mother, but felt that both women needed a rest after Luke's visit. He rubbed his red eyes, stumbled into the elevator, and pushed the black button, lettered "B." Folding both arms over his stomach to keep it quiet, he silently hoped that the hospital cafeteria food was still edible.

"Let's see," he thought outloud, doing a quick survey of the salad bar and the chalkboard listing of hot cooked items. "If I remember right, the vegetarian lasagna was especially good, that is, if Rosie is still around." Absentmindedly, he loaded up his tray and walked over to a familiar table. He remembered back to the many nights he had eaten a meal at this very spot. Jack clinched his teeth, rose, and quickly crossed to the other side of the room.

"Jack! Jack!"

Surprised by the sound of a woman's high-pitched voice, Jack turned suddenly. The tilted tray sent a shower of food and utensils across the recently cleaned floor. Marinara sauce and creamed peas covered the front of his newly laundered shirt. He bent down to wipe part of the mess off his shoes and met the eyes of a friendly face.

"Rosie!" Jack said excitedly.

"Jack!" Rosie said with a smile. "I didn't know I could cause such a stir in you." Rosie stood with her hands on her wide hips. She wasn't the type that could cause a man's heart to tumble unless you knew her very well. Kind and motherly, she had led him through the worst time of his life. "Sit down, and

I'll fix you another tray. Still no meat, right?" she asked as she disappeared behind the swinging door.

Jack wiped off his shirt and tried not to let Beth's face creep into his mind. Her funeral seemed like yesterday. They had been married just a few months when his lovely bride began to feel tired all of the time. "Maybe we're going to have a baby," Jack said softly to her one evening.

Constant spring rains had coated the roads with a slimy mixture of water and oil. One day on her way home from a long afternoon of classes, she passed out, spinning her car several times, before it landed on its top in a farmer's muddy cornfield. "The brain is so funny," thought Jack as he waited on Rosie's return. He could still remember the scent of mud that had covered Beth's body. Later, at this very hospital, the cause of his young bride's continual complaint of exhaustion was revealed. Secretly hidden in her delicate frame lurked a giant that could kill even the strongest of men. Leukemia.

"How could God take away the only good thing in my life?" he thought. Nothing was left untouched. Little by little her beauty was stolen away by an illness foreign to him. Eventually, her frail body held little similarity to the woman he remembered. Only her kindness remained the same. "It couldn't destroy that part of her," he struggled to whisper.

The clanging of a tray brought him back to reality. "I added a generous slice of cherry pie," chirped Rosie happily. "You look like you could use a few pounds."

Jack sighed. She hasn't seen me in my old suit, he thought, as he took a large bite of the juicy concoction.

"Say, my old buddy, what are you doing here?" asked the plump lady sitting across from him. Never one for short conversation, Jack knew lunch would be a little longer than expected with Rosie around.

Luke parked his truck in the circle drive in front of the Reynolds' mansion, sat back in his seat, and stared at the giant house on the hill. Was it only a short time ago that the grocery delivery boy discovered the slightly decayed elderly Mrs. Reynolds, lying across the kitchen table? The authorities had said that mice had already feasted on the bits of egg left on her plate, leaving behind remnants of their visit on the soiled tablecloth. The body and the remainder of the food were removed by the coroner, and that afternoon, a cleaning crew hired by Sara's mother arrived to scrub the kitchen, bathrooms, and wash the dirty linens.

The priceless paintings and antique furnishings were left in place awaiting the eventual sale of the estate. All of the townspeople knew the house was vacant. Sheriff O'Connell suggested that he or one of his deputies make daily checks on the home. Luke tried to convince family members they could handle it themselves. "No one ever drives up here," he told them, "unless they are lost." A feeling of caution led O'Connell to hand the keys over to Sara instead.

The next day, Luke found a partially hidden forgotten doorway leading into the laundry room at the back of the homestead. He had left his car at the bottom of the drive to get a better look at the property he had planned to overtake. He held tightly onto his hat as he walked toward the house. The spring winds still blew furiously over the hillside. The combination of the cool lake breeze and the thick lush groves of trees made it feel cool even in the heat of summer. "Another reason why this property is so valuable," Luke reminded himself.

Luke turned suddenly, feeling the tug of the wind on his shirt. He could still picture Sara and the children, stretching out on the grassy hillside looking up at the clouds. They would pick dandelions for bouquets and then roll down the hill laughing. The wind tasseled their hair into tangled messes, grabbed their handful of posies, and swept the flowers into the air. "Angel wings," Sara had explained. Their young minds readily accepted the answer from their beloved mother.

A throbbing headache returned Luke to the present. He looked up at the steep gables, "Tonight we will decide your destiny."

Six cars were parked in front of Willie's Restaurant by the time Willard locked his front door that evening. With the lights glaring brightly, one could easily make out the seven figures sitting around the table. They included a young man, Luke Jacobs, who propelled himself through life by his love of money and power; his half-asleep, rigid, aged father Samuel; the carefree and determined Alistair Goodman, architect and hotel planner; a stern, middle-aged man with a sour looking smile, Grayson Locke, legal comrade of the Jacobs family business, and a recently trained expert on casino legalities; gullible and timid looking, Frederick Hudson, environmental problem solver; pristine and seemingly spotless Donald Pierceton, head of public relations; and an unpredictable and greedy Richard Cramer, the Jacobs family personal lawyer. Together, legally or illegally, the group of men planned to do whatever it took to put a little money in their pockets and reverse the economy of the little town of Wakeegon.

Sara's room became unusually quiet after Luke's visit. Peg had stroked the forehead of her young, bed-ridden daughter until she fell asleep. Peg sat back as comfortably as she could in the stiff rusty chair and dialed Roger. It was not a coincidence that had brought Peg and the mature-looking man together. Not only were they friends from early childhood, the two couples had attended the same church for twenty five years, and had often enjoyed family vacations together. Their carefree lives ended abruptly one morning when Roger rose to fix breakfast and found his wife lying on the kitchen floor. After the death of Peg's husband, they were naturally drawn together.

A busy signal brought Peg back to the present. She looked at her daughter and contemplated the reason for Sara's call. What had been the urgency? Instead of her usual tossing and turning, Sara was still. She looks peaceful thought Peg, as she pulled the chair closer to the bed and glanced around the room. No wonder there was talk about closing down the old hospital. Each passing decade had made its attempt to improve the décor of the ancient building, hoping to offset the dire ruin of the structure itself. Doors that were once newly polished and smooth were now covered with several layers of chipped paint. Curled tiles rose from the carefully polished floors. A Victorian light fixture clashed with a landscape framed in cheap gold plastic that hung over the bed. She sighed, stood up, gave Sara a kiss, and stepped out into the hallway.

A young nurse's aide clumsily ran her cart full of supplies into the wall while rounding the corner. The sound of metal objects hitting against the hard floored surface reverberated throughout the fifth floor. Peg's heart leaped painfully inside her chest. She ran toward the elevator, her raincoat thrown over her arm. She was mumbling as she ran past Jack in the hallway, almost knocking him down. Jack recognized her from the police photo, and blurted out, "Wait, I need to talk to you!" Her frightened face disappeared behind the closing doors. His introduction would have to wait.

The tangled web of vines and branches made it difficult to reach the doorway Luke had discovered earlier. He pushed aside the limbs of an ancient looking lilac bush and reached for the rusted handle on the faded gray screen door. The screws holding the iron knob in place suddenly broke free from the rotted wood. Luke cried out as he fell backwards into the sharp, piercing, offshoots protruding from the main stalk of the plant. He rolled out of the flowery shrub and noticed the red spots that appeared slowly on the side of his shirt. Jumping up, he grabbed the remains of the door and ripped it from the hinges. Climbing through the doorway, he tripped over something lying on the floor, falling on his stomach.

"What?" mouthed Luke, as he heard the "ting" of metal hitting against his silver wristwatch. Luke switched on his flashlight, the beam immediately illuminating the hallway. "Why would a shovel be in the house?" he wondered. He stood up, and noticed that the narrow band of light also reflected the images of two small shiny objects. Luke quickly realized that the small squares were not metal but foil wrappers from the Nuville Chocolate factory. He placed the papers in his pocket and set out to retrieve what he came for, the Reynolds family treasure.

Doc Thorton picked up the picture of his sister and placed it directly in front of his ledger. He sighed, and arranged the rest of the items on his desk a second time. He had left the house this morning at exactly six forty-five, leaving time to stop by the local donut shop for his usual, a double espresso, and the local newspaper. "Sorry," he mumbled as he rummaged through his pocket for his billfold. "I seemed to have forgotten my wallet again," he apologized to the owner, a former patient.

"Doc!" said Dan, rather loudly, with a huge smile on his face. "You know, I worry about you lately. What's been on your mind? You didn't leave your billfold in one of your patients did you?" Doc shrugged his shoulders. He looked so forlorn that the owner boomed with laughter.

Doc took a step onto the sidewalk and reached for a small notepad in his pocket. Squinting from the morning sunlight he jotted down, "Owe five-fifty to Dan's Donut Shop," on the slip of paper. His eyebrows rose from the top of his sharply-pointed nose and ended in a bushy-white crescendo that curved like an eagle wing toward his hairline. He drew the two brows together and frowned. Not only had he been absent-minded outside the hospital walls, but he had also missed the weekly meeting required of all doctors on payroll.

Doc rubbed his throbbing forehead. He felt most of his memory issues came from his worry over Sara's lost file. Doc knew his involvement with her case would eventually cause a problem, but the money Luke loaned him would definitely help with his current financial struggles. Several months ago, after a long debate with the hospital board, Luke had cornered Doc in the dark recesses of the parking garage. Twenty minutes later, like so many others in town, Doc had sold his soul to the Jacobs family. Forsaking his oath as a physician, he had agreed to lie about Sara's well-being.

"I want that property," Luke had spewed out with a vengeance. "If Sara is declared incompetent, the last barrier to my plan will be gone. You know you only have a few beds left on the nut wing, Doc," he added pointing his finger in Doc Thorton's face. "I have the means to send you packing from here today. Remember that small loan my dad gave you a few weeks ago?"

"Small loan?" Doc muttered to himself again later that day returning from lunch. Ten thousand dollars! His addiction to off-track betting and Luke's threat to close the fifth floor wing left him with no choice. The bumper of his older model, silver-colored BMW tapped against the retaining wall that surrounded the parking lot reserved for the resident doctors. Doc shook his head, grabbed his briefcase, and walked slower than usual to his office.

"Doctor Thorton! Where were you this morning? I almost called out the marines." Doc turned to see one of the other doctors on staff.

"Didn't you get my call?" asked Doc Thorton.

"A bit late," the other man responded.

"Sorry. I have a lot of things on my mind right now," Doc replied.

"Anything I can help you with?" the man added, looking at him closely.

"No, no." said Doc. "But, don't you think six a.m. is a little early for a meeting? Especially, for a man with too little sleep? You know how it is."

"Well, pick up the information you missed on my desk this afternoon," said the other man.

Doc quickly exited before any more questions were asked. Sara's missing file left him feeling paranoid and edgy. Why would anyone want her medical information? There wasn't any profound information written within the thick stack of pages. Only professionals trained in psychiatry could understand his jots and abbreviations. He was pretty sure that no one knew of his shady dealings with Luke. At least, he hoped. Had Luke opened his mouth a little too often when he was drinking, and divulged their private plans?

Arriving at his office, Doc sat at his desk reviewing Sara's history of depression that had begun soon after the death of her father. A few days prior to her accident, Sara's struggling marriage to Luke had brought her back into his office. A cold front forecasted for the last weekend of March, had promised to bring an unseasonable snowstorm after midnight. Doc was to leave early that afternoon to spend the weekend with his sister at her farmhouse outside of Hyattsville. Instead, Sara arrived at his office at exactly five minutes to four, changing his plans.

"Sara, come in," said Doc. She sat down on the chair closest to his desk. Flushed, Sara rested quietly with her hands in her lap and uttered not a word. "Let me get your file. Let's see. It's been a while, hasn't it?" inquired Doc. He noticed the white tinge around her pinched, lightly-tinted pink lips. "Sara?" Doc asked again.

Unresponsive, she pulled from her purse a tiny piece of paper, crumbled from too much handling. "This morning," she paused, taking a few breaths, "when I was doing the laundry . . . I found this in his pocket. I think the person it refers to . . . is me." Her hands trembled as she slowly unfolded the food-stained paper. She lost her grip on the note and it fluttered to the floor. It landed right side up, making the large-typed print easy to read. Doc removed his reading glasses, rose from his chair, and bent down to retrieve the paper. It simply read, "Luke. It will be your responsibility to get rid of our last obstacle." The sentence was followed by a penciled in "S." Neither knew that the chill in the room would soon be overshadowed by the storm to come.

CHAPTER 5

Jack barely noticed the portly gentleman entering the elevator. He couldn't get his mind off of his conversation with Sheriff O'Connell. What did O'Connell say about the family? Something about the *Twilight Zone*? Quietly, Jack entered Sara's room. A white-haired man in a doctor's coat was bent over Sara, lying in her hospital bed, still in deep sleep. Jack cleared his throat with a loud "herumpfffff," causing the doctor to turn suddenly, his stethoscope hitting an unaware Sara directly in the nose. Startled awake, she sat up and screamed. Doc Thorton backed up awkwardly, knocking the phone from its resting place on the bedside table. Two floor nurses came running into the room expecting an emergency by the look on their faces. The whole scene happened so quickly and unexpectedly, that everyone in the room looked bewildered.

After a period of silence, a loud "Haw!" escaped from Jack's mouth. It was followed by a stream of high-pitched laughter from the young nurses. Doc's lips slowly curved into a nervous looking smile, and Sara, for the first time since the accident, began to giggle uncontrollably. Everyone turned toward Jack at the same time with questioning eyes. Stepping forward, he offered his hand to Sara.

"Hi. I'm Jack Wilder, the private detective assigned to your case. Sheriff O'Connell sent me." Sara stuck out a small cold hand and placed it in his. Jack could feel the rapid beating of her heart. Could it be fear, and possibly something else? Perhaps, a slight interest in him?

No one noticed Doc Thorton leave the room. Breathing heavily, he stopped just outside the door, unconsciously buttoning and unbuttoning his jacket. Doc knew O'Connell was a friend of the family, but he never realized his report to the sheriff would go this far, not with the town's pathetic budget. O'Connell's predecessor rarely followed through with anything.

Shaking uncontrollably, Doc leaned against the hallway wall. "What was he going to do now?" he thought. What little respectability he held would soon disappear. Surely, his part in Sara's health condition would eventually be discovered. He had toyed with the idea of confession. He could have told Sara's mother everything; his involvement with Luke, his addiction to gambling. But now, it was too late.

Pushing himself away from the cement surface, he felt a sudden need to escape as far away from the hospital as possible. Distraught, he ran smack into Sara's mom, knocking her purse out of her grasp. The clatter of coins broke the eerie solitude hovering over the darkened corridor. The contents of her black purse lay across the newly polished tile.

"Doc? I need to speak with you!" said Peg, ignoring the mess on the floor.

"Sorry!" he said, hurrying down the hall. "Can't stop now! Emergency!" Doc glanced up at the clock on the cracked plastered wall. His plans for confession had been changed within a matter of minutes.

Luke sat in his newly-polished truck rehashing the night before. The small flashlight had discouraged his plans for a more intense search of the old Reynolds' home. The mansion seemed to hold a darkness that could not be illuminated by such a narrow beam of light, he had thought. His curiosity of the fabled Reynolds family treasure had led him back to the deteriorating house on the hill. An emerald as green as the Irish hills it came from, it was said. "Where could it be hidden?" he wondered. Some of the elder residents in town suggested that old lady Reynolds took the secret of the jewel's hiding place to her grave. "Perhaps that would be a great place to begin," laughed Luke.

Other townsfolk scoffed at the stories about the emerald. "Never anyone saw it," said an acquaintance of the family's former farmhand.

Sara had told Luke that the family never really knew the truth about the emerald. They did a lot of joking about how they would spend the money if they ever found the valuable jewel. "If I had that gem," thought Luke, "I would have enough to invest in the casino without the help of Dad's old cronies. All the income would come right back to me." He decided that the search was too risky at night by flashlight. It would be safer to do his treasure hunting in broad daylight.

On the fifth floor, two fresh-faced nurse's aides picked Sara up from her bed and sat her in a wheelchair. Surprised by her request to get out of her room for a while, they were more than glad to help. They excitedly talked about the upcoming regatta, as they wheeled Sara into the large vacant lounge. Last summer's boat race competition had brought a number of interesting visitors to the quaint town of Wakeegon, they had said. Laughing, they admitted they were more interested in the young male participants than in the event itself. Placing Sara in the chair closest to the large sunny window, they left without saying goodbye, discussing the new outfits they had planned to wear.

Sara stared out the barred window of the building that had become her prison. Today, though, she felt different, almost giddy as her mother would say. Jack Wilder. Who was this man who unwittingly captured her attention? What time did he say he was coming tonight? Seven o'clock? Maybe, she could have one of the aide's fix her hair a little different. She giggled. Other than an occasional wash and dry, a few strokes with a brush had been her best attempt. Relaxed, Sara sat back in the chair and let the rays of the sun bathe her in warmth. She picked up the latest novel, a gift from her mother, and wiggled her toes in delight. The book bounced off the wheel of the chair as it slipped from her fingers. She glanced down at her feet and wiggled her toes again.

The early model sheriff's car had as many wrinkled and faded spots on its exterior as the man sitting behind the wheel. O'Connell reached for the envelope sporting the town's seal, opened it and groaned. Every year he received the same paper in the mail expressing apology from the town board. The words "too little funds" described everyone's dilemma in town. He wadded up the paper and threw it on the floor.

The sheriff opened the car door, and with the aid of the armrest, attempted to lift his heavy frame. He tried juggling his iced coffee and a stack of folders from his right arm to his left and realized he could not close the door. Backing into the car, he heaved his large frame against the side and succeeded by closing the door with a bang. Exposed skin sticking out from under a too-small shirt touched the metal warmed from the hot afternoon sun. A loud yowl escaped from his lips and scared old Mrs. Meadows across the street walking her dog. "Sorry," he called out. The old lady picked up her toy poodle and gave it a kiss while sending a look of distain to the sheriff.

O'Connell tried to wipe his forehead with the back of his hand and cursed at the temperature sign that flashed 88 degrees in bright red letters. "88 degrees this time of the year?" he said aloud. "No wonder I feel so cross." He walked around the side of the car and gave the left tire a swift kick, spilling the remaining cup of coffee down the front of his newly laundered shirt. He kicked the tire again, crumpled the empty cup, threw it on the graveled parking space, and walked toward the police station. Halfway there he turned, walked back, picked up the offending cup, and threw it in the garbage can close to the entrance.

"Need to be a model citizen," the sheriff muttered, remembering Jack's constant reminder to recycle. "Women!" he added. O'Connell was still upset over the letter he had received that morning from his ex-wife. "What more can I give her?" he asked out loud to a disheveled looking man standing by the door.

"Don't ask me, Sheriff," he responded, shrugging his shoulders. "They said I served my time in the drunk cell and I could leave now."

O'Connell waved him on and was still mumbling to himself when he sat down on the rickety office chair. He rose, and walked over to the closet to retrieve a small cylinder-shaped pillow. "It gives me a sore back every day," he had complained to the council about the torturous piece of furniture, but like all his requests, it was refused again. He could survive without a decent car or a new chair, but how was he supposed to run his station on the little funds they gave him? Thank heavens, Jack was self-supported! O'Connell paused. What did the doctor tell him to do when he felt his life was out of control? Close his eyes, count to ten and breathe slowly. He began to count out loud, "One, two . . . ."

"Three, four. Glad to see they at least hire educated men to work here," said a familiar voice.

"Jack, my boy! Come on in! I was just getting ready to call you, and Doc," said O'Connell. "By the way, do you know what's wrong with him, lately? I saw him the other afternoon at the post office. Barely looked at me. When I asked how he was, he squeaked out some answer I didn't understand, pushed past me, and hurried out the door. Strange fellow he's become," remarked the sheriff with his country drawl.

"I really don't know him well enough to tell if he's acting any different than normal," answered Jack. "He did seem a bit nervous at the hospital today."

"He has become rather sullen. Wonder what's going on with him? He used to be such a likeable guy. Now, Son, what are you doing here this late in the day?"

"I need you to answer a few more questions about Sara. I admit I'm a little apprehensive about meeting with her tonight. Does she know someone tried to kill her?"

"How much time do you have before you leave for the hospital?"

"I told her I would be there at seven."

"Then, have a seat, Son. This might take awhile."

Jack was pulling his chair close to the desk when the sheriff said, "Better close the door. Never know who is lurking around in this town." Both men glanced out into the hallway before the door slammed shut.

Luke threw his heavy, overstuffed backpack onto the bed of the truck. Loaded with tools, it produced a loud clang when it collided with the metal surface. He sat in front of Willie's, his thoughts reflecting back to the meeting just a week ago. Seven men trying to change the future of the little town of Wakeegon. It seemed to be such a good idea. Or was it? "A time of economic woe provides a great opportunity to squeeze in a casino in any community. The promise of many jobs, and an end to the town's budget problems. Who would object?" commented old Jacobs, who received an "amen" from his financial companion, Grayson Locke.

Luke knew most of the men, like him, were in the deal for themselves. "All except Frederick Hudson. What on earth had gotten into him, lately?" wondered Luke. At the last meeting, Hudson had stood up at the end of the long table and voiced rather strongly, "My fellow men. Is there a different project we could be working on together to solve our financial problems? We've all seen from our past ventures the destruction gambling reeks by making the poor poorer, not to mention, the deterioration it brings to the values and morals among the townspeople. Sure, we can spruce up the downtown and fill the area hotels, but is it worth sacrificing the charm and ambiance of this little town?" he finished as he sat down.

Old Jacobs had coughed to hide his anger but Luke had jumped up and grabbed hold of Hudson's collar. "There won't be a town if something's not done. If you don't like our 'venture' together, then leave."

Hudson, bent-over and defeated, slunk back to his chair while Locke took his place at the head of the table. Luke gazed over at Hudson. Of all the men, Hudson worried Luke the most. We've been in business together many times, thought Luke. He's never acted this way before. As for me, I could care less about the environment. I only need Hudson on the committee to fool the community that we're concerned enough about the town to hire someone like him.

Locke cleared his throat. "Plans are coming right along. I'm a little disturbed about the state's ever-changing gambling policies. A huge developer's decision to pullout from the proposed plans for a gaming facility in West River has made everyone on edge. Although," he added smiling, "on the other hand, it could be the best thing that could have happened, at least for Wakeegon."

After a few more reports, Luke paid Willie for the bills left on the table and followed the other men to the parking lot. Locke watched Hudson drive off, and then walked over to Luke. "Do you want me to put pressure on him, boy? Cause I can. I'm sick and tired of his sappy speeches. I'm afraid he might blow this thing for all of us."

"Leave him be for now," replied Luke. Locke shrugged his shoulders and got into his old station wagon. Locke definitely was frugal, as he called it, thought Luke. One would never believe he was one of the wealthiest men in the area.

Luke pulled out of the parking lot and took the road that wove through what was left of the main part of town. The smell of lake water filtered through his partially lowered window. Despite his motivations, he really did love the area where he grew up. He knew the town had become as worn and tired as the people who lived there. Most of the residents never noticed the gradual deterioration of the buildings, he thought. Some had chosen to stay on and weather out the economic storm. They stayed for the same reason their grandparents never left. Hope. A force stronger than any dollar could buy.

CHAPTER 6

Richard Cramer stared at his empty cigarette pack. Reaching into his pocket he withdrew a mint toothpick, chewing on it until it broke in half. The sodden, splintered mess missed his shoe and landed on the ground. He had unexpectedly met Luke in the parking lot of Willie's that morning, and was still seething over the confrontation.

"Hey, Cramer, what are you doing up so early?" Luke had asked with a slur. "I thought you never rose before ten?

"I do have a job other than setting up the casino, Luke," answered Cramer, his lips tight and drawn. "So, I see you've been drinking already this morning?"

"Why does it bother you so much?" asked Luke, stepping closer to Cramer. "I'm sober when I need to be. By the way, I heard you don't like how I'm spending the planning money. Think you could do better, Mr. Lawyer?"

Cramer backed up and twisted his lips. "I only remarked about Hudson. He's trouble I tell you."

"Why he has turned all goody two-shoes, lately? You'd think he doesn't care about making money," remarked Luke.

"Or maybe, he just wants a bigger share of the profits. Six Pines needs a very costly sewage system. I guess we'll have to make it worthwhile for him to look the other way. He knows if someone at his office finds out what he's doing, it'll cost him more than just his job. The guy won't find work from here to Alaska," said Cramer. "Then, there's the other problem."

"What other problem?" asked Luke.

"If we silence the discovery of those Indian artifacts Hudson's men found, the town's Historical Society will be very upset with us. Once the word leaks out, the plans for the casino will be halted," he added.

"I suppose we'll have to pay for that, too. You know? Money to keep someone else's mouth shut. Where did you say he found them?" asked Luke.

"His men found a few pieces of broken pottery and part of a clay pipe in the small hills surrounding the back lot of the mansion. They were in the process of taking core samples for the sewage and drainage system for the hotel," answered Cramer.

Luke grabbed hold of Cramer's arm. "Tell him to put the artifacts back where he found them," replied Luke. "Pay him well. Money is always the answer. We need to keep Hudson on the team, if only to do some sweet talking to the townsfolk. You know, let them think that we hired him because we're concerned about the environment and the welfare of the people." Luke added with a forced grin, "A little sincerity wouldn't hurt now, would it?"

The stench from Luke's breath, along with Cramer's own full stomach of greasy breakfast food from Willie's, brought a sudden wave of nausea to the young lawyer. He broke from Luke's grip and bent down to retrieve a smoldering cigarette butt from the car's ashtray. Luke flinched as if he'd seen a ghost.

"You stupid idiot!" screamed Luke as he stepped back. "What are you trying to do?"

Cramer tried to hide the smirk on his face as he crushed the remains of the cigarette with his leather shoe. Everyone knew of Luke's phobia with fire. It began the day of Luke's tenth birthday. The family had planned a quiet backyard barbecue with a few friends. All went well until Luke's overly-friendly dog, knocked over a plate of newly-grilled hamburgers, and was leashed and hauled away to an empty stable by a furious looking Samuel. Later that evening, the family awoke to the sound of someone pounding on the front door. A fire had broken out in the largest of the family estate barns. It burned to the ground, killing not only eight of their prized horses, but the young boy's beloved pet American Eskimo dog, Baxter. Even now, the smell and sight of smoke could send Luke running like a scared rabbit.

Luke kicked a few stones with his shoe toward Cramer and turned toward the restaurant, swaggering as he walked. "Like father, like son," whispered Cramer. He shuttered when he thought of his connection to the Jacobs family. Samuel Jacobs, Luke's father, had married Cramer's mother shortly after Cramer's father died. Cramer never really understood why such an influential man would ask his mother, a tenant, to become his wife.

"Your father was a good man, but he left us nothing to live on, dear," his mother replied. "Besides, we need the protection Mr. Jacobs can provide for the two of us. The Jacobs name is well known, you know. You'll get the same respect from the townspeople, just like his son does."

The day after the marriage vows were spoken, Samuel parked a flatbed truck in the drive of the cottage. "Listen," he said crossly, "people won't want to do business with me if they know you and your boy are living in this rundown dump. They'll wonder what's wrong." Cramer never understood why his mother refused to move into the Jacobs family home.

One night when the two boys, Luke and Cramer, were playing hide and seek in the large attic of the Jacobs' house, Cramer ended up in the downstairs hallway at the entrance of the old man's study. Samuel and one of his business partners were discussing a deal they had closed on that day. "Values get tossed aside Jenkins when a good opportunity comes along. Don't let your momma's preaching, cloud your thinking." Looking up, he saw young Cramer leaning on the stairway intent on his words. Pointing a finger at the child he said sternly, "Don't you forget it, boy. You're a Jacobs now."

Horrified, Cramer ran home to the cottage, crawled into bed with his clothes on, and pretended to be asleep. Early the next morning, he went to his mother's bedside and shook her softly awake. She pulled him close in her arms and inquired what was wrong. He had asked her, "Am I really a Jacobs?" His mother looked sad as she try to explain to him that she was a Jacobs by marriage, but he could decide if he wanted to be known as Richard Jacobs or stay Richard Cramer. He pleaded with her that he didn't want to forget his real father, and could he keep his family name? "Of course," his mother had replied, "such a loving request from such a small boy."

"How ironic," he thought, returning his thoughts back to the present. Shaking his head in disgust he whispered, "I'm becoming just like the Jacobs men I despise."

Sara's mother braced herself for the coming eruption. The visits with her daughter had been interrupted twice this week. First, it was the abrasive arrival of Luke, and later came the unexpected appearance of Jack Wilder. "What was O'Connell thinking?" thought Peg. She had seen the admiration in the eyes of Sara when the young detective had introduced himself.

Sara had left a message on Peg's phone, her voice rising to a high quivering crescendo. Peg had dressed quickly and had broken the speed limit more than once to arrive at the hospital fifteen minutes later. Her heart was beating wildly. She stopped in front of the hospital Coffee House to purchase a double espresso. "Maybe I need to sit down and practice what I'll be saying to Sara," she thought justifiably. She knew the inevitable question would come from her daughter, eventually.

Doc Thorton was standing in front of the cash register searching through his jacket pocket for his wallet. "Never mind, Doc," said the smiling girl behind the counter. "I'll put it on your tab."

"Thanks, Debbie," he called over his shoulder as he turned to leave.

"Doc! Doc!" shouted Peg, excitedly. "Wait!" Doc, recognizing the voice of Sara's mother, began to walk faster. He dropped down to a slower pace when Peg caught up with him. "Doc, why do you always seem to be avoiding me?" she questioned him. "I need your help. I think Sara has remembered," she added, with a grave tone.

Doc stopped immediately and turned toward Peg, spilling some of his steaming drink onto the floor. He muttered something inaudible and rested his folders on the edge of a nearby table. He didn't need to ask what Sara remembered. He already knew.

Peg ran back to the counter, grabbed a handful of the thin napkins, and bent down to wipe up the brown puddle. "What should I say?" she asked with desperation in her voice.

"Peg, we have discussed this many times," replied Doc.

"I know. But, Doc. I'm not a very good liar."

"Well, you will be when you keep in mind the frailness of your daughter," reminded Doc. "Just tell her not to worry and that you have it all under control." He was glad Sara had asked for an explanation from her mother and not him. "Let me know how it goes," he added. Quickly, he picked up his belongings and took off around the corner, leaving Peg standing in the middle of the hallway with her mouth partially open.

Doc stepped into the elevator, grateful to escape more questioning. The bulge in his overcoat reassured him that the notebook was still there. He removed it from his pocket and opened it to the last page.

"Excuse . . . me," stuttered the stout man, entering the elevator just before the door closed. "Are, are, you . . . you Sa . . . ra's doc . . . tor?" he asked in a string of broken words.

One light was burned out in the ceiling of the minuscule space, making it hard to see. "Who are you?" asked Doc, narrowing his eyes to get a glimpse of the man's face. The occupant's clothes were covered with short gray hairs and left the small volume of air permeated with mice and mothballs. When Doc stepped closer, the foul smelling man backed deeper into the corner, emitted a piercing shriek, and pulled his stained jacket over his head. The door creaked open when the elevator reached the fifth floor. Without warning, the man shoved Doc, who dropped the tiny notebook on the floor. The man turned, pushed the elevator button sending Doc to the main floor, and exited. Astounded, Doc was unable to move, or speak.

Peg drank her coffee quickly, relying on the jolt of caffeine. "Could she lie to her own daughter?" she contemplated. The subject of her grandchildren was still a tender wound in her own life. Dropping the empty cup in the trash can, Peg was suddenly anxious to get the whole confrontation over. The light blinked, signaling the elevator's arrival. Chilled, she wrapped her cotton sweater tighter around her shoulders. The awaiting crowd backed up to allow the passengers to exit. The door opened revealing one man with the look of bewilderment. Peg's eyes locked with Doc's as she followed the crowd. "Excuse me," she said as she pushed her way to the back and found herself beside him.

"You look like you've just seen a ghost. What's going on?" asked Peg. Doc opened his mouth to speak, and then closed it again. Peg looked at him with curiosity.

"The weirdest thing just happened," he replied after a few seconds.

"Fifth floor, thanks," said Peg to the woman standing closest to the elevator buttons. Slowly, the elevator emptied, leaving only the two of them behind. Doc stood rigid, twisting his sweaty hands until the bell sounded their arrival at the floor reserved for the mentally ill, Sara's home for the past couple of weeks. Doctor Thorton stepped out onto the floor, straightened his tie and began to search through his pockets.

"That little creep stole my wallet!" he snarled.

"What little creep?" asked Peg.

"The one in the elevator who pushed me," he answered.

"Remember Doc, you never had your wallet to begin with," stated Peg. "The coffee shop?" she reminded him.

"Oh, yeah," he muttered.

"Now tell me about this . . . creep," said Peg, "but wait until I check on Sara first." She followed Doc to Sara's room. Halfway through the doorway, he stopped abruptly, causing Peg to slam into his back at full speed. The noise that came out of his mouth startled the man bent over Sara's sleeping form. In the soft light over Sara's bed, Doc recognized the same offensive man from the elevator.

Doc stepped out into the hallway and yelled, "Security, security!" to the lone nurse sitting at the station. The intruder pushed past Peg, who was standing outside the door.

"What's going on?" she asked, as Doc leaned over, his chest heaving from heavy breathing. Peg, unsure of what had just happened, stepped inside Sara's room and switched on the lights. Sara, always a light sleeper, opened her eyes, sat up, and pulled her nightgown with the missing buttons together.

"Mother?" she asked with a look full of questions.

"Sara? Are you okay?"

"Why wouldn't I be?" she asked.

Peg bent over and gave her daughter a lingering hug. Just as she straightened up, Doc entered the room looking rather pale.

"Doc? What's wrong?" asked Sara.

"Nothing important, Sara." He rubbed his forehead, still throbbing from what had just taken place. Or maybe, he wondered, was it the conflict between right and wrong going on in his head? Doc opened his mouth to say something, closed it, and ran from the room, leaving Sara and her mother speechless.

Still not aware of what had just happened, Sara regained her composure. "Mother, why didn't you tell me?" Peg stared at her daughter, and sat down on the uncomfortable metal chair, her head in resting in her hands.

"Sara. I'm so . . . so very sorry. I didn't know what to say. Doc said we couldn't discuss it," Peg ended with a sob.

"Mother? What on earth are you talking about?" Sara asked, as she leaned back into her pillow. "So, my little ones, how are they doing? Can you bring them by later? I've missed them so," she trailed off with a sigh. Peg sat up. A look of confusion filled her face.

CHAPTER 7

Jack stood in front of the bedroom closet examining his worn-out wardrobe. Faded jeans with ragged bottoms, t-shirts from his college days, and grass-stained running shoes hardly seemed suitable for his visit to Sara. What time did he tell her? Seven? Again, the unfamiliar sense of excitement cluttered his thinking, "What will I say to her? Sorry that your whole world has turned upside down?" How much had she remembered the last few days? he wondered. He had wanted to talk to Sara before Doc found out she was being questioned. He couldn't exactly put his finger on it, but there was something about the mousy-thin man with the white coat that didn't seem quite right.

Jack carefully chose a pair of newly-ironed brown pants and a short-sleeved yellow shirt. He struggled into his father's slightly too small overcoat, and gazed into the mirror. The coat had faded to a light brown from repeated cleaning, and still bore a slight tear at the inside pocket where his father had kept his pen and money clip. Jack rubbed his fingers softly over the smooth material. His childhood friend, Luis, thought the outerwear made Jack look like a detective on TV. He glanced at the mirror again, removed the overcoat, and placed it back on the hanger. It was too hot to justify wearing the treasured garment for his meeting with Sara today. What had she thought of him? he wondered.

Jack added a splash of Beth's favorite men's cologne to his cheek. When he reached the foyer, Jack suddenly turned, ran back to the bathroom, grabbed the nearest hand towel off the rack, and proceeded to rub his skin until the offensive smell diminished. Muttering, he reached for his keys and a cinnamon-scented handkerchief by the front door when his eyes met with a picture of Beth's smiling face hanging on the wall. His jaw tightened as he turned off the light and slammed the door.

Jack pulled into the parking space closest to the hospital entrance. The weather man had reported that the evening sky would be clear tonight, except for the billion stars scattered about, some randomly, others in intricate patterns. Beth had always been fascinated with the heavens. "How could anyone not believe in God?" she had asked in her childlike voice. On her twenty-sixth birthday, Jack had named a star after her. That evening, he had pulled her out to the tiny lawn at the back of the house, placed his arm around her tiny waist, and pointed up to the eastern sky.

"See? Right there? That one is you," he informed her, then bowed down as to a queen.

Beth laughed. "Now I can watch over you every minute." He had grabbed hold of her and playfully waltzed around the grassy green ballroom floor, gently dipping her down to the ground, her head touching the newly planted geraniums. He plucked one and placed it in her soft brown hair.

"My queen of the universe. Shall we go in to our elegant supper of scrambled eggs and potatoes?" he had asked. She grimaced, and then curtsied, "Thank you, kind sir." Beth had succumbed to her husband's no meat vegetarian lifestyle, although she said she still missed the smell of frying hamburger.

Jack looked up at Beth's star and hoped she was still watching over him. He walked over to the double doors of the hospital, grabbed his handkerchief from his pocket, strolled past the front desk, and flashed a smile to the matronly figured woman.

"Evening, Mr. Wilder. Nice to see you again," she added, her eyes resting on the handkerchief. Jack smiled. He was used to the familiar stares. Jack pulled the white material closer to his nostrils, pushed the elevator up button, and waited.

Anguished over the conversation with Sara, Peg rushed from the fifth floor room unable to speak. Nurse Daly saw her ashen face and ran after her all the way to the elevator doors. After a few words with Sara's mother, the middle-aged woman walked back to the nurse's station with a distraught looking Peg close behind. Sara, puzzled about her mother's behavior, waited alone. Jack chose that very moment to step into the room.

"Jack!" said Sara excitedly.

"Hello again, Sara," replied Jack. He started toward the bed and paused. He stepped backwards through the open doorway to get a glimpse of Sara's mother and the head nurse who were taking turns conversing to someone on the hospital phone. The plump, professional-looking uniformed woman had her arm around Peg's waist in a consoling gesture, while Sara's mother talked animatedly with the person on the other end.

"What's wrong with your mom?" asked Jack, as he skirted the bed and landed on the worn chair.

"I don't have any idea. All I asked her about was the children."

Jack stared at Sara, his mouth forming words, but no sounds were coming out. He remembered reading about the children in the police file given to him by Sheriff O'Connell. "So," he said calmly, "You must be a chocolate lover."

"Why do you ask?"

"Your room is permeated with the smell," he said as he sniffed the air. "It must be my favorite. Dark chocolate with a raspberry center." He pointed his nose toward the direction of the enticing delicacy. "So, are you going to keep them all to yourself?"

"Keep what all to myself?" asked Sara, still confused.

"These," he replied reaching down and picking up two small foiled-covered squares from the bedside table.

"My mother must have brought them when she came to visit."

"Hmmm," he said, "Nuville chocolates. The very best."

"How did you do that?"

"Do what?" asked Jack.

"Know what kind of chocolate it was before seeing it?"

He pointed to his nose. "My mother thinks my sense of smell is a gift, but I think it's a nuisance." Jack laid the two candy pieces on Sara's blanket. "May I?"

"By all means," answered Sara, handing him a chocolate while unwrapping the other and placing it on her tongue.

Jack opened the foil-wrapped square, placed the creamy confection between his teeth, making a snapping sound. "Now, let's talk about you. I have two questions. First, did the doctor say why you are here on the fifth floor usually reserved for patients with emotional problems, when you clearly have physical injuries," he added pointing to her leg swathed in bandages. "And secondly, tell me how you first met your husband, Luke Jacobs." Sara stopped chewing, her eyes widened.

Richard Cramer slammed his fist on the table, knocking over a bowl of freshly popped corn. "Holy cow, Cramer! Could you watch what you're doing?" retorted the senior Jacobs, throwing a few pills down his throat and washing them down with his favorite bar drink. "Some of us plan on eating that!"

Cramer made no excuse for his behavior. "For crying out loud, Luke, no one is going to make any money with this deal!" he spat out, throwing the new report on the table. "Except you, that is," he added. "It seems you have yourself well taken care of." Luke's face went from a palette of ghostly white to sunset red, as he walked around the table pointing a finger at Cramer.

"You . . . due to your own multiple, soured, real estate deals," Luke paused, "have the smallest amount of money of anyone in this room invested in the casino." He stood beside Cramer's chair and leaned in close to his face. "You never did like me being in charge, did you?" he bellowed. Cramer stood up and pushed the younger Jacobs back against the white-washed wall. The voices of the two men continued to rise until the elderly Jacobs rose, raised his arm, staggered, and fell to the ground. For a moment, no one moved. Cramer walked over to the stilled body and bent to take Samuel's pulse.

"He's dead," said Cramer, an edge of gladness to his voice. The remaining men showed no emotion. Not even Luke.

"Heart attack," stated the paramedic, rising from the floor. Luke stood by the picture window, his reflection revealing an angry face. Two men from the ambulance service lifted the deceased man onto the mobile stretcher and covered him with a gray blanket from head to toe.

"Stupid old fool," said Luke with a raspy voice.

"What will we do now?" asked Cramer twisting his hands. He looked at Luke. "I guess I can cut corners in the law office over the old man's will. Remember, the deadline for the casino permit is the 25th of May!" The lawyer reached into his pocket for a cigarette. He could feel Luke's eyes boring in the back of his head. Silently, Cramer crossed over to the door leading outside.

"You know my father would want us to go on with the plans. Same time tomorrow night, men," Luke added, as the group filed past him expressing their condolences.

Luke drove to the modest, completely remodeled, ivy-covered cottage located at farthest corner of his father's property. He stepped from the car and stared at the back of the Jacobs' homestead. Was it sadness or excitement that stirred his heart? The evening had started out like any other. Samuel Jacobs had stood up, leaned on the back of the chair, and opened the meeting with his usual toast to the future of Six Pines Casino and Hotel. Eager to get on with the meeting, Luke had refused to participate in the ritual. "Cripes, Luke. Loosen up. Just remember, if you hadn't run the family business down to almost nothing we wouldn't have to have so many meetings to talk about the money, or lack of it to fund this project," stated the senior Jacobs, already tipsy from his early arrival at Willie's.

At the start of the evening, Goodman had arrived carrying a long cardboard tube. The intense smell of ink aroused Cramer, who was sitting on a chair in the dark shadows of the private room. He rose and crossed over to the table just as Goodman centered the freshly printed blueprints across the newly-washed wood-topped surface. The architect stepped back and awaited the approval of the men. Immediately, the room was filled with chatter. The expertly drawn plans, showcasing the exterior of the casino, had shown the Reynolds mansion still visible within the expanded structure.

"As you can see, the Victorian-styled complex blends in well with the view and will definitely appeal to those in the local rural area," said Pierceton, who was in charge of public relations. He slapped the architect on the back. "I smell money," he chuckled. They spent the next half hour bent over the prints, giving their opinions of the plans, until Hattie, the head waitress, announced that their fish dinners would be arriving in five minutes. The plans were rolled up and placed back in the tubes.

After dinner, Grayson Locke, the expert on the legal workings of the casino, pulled out a thick stack of serious-looking papers. "Okay boys, let's get on with the boring but necessary part of this deal," he stated. The men groaned, and took their places at the cleared table. Just at that moment, Frederick Hudson, hired to assess the environmental problems of the complex, opened the door and stepped into the room.

"Sorry I'm late. I must have missed the announcement about the meeting tonight. Good thing I saw the cars on my way to the store. Luckily, I have all the statistics in the trunk of my car," he said as he passed out a neatly written report to each man. The men looked at each other. No one spoke. They had secretly voted to continue to pay Hudson as a ploy, to portray their sincerity concerning the environmental issues of the community. Hudson would be paid off for his slightly adjusted projections. The townsfolk would never know.

"The artifacts from the Indian mounds will definitely shut down construction until something can be worked out for their protection," he began. "We all know the projected cost to protect the area will almost double the cost of the estimated plans."

"I thought we agreed to look past a few things! You were paid well for your time!" complained Luke, standing up.

"Men, we can't look past the problems or the opportunities this project will present to the community. Can we schedule a time to discuss the issues further?" asked Hudson.

"We'll let you know when the time is right, okay?" said Luke as he guided the man to the door. "We'll schedule a meeting just for your business only. How about Wednesday night?"

"Wednesday? Uh . . . that would work I guess, thanks! See you guys then," he added as Luke returned to his seat.

"Is there something wrong with that man's head? You need to remove him from the group! I told you it was a mistake to keep him on, Jacobs!" Cramer sneered at Luke from the other side of the table.

"Cool it, Cramer!" replied Luke. "I'll take care of it. You're such a worrier." Cramer rose and shoved his chair under the table with a bang. Although Luke had disagreed with Cramer over many details, he knew Cramer was right about one thing. Somehow, they had to get rid of Hudson.

CHAPTER 8

Doc hung up the phone and cleared his throat. His hands shook as he unconsciously patted his pocket for Sara's bedside notebook. Yes, it was still there. His breathing quieted. The tightening in his chest diminished. Now what? he thought. That meddling amateur detective said he wanted a word with him. A word with him! The way the man spoke, made Doc feel as if he'd done something wrong!

The notebook. He had promised Sara he would destroy it, but the written evidence may be his only way out someday. The earlier pages had described over and over her disillusionment of her marriage to Luke. Toward the end, the passages had begun to be filled with . . . could it be, wondered Doc, Sara's fear of her own husband? Was he the person she thought had wanted to kill her? Would Luke want to kill him, too? He wished again that he had not given in to Luke about falsifying Sara's condition.

Doc thought back to earlier that day. Who was that little man in the elevator? Was he trying to steal the notebook? He had looked strange enough. Doc's wild imagination drove him to unlock the file drawer in his desk and place the notebook with the valuable information in its deepest hollows. A knock on the door jarred him back into the present reality.

Uninvited, Jack stepped in and looked at Doc. "I'm Jack Wilder. I have a search warrant for the file on Sara Jacobs," he stated as he laid the official paper on the desk. "I need to know everything about Sara's condition and what you're doing about it."

"So. You are Mr. Wilder?" asked Doc. "Why didn't you introduce yourself the other day? You know, you should have come to see me first, before you spoke to my patient. Confidentiality, you know." Jack walked across the room and peered at the photos displayed on Doc Thorton's bookshelf. He clicked his tongue as he reached down to pick up the picture of a smiling redheaded lady.

"Your wife?" asked Jack.

"No, my sister," Doc replied. "So what do you think?"

"She's very pretty," stated Jack.

"No!" said Doc impatiently, turning his chair toward Jack. "What do you think about Sara?"

Jack plopped down on the nearest chair. "She's great, but it seems she has been given the wrong information about her injuries."

Doc squirmed in his seat. "What do you mean . . . wrong information?"

"She said she wanted to surprise you."

"Surprise me? With what?" asked Doc.

"Her toes," said Jack. "She can wiggle her toes."

Doc's cheeks flushed as he turned toward his desk. Jack continued, "Could I see the file that contains the report about her diagnosed paralysis?"

"Listen, Mr. Wilder. You can't barge in here and ask for private information."

"My search warrant grants me permission."

Doc frowned and then placed a smile on his face, "Sorry to inform you, Mr. Wilder, but the file you want has either been misplaced or stolen. I reported it to the hospital security. They'll take care of the matter now. You know? The Privacy Act? I can't just give out information to just anybody."

"Well," said Jack, "That doesn't mean Sara can't discuss her treatment with me."

"Be assured, Wilder, if you cause any distress to my patient, I'll ban you from the hospital."

"Are you really concerned about Sara, or are you afraid of what I might discover, Mr. Thorton?" Jack stared at him a few seconds and walked out.

Dazed, Doc grabbed a briefcase and began filling it with papers containing any information that had to do with Sara's case. Satisfied, he sighed and sat down on his desk chair to retrieve the notebook when the phone rang. "Yes, yes, he was here, Sheriff O'Connell." Doc listened. "Well, he's an interesting man," he added, while trying to keep a positive tone to his voice. "Sure, sure," said Doc. "I'll fax the information right now." He stood up and absentmindedly shoved the unlocked desk drawer closed, forgetting about the small pad of paper still inside.

The next morning, Jack looked at his watch, and dialed the number of O'Connell's office. A gruff voice answered the phone with a blunt, "O'Connell."

"What did you do? Make the cleaning lady mad?" laughed Jack.

"Jack, old buddy," said the sheriff. "What did you think of the Reynolds girl?"

I think of her a little too much, thought Jack. He cleared his throat and blurted out something that had been bothering him since his talk with Sara. "You were right, Sheriff. Something is definitely wrong with this case."

"What do you mean?" asked O'Connell.

"Sara has been given the idea that she is partially paralyzed from the accident. She has been confined to her bed on the fifth floor since she entered the hospital," replied Jack. "The other afternoon she requested a trip to the patients' sitting room. The young aides working that shift slipped up on the fact that she is not to leave her room, Doc's orders. While she was sitting in the sun, out of the blue, she wiggled her toes. You know? The ones on the leg that was supposed to be paralyzed? When I mentioned to Doc what had happened, he sounded more perturbed than shocked. Now get this. Last night Doc came into her room and told her to remain in her bed and not to move if she ever wanted to get better. He told her she probably just imagined the whole wiggling toe incident and proceeded to prescribe her a new medication. Sara said it made her feel weak after she had taken it . . . like it could have been something to knock her out. Anyway, she was frantic when she called me this morning. She said she awakened to find her leg in a cast. Can you believe it? Her mom visited the hospital and seemed fine with the whole situation. I don't like it," he added. "I don't like it at all."

O'Connell pushed back his chair, expelling a large amount of air from his lungs. "What else did you talk about, Son?"

"Well," he added with sadness, "her children. She wants to see them this afternoon."

O'Connell's donut fell from his hand and left a trail of sugar as it rolled under the desk.

Spring arrived in a huff. It settled in with hotter than normal sunny afternoons. Torrential storms dropped buckets of warm rain that bounced off the tree tops and quietly slid down the deep crevices of the rough bark. It eventually landed on the fragrant undergrowth of the thick woods surrounding the old Reynolds' homestead. Excess water quickly filled the shallow stream that wove through the private grounds. Small animals and shiny-skinned reptiles spent the warm days quenching their thirst while sunning on the sporadically spaced stones. Air bubbles sprang up from the algae-tinged water, revealing a partially submerged, minuscule frog that crawled to the surface and began resting on a fuzzy moss-covered rock. It closed its eyes into tiny slits as it contentedly enjoyed the warm rays of the sun.

Jack reached for the camera on the backseat of his car and removed his bright red college sweatshirt. He paused and took in a deep breath of fresh air. The hospital smells gave Jack a continual headache. O'Connell had insisted that he take a break and clear his mind. When he had mentioned to the sheriff that he had never seen the Reynolds' property, O'Connell suggested a trip to the house on the hill that morning.

"Whew!" Jack blurted out to two fat squirrels chasing each other under the nearest tree. "It's going to be a hot summer."

The squirrels stared at Jack, cocked their heads sideways, and darted off. Jack laughed at their antics and placed the strap of his father's old camera around his neck. The camera was the top of the line in its prime and was one of the first waterproof experimental models invented. "EJ Wilder" was inscribed on a bright red plastic label on its underside. An environmental lawyer by trade, his father was often rewarded with picturesque moments only a patient cameraman could capture. Jack would lay on the carpet of the home library for hours studying the glossy pictures of a mother deer bringing her twin fawns to the sweet grasses of the field for the very first time, a family of groundhogs rubbing sleep from their eyes after emerging from a long winter nap, and a tiny spring violet bursting out of its green cocoon to feel for the first time the coolness of the forest floor upon its petals.

The young detective leaned against the fender of his vintage Thunderbird and slid on an old pair of brown knee-high rubber boots borrowed from O'Connell. He placed his shoes on the back floor of the car, locked the door, and then unlocked it again. "No need to lock the doors," he thought. The house had been abandoned since the old lady's death. Intent on snapping a few good pictures, Jack quickened his pace. He had overslept this morning, something unusual for him since his wife died. Could it be his acquaintance with Sara? He thought about the dream he had the night before where he rushed to Sara's side when he heard her scream. O'Connell had talked about his premonitions of the little town. Could O'Connell's gift of intuition be rubbing off on him?

A flock of Canadian geese skimmed the top of the tallest sycamore tree, the leader honking his command for the rest of the group to keep up. Climbing the hill, he eyed the small stream that encircled the property. The early heat along with the heavy rains had transformed the brown grass into lush green carpets already in need of a lawnmower's blade.

Jack continued to scan the area until his glance settled on the flower beds directly in front of the monstrous house. "Hmm," he thought, "they must have kept on the gardener." Freshly overturned shovels of dirt indicated a recent spading, and the dead brush of the winter's past had been cleaned out and hauled away. Through the lens of the camera, he spotted what looked like the same two squirrels pursuing each other along the stream's edge. Jack took a few landscape shots. Feeling like a child again, he held on to his cap and ran down the hill toward the stream. Nearing the bottom of the hill, he slipped on a wet patch of grass and tumbled headfirst into the warm water. He laughed as he struggled to get up.

The bottom of the stream was lined with small pebbles that had become slippery with algae and mold. Jack placed his hand on a large green stone protruding from the water and tried to push himself into a sitting position. "This is no rock," he told himself, as it disappeared beneath the surface. It felt soft and squishy. Rolling to his side, he squeezed the object under his hand and let out a small cry. As it rose to the surface, two eyes appeared, then a nose, and finally a gapping mouth showing a set of straight teeth coated with green slime. The face bobbed up and down with the current. Jack leaned over and expelled his lunch alongside the body. He heard the sound of a cracking branch behind him before everything became black.

O'Connell took off his hat, wiped his brow with his sleeve, and walked over to Jack, who was leaning against the side of a tree.

"Please, sir," said the young woman to Jack. She wore the red emergency insignia on her sleeve. "You must sit down!"

"I tell you, I'm fine!" stated Jack roughly. "What time is it?"

"Late morning," she replied. "Now sit down!"

"Jack," said O'Connell, "just do as she says." Jack sighed, walked over to the back of the ambulance, and climbed up on the stretcher. The sheriff's face looked pale and weary. "How are you feeling old boy?" O'Connell asked as he climbed into the back with Jack. He had come looking for his friend when Jack didn't return to the station for an early lunch meeting. O'Connell felt the blood drain from his face when he saw Jack lying on the bleached white sheet. Having no family of his own, Jack was as close to a son as he could get.

"Hey, old boy yourself," mumbled Jack. "What have you found out about the victim?"

"They found a plastic card lying underneath him in the mud. It must have escaped the killer when he cleaned up the evidence. The unlucky stiff was registered with the Environmental Protection Agency. Name was Frederick Hudson." Jack sat up, his eyes full of interest. "Don't know why he was here, though. The agency said he wasn't working on anything around this area. In fact, he was on a month's sabbatical, suggested by himself. Emotional problems, they said. Perhaps he was here on a fishing trip. Wakeegon is a vacation town, you know? I've got a few of my buddies searching for a boat permit or a fishing license."

"What about a car?" asked Jack. O'Connell shook his head.

"No abandoned vehicles anywhere within five miles of the place. Really fishy, if you ask me," the sheriff added. Jack laughed at the sheriff's observation.

"Ouch!" complained Jack, holding his head.

"Sit still!" said the nurse, again. "I'll have to patch that nasty cut above your ear." Jack reached for his hankie and found it missing. He winced as she covered the wound with a bandage.

"My hankie, Sheriff. It's missing," said a panicked Jack. "And my camera . . . can you locate it for me?"

"Hold on, Son," said O'Connell. The sheriff walked over to one of the newly appointed temporary deputies. "Sorry," he said when he returned. "No camera was found. Sure you're thinking straight?" Jack tried to get up from the stretcher, rubbed his throbbing head, and lay down again.

"We combed the stream at least a 100 yards on each side of the crime scene," the young deputy told the sheriff. "All we found was a set of car keys belonging to Jack's car."

"My dad's camera," said Jack, attempting to sit up again. "It still worked great, although the film it took was getting harder and harder to find."

"What was on that roll of film, Son?" O'Connell asked.

Jack gave him a look of puzzlement. "Only a picture of a couple of squirrels and a few shots of the landscape," he added. "Why?"

"Brady!" yelled O'Connell to the man putting on his boots. "The situation has changed. Look for fresh footprints and something that could have been used as a weapon against Jack. Probably a man's prints," he added, turning toward Jack. "It took a strong arm to produce the deep gash on the back of your head. Nurse, check Jack's hair and the wound again for bits of wood fibers, okay?" Jack's eyes widened as he listened to his friend.

"What do you . . .," whispered Jack as he turned a sickly shade of gray. "Bleeding," he added as he lost consciousness and fell back on the damp, green-stained sheet.

Earlier that day, just a short distance away, a small flock of birds scattered and flew to the top of the tree as the van screeched to a halt. A middle-aged man wearing an orange hat and tall rubber boots jumped from the driver's side, tripped on a clump of twisted vines and old rotted tree branches, and fell forward landing on his knees. Grumbling, he stood up, ran to the water's edge, and continued out to the end of the wooden pier. His hands trembled as he bent down to wash away their red stain. Shaking off the water, he withdrew an object zipped up in the front of his jacket. His hands caressed it gently before he threw it into the shallow inlet. He turned, ran toward the van, paused for a moment, and ran back to the lake removing one heavy boot, then the other. Both were thrown into the lake. He stood quietly for a couple of seconds and watched as they filled with water and sank. Moving his head back and forth he searched for the occasional vacationer who might be watching his strange behavior.

Convinced that he was alone, he ran to the path's edge and tore a large leafy branch from a nearby tree. Moving quickly back and forth, he removed the traces of his boot prints in the sand. Satisfied, he drew in a giant puff of smoke and absentmindedly flicked his cigarette butt on the ground. In his stocking feet, he again walked to the edge of the water, threw the branch into the lake, and calmly walked up the trail to his vehicle. Mud flew from the tires as he sped away. A bird fluttered down to investigate the still smoldering cigarette as the van's driver rounded the corner heading toward town.

CHAPTER 9

Luke sauntered down the hospital corridor, the usual tight-lipped expression spreading across his face. "Where does she get off talking to me like that?" he muttered. "That's not her usual mouse-like response. It must be the medicine or something." Sara had become quiet after their last conversation when he told her he didn't want her attending the elder Jacobs' funeral.

"What about his grandchildren?" she had asked. "Don't you want them to attend either? I know your father didn't have much of a relationship with them, but I thought that at least you would want to introduce them to his friends." Luke had bitten down hard on the tasteless lump of chewing gum in his mouth and let out a yelp. "Luke! Luke! Come back here! I need to talk to you!" she had shouted as he fled down the corridor.

Luke glanced at the elevator, groaned when he noticed it was stopped on floor one, and kept walking toward the door with the bright green exit sign beaconing from above. His steel-toed work shoe made a resounding thud as it hit the metal doorplate. Silently, Luke grabbed his hat labeled, "Jacobs Construction" from his head, and tucked it under his arm. He leaned against the wall of the landing, opened his mouth, and swallowed the remaining contents of the small bottle he kept inside his vest. He had wanted the Reynolds' property more than anything, but not this way. It had been a little over three weeks since the last funeral, hardly enough time to mourn. He placed the empty container in his pocket and reached for his vibrating cell phone.

"Yeah? What do you want?" Luke answered in his usual manner.

"Luke? It's Doc," said Thorton.

"What now, Thorton? You know, you're becoming a real pain," he trailed off.

"I'm in big trouble. You're in big trouble. That guy Wilder came to my office today. You know, the detective? He's going to be trouble," he added.

"Do you know any other word besides trouble?"

Doc paused for a second, "Sara wiggled her toes today."

"Great. Call me when you have some actual news to tell me," replied Luke.

"You're not thinking, Jacobs. Remember? I've kept her medicated and the leg wrapped up in bandages. And now, the cast? She actually believed her leg was paralyzed. At least, that's what I've been telling her. I've never let her get out of bed. Those stupid teenage volunteer girls took her to the lounge the other day at her request! I'm afraid she'll ask to go home. Her mom has gone along with my judgment so far, but I don't know how much longer. You were the one who wanted to keep her in the hospital until we signed the papers stating that she is incompetent!" Doc stopped talking, suddenly out of breath. "Listen, Jacobs," he began again. "I'm getting a little nervous about this whole deal. Is there any other way I can repay my debt to you?"

"You're kidding, right?" Luke asked with a laugh. "I'm afraid you're too deep in the muck, Thorton. Your gambling habit will put you in debt to my family for quite some time to come."

"We have another problem," said Doc. "She had a witness to this toe wiggling."

"Who?" asked Luke angrily.

"The one and only Jack Wilder," said Doc. "I can tell he really cares about Sara, if you get my message," he added, smiling to himself.

"I'll meet you in a half hour at your office, Thorton," said Luke, his voice becoming quieter.

"No!" said Doc sharply. "It's not safe. Someone broke into my office this week."

"Why didn't you tell me, you idiot? Meet me at the Coffee House, then. Make it look like a casual meeting to discuss Sara's condition," he added as he placed the phone back into the pocket of his jeans. No sweat, thought Luke. Just a little change of plans. We'll just have to do something a little more drastic.

He bounded down the stairs two at a time. When he opened the stairway door at the first floor, he bumped into a round little man who smelled of mud, and what was the other smell? Chocolate?

"I want out of here! Now!" said Sara, with a tone of authority. Peg walked over to her bedside and tucked the frayed blanket under Sara's elbow.

"Sara, stop it!" shouted Peg. Sara jerked away from her touch. "What will Nurse Daly think of you? You're acting like a little child!"

"Speaking of children," said Sara angrily, "Where are they? I asked you to bring them with you today!"

Peg held her breath. "Sara, a hospital is no place for a child."

"So, call them on the phone so I can speak to them. Are they with their father?" asked Sara. Peg turned away and faced the window.

"Sara," her mother began when the phone rang at Sara's bedside.

"Hello?" said Sara.

"Sara, this is Sheriff O'Connell. Jack told me what's been going on. Can we come over right away?"

"Yes, and please hurry," she added. Sara hung up and looked at her mother. "What is happening to me? Did they talk to you about this cast?" She pointed to the clumsy wad of stiffened bandages.

"Sara, you know Doc wouldn't do anything to hurt you." Peg stared at her daughter. "Who was on the phone?"

"Sheriff O'Connell," she stated bluntly. "He's bringing Jack."

"Oh, it's Jack now?"

"Listen, Mom," she said in a softer tone. "They both think something funny is going on. This cast," she added, pointing to her leg. "You'll see." Peg hesitated to respond and turned toward the door.

"Where are you going? Can't you stay until they get here?"

"I'll be back in a little while," she said as she walked back to the bed and kissed Sara on top of her head.

"Mom," asked Sara with pleading eyes, "if you're going home, please bring the children with you when you return. I can't go any longer without seeing them!"

Peg almost fell as she rushed out the door. Was Doc to be trusted? she wondered. He had brought her daughter through this ordeal so far. Why would he want to deceive her? No. Sara was just ill and confused. Peg knew she must believe in Doc even though no one else did.

Jack flung open the door of Dan's Donuts, revealing a guilty looking Sheriff wiping powered sugar from his face. "Sorry, Jack, I was running a little late. Thanks for meeting me here. I needed something to eat," he added. "Did you hear about the brushfire down by the lake? It was pretty small, but it could have been worse. They found a cigarette butt in the ashes. Must have taken a while to smolder into a fire. Thank goodness for the early spring rains." He paused long enough to take another bite. "Cripes, these things are messy," he said as he wiped a spot on his shirt.

Jack smiled, and then put on a stern face. "My friend, you need to lay off those things for awhile. Why can't you just get coffee?" asked Jack, as he placed his order for a venti light-roast with low-fat milk, no sugar.

"I can't help myself," said O'Connell. "It's been worse since my wife left me," he added sullenly. "How did you handle the pain, you know, after Beth died?"

"How did I handle the pain?" repeated Jack. "It's ongoing. Don't ever think it will stop. You just learn to deal with it. Now, back to the subject of donuts. It seems I can't get into my best suit," added Jack, smiling. "And, I'll be danged," he added in his newly acquired rural slang, "If I'm going to buy a new one."

O'Connell looked at Jack closely. "You look great, kid, except for that nasty cut on your head. Can't you cover those stitches with a bandage or something?"

"The nurse said I had to air it out, whatever that means. It makes me ill to look at the dried blood. By the way, any news about Hudson?"

"Not yet," said the sheriff. "The state's involved with the case since he was employed by them. That means it will be slow goin'. Anyway, getting back to the previous conversation," he added. "What the heck do you need a suit for in this town?"

"It's the principle of it, Sheriff," said Jack. His friend picked up the remaining half of the sugary mess and reached for the white bag containing extra donuts for breakfast tomorrow. O'Connell, still intent on finishing his morning's delicacies, turned toward the door and ran head long into Luke Jacobs.

"For crying out loud!" yelped the sheriff, dropping the mashed confection down the front of his newly-laundered dark brown uniform. "I spent all of last night doing my ironing," he grumbled. Both men stood back to face each other.

"Hmmmm. Here again, Sheriff?" Luke muttered. No "sorry," or "excuse me," came from his mouth. The two men knew not to take the conversation any further, especially in a public area. Luke made a bow and stepped aside for the two men as they exited the room. Jack followed O'Connell to an outside overstuffed trash container.

"Stupid garbage company!" O'Connell said, grumbling. "This is a public health violation. Remind me to call them this afternoon," he added.

Jack looked at his friend. "Well?" he asked.

"Well, what?"

"What was that all about?" asked Jack. "Why didn't you say something to that creep?"

O'Connell stared at the ground. "Jack, I can't say just anything I want to just anybody." He didn't add the fact that the Jacobs family had been spreading rumors about him, that he was incompetent and incapable of running the town the way it should be.

"Well, I can," said Jack.

"Listen, Son," said the sheriff, pulling Jack aside. "Watch your step with that family. Don't forget what happened to you out at the Reynolds house," he added, getting into the car and adjusting his seat belt. "I'm telling you from experience. Don't trust any of them!" Both men became silent. Jack looked at his friend as he pulled the car out of the parking lot. Why did O'Connell fear the Jacobs men? Had they threatened him, too, like many others in town? he wondered.

Luke sat in his vehicle and watched the sheriff's car drive away. He laughed as he drove toward the hospital. Who does O'Connell think he is? The Jacobs family has been running this town since the late 1800's. If only the former sheriff didn't take to beating his wife, O'Connell would never have been voted in, he thought.

Luke glanced at his watch and turned toward the mansion instead of heading to the hospital coffee shop for his meeting with Doc. "I'm a little early. Might as well drop off my tools first," he muttered. Taking the drive at his usual speed, he sent a shower of gravel through the air and ended with a screech at the circle drive. He got out, stretched, and unconsciously looked up. The mansion's high turrets always commanded the attention of any visitor.

"Shoot, it's going to downpour any minute," he said, noticing the darkening sky. Grabbing his tools from the back of the truck he saw a black shadow cross the upper story window. "Great," he shouted crossly. "It looks like those bats Hudson was talking about are back." As he rounded the house, he never saw that the turret curtains fluttered slightly, and were quickly stilled by a pale-looking hand.

CHAPTER 10

Peg was oblivious to the stares as she ran down the hospital corridor. Should she go along with the instincts of her daughter or trust the advice of Doc Thorton? After all, she thought, he was not only Sara's longtime medical practitioner, but a friend of the family for many years. For goodness sake, he knew more intimate details about the Reynolds clan than anyone in town! So, why did she feel a chill when he was around? She had to agree with Sara somewhat, she admitted. Putting a cast on her daughter's leg was pretty drastic.

After her visit to see Sara, she had called Doc at the hospital expressing her concern about the cast. He explained that Sara would heal quicker if he kept her in one place. "Probably just felt some electrical nerve charges," he said. "They do that sometimes when they are damaged."

"But Doc," she had exclaimed into the phone. "You said her right leg was paralyzed!" she added, her voice rising along with the wind outside the window.

"Can't hear you very well," he said, as the phone cracked and became silent.

Peg's mind was still full of questions when she reached Doc's office. The crack under the door was dark. Catching sight of a floor nurse she asked, "Where is Dr. Thorton? Did he leave early?"

"No, madam," she replied. "He just wanted to take a break and get a cup of coffee at the Coffee House."

Peg reached the elevator and pressed the number one. The Coffee House, a gift from the Jacobs family, was added last year to improve the look of the hospital. Three walls of glass gave visitors a beautiful view of the garden area behind the ancient building. "Anything," Peg muttered, "to boost their reputation with the community."

She spotted Doc sitting in a corner booth, engrossed in a very intense conversation with the person facing him from the opposite side. Peg grew closer and saw that it was Luke Jacobs. Quietly, she slipped behind a dessert display loaded with apple and cherry pie.

"Sara," said Doc, "She will find out . . .," was all that Peg heard when someone across the room dropped a tray of food. Startled, both men turned to see what had caused the commotion. Doc rose and knocked over his water, which ran across the top of the table and onto Luke's pants.

"Thorton! You idiot!" Luke spewed out as he jumped from his seat.

"Sorry!" said Doc crossly. Coffee drinkers nearby turned their eyes toward the heated voices. Wiping himself with a napkin, Luke turned to leave.

"Luke, what do you want me to do?" asked Doc to the retreating figure.

"Use your head, Thorton. You're on your own. You owe me. Remember?" he added.

Peg stepped out from behind the racks of pies. She had never seen Doc this way before. His voice had been laced with hatred and venom. "What was Sara going to find out?" she wondered. Shaken, Peg walked toward the lobby. Could Sara be right? If so, should she be left alone?

Luke roughly pushed aside the new growth of the flowering bush concealing the back entrance to the Reynolds home. He froze, and stared a few seconds at the wooden door that had been recently repaired with two shiny aluminum hinges. A trail of goose-bumps ran up his shoulder blade and climbed the side of his neck. Except for his phobia with fire, fear was a stranger to him. If someone was watching out for the condition of the house, they could be watching him, too, he concluded. Opening the door, he covered his nose as the stale musty air escaped the mansion and penetrated his spring allergy-inflamed sinus cavities.

"Yechhh!" he complained. Thump! He turned his head toward the muffled sound. It came from one of the upper floors.

"Those stupid bats!" he remarked softly. "I'll take care of them," he vowed, climbing the dust-covered stairs. The grand stairway curved up one wall like a twining vine to a tree. Beautifully polished oak railings and steps were surrounded by carved faces of gargoyles that graced the thick round posts. Century old brass rods held the rose-flowered carpet tightly to each step. The stairway grew darker as he climbed to the second floor. Even in the daylight, the hallway between the upper rooms was dismal and gloomy.

Screeech! "What on earth?" he started to say. Scrape! The sound was so irritating that Luke covered his ears. He stood before the third set of stairs. They were neither imposing, nor inviting. Cheaply stained and covered with scratches, they extended up to the top floor that was once reserved for storage and living quarters for the servants back in the late 1800's. Luke bent down to observe the wooden steps closer. Shining the light on the second step, he flicked his finger through a footprint of mud. The mud was still wet.

Jack and O'Connell stepped through the door of Sara's room at the same time. "Umpfff," complained O'Connell.

"Watch out!" said Jack to his plump friend. Both were stuck sideways in the opening of the antiquated narrow passage. Neither one could go forward or backward. "Hold your breath," suggested Jack.

"Hold my breath? Are you assuming that the problem is all mine?" asked the sheriff, turning a light shade of red beginning at the bottom of his neck and finishing at the tips of his earlobes. Both men turned toward Sara who was holding her side and laughing hardily.

Embarrassed, Jack counted, "One, two, three," at which they both sucked in their stomachs while leaning toward the room. O'Connell landed on the floor while Jack ran into the end of the bed. He looked at the young girl with tears streaming down her face and a jubilant smile.

"You two are crazy," she said, as Jack helped the sheriff from the floor. Sara's cheeks were lightly flushed, and her eyes twinkled brightly.

"I'm sorry you had to see that, Sara," said Jack. "Do you know this is only the second time you have laughed since I've met you? What does that tell you, O'Connell?" Jack asked his friend. All three began laughing again. Jack glanced at O'Connell and cringed. The sheriff had rolled up his pant leg, and was gently rubbing the reddened area. "Perhaps you had better sit down and rest that knee." O'Connell hobbled over to the bedside, looking questionably at the rickety chair.

"So, Sara," began Jack, "It looks like your mother was just visiting you."

"Why?"

"Because there are those chocolates again," he said pointing to the shiny covered delicacies on the nightstand. "And the big clue is . . .," he paused as he reached down and picked up a large black handbag, "this. I think it's hers."

Sara clasped her hands together and giggled. "She'll be back, eventually." She became quiet, deep in thought, and then, the words began rushing forth. "She ran out. I guess I've been too hard on her lately. It's not like me, you know, being harsh with her . . . or anybody." She stared at her hands on her lap, "No one will help me to see my children." Looking up, she asked, "Jack, could you bring them to me?"

Jack's face turned ashen. "Sara, can you remember anything about the accident, anything at all?"

"Sometimes. I don't know if it is reality or just a dream," she answered.

O'Connell cleared his throat. "Well, Sara, Jack is here to help you."

Jack sat down on the edge of the bed. He wished that he was still in Chicago, or anywhere, but here. "Tell me what you know about that night, Sara," he began as O'Connell soundlessly slipped from the room.

Heads turned to watch Doc leave the Coffee House. Doc's face looked as if he had spent the day in the sun. His chiseled jaw was tightly clinched and his narrow eyes stared straight ahead. "Hey Doc!" inquired a young intern. "Is everything alright?" Doc brushed past without noticing him.

Doc remembered Luke's final words and shuddered. "On my own? What did that mean? If only I hadn't accepted the $10,000 loan to pay off my gambling debts." Not only did he threaten me, thought Doc, but what about his threat against the hospital? Luke would make sure Doc's unit would be closed down if he didn't do things his way.

Doc knew that Luke had quickly moved forward with his plans soon after Sara's accident. What did she know about the future of the old Reynolds' homestead? She had never mentioned anything to him in her sessions. Luke had wanted him to declare Sara incompetent. What am I going to do? he wondered. How can I destroy her with a lie? If he was really on his own, like Luke said, what could he do to make Luke satisfied?

After a few minutes of rummaging in his office, Doc calmly walked back to the elevator and pushed the button leading to the basement floor. A pair of surgical gloves were removed from his pocket and placed on his sweaty hands. "Thank goodness," he reasoned, "I found my keys." He started down the hallway and stopped. His prickly skin suddenly burst out with a rash of tiny red bumps. He paused momentarily, glanced around the area, and continued walking until he stood in front of the door marked "Pharmacy." The key fit precisely into the old lock. The smell of rubbing alcohol and vitamins laced with iron rushed from the room, making his nose itch.

Doc hurriedly searched the rows of pill bottles until he found the right one. The combination of the drugs in the bottle and the ones he had just prescribed for Sara would be catastrophic for the bed-ridden girl. "This medication can cause slow heart rate, coma, and," he shivered as he read the final warning from the drug company, "possible death." Doc pushed his glasses up on the clammy, damp-skinned ridge of his nose. He put the pill bottle label through the shredder, quickly replaced it with a new one he had printed up in his office, and shoved the bottle into his back pocket. Silently, he moved toward the door, checked the hallway, and exited the room. Doc never saw the shadow around the corner.

"Well, go on, Sara," urged Jack. "Tell me what you know." Jack sat at the far side of the bed, carefully avoiding the leg enclosed in the hard cast. Sara looked away, trying to escape the intensity of his green eyes. "So," he said to get her talking, "Do you have a picture of the children?"

"All of my things have been taken from my hospital room locker," she replied. "Whatever I had with me the day of the accident is gone, purse and all. I think my mother took everything home."

"Tell me what happened that day, Sara."

Sara grew quiet, her complexion matching the pastel pink of the faded sheet. "I had shopping to do in the morning," she started weakly. "It was also laundry day. I was sorting clothes. The children . . . they get so dirty." She paused, and asked cautiously, "Do you have children, Jack?" Jack shook his head. She continued, "Luke had just returned home. We had a big argument."

"What about?" asked Jack.

"The usual. He leaves the house and never tells me where he's going," she choked. "The children never get to see him. They are both asleep long before he returns, if he gets home, that is. He'd been drinking. He promised me he would stop," she said, looking at Jack for support. "I had just gotten them to sleep. The shouting woke both of them up. They go to bed pretty early since they're so young, you know?" she paused, then, continued, "He staggered into our bedroom. It was the first time he ever hit me," she said quietly, her head down and her eyes closed.

Jack fought the urge to comfort her. She looked up at him. "When I do the laundry, I always check his pockets for papers and coins. There . . .," she paused, "have been notes in his pockets before. Some even had the numbers of his lady friends," she added heavy-heartedly. "This time the note was different from the other ones I've found. It was in bold print and contained only one sentence. It read, 'You have to get rid of the last obstacle.' It ended with a penciled in 'S', Jack. When I questioned Luke about it in our bedroom, he hit me so hard I fell. Guess I shouldn't have brought it up, huh, especially when he was drunk?"

Jack looked at the dark circles under her eyes. "Sara! He should have never hit you, regardless of when you brought up the question! Do you understand that?" he said angrily. After he had calmed down, he continued, "Sorry for my outburst, Sara. Do you want to go on?"

"Yes," she began softly. "After he struck me, he fell asleep right away. The alcohol, you know? Anyway, I wanted to talk to my mom, so I called her. The line was busy. I couldn't calm the children so I thought I would drive to her house. A car ride always puts them to sleep. I bundled them up, put them in their car seats, and gave them each a cup of warm chocolate milk. It makes them sleep better," she added. "When I opened the garage door, I noticed it was snowing heavily outside. I almost changed my mind but thought, it's only fifteen minutes to her house, right? I could stay overnight if I had to."

"Go on," said Jack, leaning his arms on the bed.

"Oh!" she paused, "Did I say that I was driving Luke's car? Mine was getting new tires."

"Did Luke give you his car for the day?"

"We switch vehicles sometimes. Anyway, I was glad to be driving the SUV that day." She continued, "I was so upset, I couldn't see straight. The roads were pretty good until I got to the edge of town. The wind had started to blow harder, and they were beginning to ice over. I could see his car in the driveway."

"Whose car did you see?"

"Roger's. The man my mom is dating." Sara continued, "I slowed down, stopped before I got there, and turned off the headlights. I didn't want to scare her. He . . . was parked in my space," she said, her voice becoming

THE SECOND DOOR | 71

agitated. "My dad wasn't gone six months before he started showing up every night." She wiped a tear from her cheek. "I parked there for awhile, until I saw Roger walk past the picture window, the one that my father put in, with his arm around my mother's waist."

"It made me furious, Jack. I started the car, accelerated, and drove right past the driveway. I turned to check on the children. When I faced forward again, I saw a shadow zoom across the road. That's all I can remember. I don't remember coming to the hospital." She paused. "Have you seen my children, Jack? Were they hurt, too?"

When Jack didn't answer, she said, "This cast. My memory. I'm so confused. They say I have to remember things by myself," she trailed off. Her voice had become subdued, reversing into a tone of meekness and uncertainty.

"Sara," said Jack, "I think we'll stop for today."

"But," she began to yawn, "We never talked about the children."

"Plenty of time for that," said Jack. "We'll be back tomorrow," he said as O'Connell peered around the door. Jack took her hand and held it tight.

"Get some sleep, Sara," he said as he gently let go of her hand. Her eyes were partially closed when he turned around for one last glance.

"Please, my children," she mouthed silently to Jack before she fell asleep. Neither of them knew that the events of the following morning would make this conversation their last for a long time.

CHAPTER 11

"You're on your own. You're on your own." The words kept repeating themselves over and over in Doc's head as he held tightly onto the brown bottle. Doc paced back and forth in the room, languishing over the idea of harming the daughter of his longtime friends, until he succumbed to a decision. "I have no choice. Time is running out," he told himself. "There's no other way out if I have to keep my bargain with Luke. Besides, why should I feel so bad? He has regard for no one," whispered Doc. "Not even his wife."

Doc opened the door, checked the hallway, reached into his pocket, and pulled out a handkerchief to wipe the perspiration from his forehead. Gasping, he ran to the elevator. The door shut just as he heard voices in the outer passage. He was fingering the smooth bottle when it slipped from his grasp, its contents spilling across the dusty tile floor. Doc quickly scooped up the white capsules and placed them in the front pocket of his medical jacket. The floor numbers lit up one by one. He was breathing heavily when the elevator reached floor number five. The doors opened to an empty corridor.

Sara was sleeping, her delicate form tucked tightly into the blanket folds, when he entered the room. Cautiously, he inspected the hallway once more, walked silently toward the bed, and lightly placed his hand over Sara's mouth. She squirmed and grabbed his arm.

"Doc?" she asked anxiously.

"Everything will be fine, Sara," he answered. "The nurse is busy with another patient. I have a new medicine for you to take. I think it will help your memory."

"Shouldn't . . . ?" she began.

"We need to start now. Too much time has passed already."

"Well," she said slowly, her mind still fuzzy from sleep. Doc slid the handful of pills unto her palm and held the glass of water close to her lips. Sara raised her hand, took a sip, and let them slide down her parched throat. She held onto the glass and continued to drink. Fidgeting, Doc pulled the glass away from her lips, spilling the liquid on her nightdress. She winced as its coldness touched her skin.

"Wait!" said Sara weakly, as Doc turned to leave.

"Shhhhh!" said Doc. "We must be quiet," he added roughly.

"But," Sara said sleepily as she laid her head back against the pillows. Doc glanced at the clock. Midnight. He stepped back into the shadows and waited until the minute hand reached four.

"There, that should do it," he said in a business-like tone as he approached the bed. His heart pounded loudly, as Sara's pulse slowed to a faint beat. Doc stepped toward the door. A flicker of light at the end of the hallway made him flinch. He walked steadily toward the closed elevator doors. When they opened he stepped inside, pushed the button, and placed his shaking hands in his pockets to keep them still. The doors were slowly closing when he heard the nurse's scream.

Richard Cramer pulled the perfectly preserved vintage white, 1970 VW Beetle, a gift to himself after law school, into the handicapped slot in front of the display window of Ray's Bait Shop. The shop's exterior had weathered to a soft gray, similar to the buildings on the cover of the seaside calendars sold at the front of the store. A lopsided sign shaped like a fish hung from a post by the sidewalk. "The Only Bait Shop in Town," was sloppily painted on both sides. It swung gently in the moisture-laden breeze by only one hook. "Meaning to fix that," was Roy's answer to why it remained broken for the past two summers.

Cramer glanced toward the small pier surrounded by burnt blackened grass, jutting out into the lake. He searched for a cigarette, found a stub in the ashtray, and lit it with his last remaining match. Although fishing was his favorite past-time, he didn't plan on buying any worms today. He was waiting for a vehicle that passed by the shop early every morning, at least that's what Ray claimed. "What was Luke up to?" Cramer wondered, sleepily. "What was he doing at the Reynolds' house that early in the morning that he could not do any other time of the day?"

The shrill call of the killdeer, and the sound of tires making the transition from paved road to gravel, awoke Cramer from his shortened slumber. A black pickup advertising the "Jacobs Construction Company" whisked past the shop, the driver only a blurred image to the observer. Cramer started the VW, pulled out onto the road, and stayed a safe distance from the vehicle in front of him.

The sight of the Reynolds' house always brought the same response from Cramer. It began with remorse and brewed into a full blown anger that cooled to a sick feeling of disgust. He absentmindedly reached for the cigarette case lying on the seat beside him, remembered it was empty, and grumbled. Cramer rolled down the window and hoped the cool, misty air would settle his nausea. Gritting his teeth, he acknowledged his hatred of the Jacobs men. But Sara . . . she was different, he concluded, rubbing the moisture from the corner of his eye.

Cramer pulled close to the towering pines. Luke had parked his vehicle behind the tall forsythia bushes that lined one side of the drive, and was pulling a black duffle bag from the bed of the truck. Cramer watched as Luke placed the bag on the ground, took out a large metal flashlight, flicked it on, then off, then on and off again. Satisfied, Luke put the flashlight in the pocket of his jacket, zipped the bag shut, placed the straps over his shoulder, and walked to the back of the house.

Cramer waited awhile, stepped from his car, and stood on the thick pine needles carpeting the ground. He began to walk toward the house, stopped, and stared at one of the pointed turrets. A flash of light from the right tower caught his eye. What was Luke doing on the third floor?

Cramer drew in his breath. Was his imagination overcoming him? The sun was burning full-force as he backed the car around to leave. The golden rays caught the whites of two eyes staring back at him from the second-story window.

Luke descended the stairs of the mansion to the second floor and stopped by the first of three windows. He lifted a cushion from the window seat and ran his hand over the carved woodwork. Faded red brocade velvet matched the color of the roses in the floral carpeting. Luke had spent his childhood in a house with similar interior and had grown to appreciate fine furniture and décor. He took note of the pieces that would be kept to maintain the ambiance of the past within the new casino entrance, projected to run through the remains of the old house. The rest of the furnishings would be sold before the construction began, the profits benefitting the new building.

A cushion was admired and put back into place. This morning he had driven to the mansion for another reason. Irish treasure! The tale of the Reynolds' emerald began back in the 1800's with the arrival of the wealthy O'Donnald family from Ireland. For months Mr. O'Donnald had been corresponding with the young enterprising Reynolds family about purchasing a small waterfront building, where his family could reside and conduct their business. The youngest O'Donnald, Katrina, had married into the Reynolds family line, and there the story of the green jewel began. Tales of the emerald and its previous owner, old lady Reynolds, were spread about the town, more after her death, than when she was alive.

"Let's see," Luke reviewed out loud. "They say it's hidden somewhere in this house, but where do I start? Old lady Reynolds was a tough old bat," he laughed. "Speaking of bats, I think I'll check out those turrets one more time . . . and the mud on the steps." He had been at the mansion several times this week but had found no more muddy footprints. Ever since they began to plan the casino and the reconstruction of the house, there had always been something amiss, he reflected. A few candy wrappers here, a shovel there, the occasionally moved furniture and the weird sounds. The sounds had freaked him out the most, but now the footprints added a new twist to the situation. "Could be kids from town or maybe a small animal had found an entry-way tucked away under the eaves? No," he had to admit. "The footprints were definitely human."

Luke soon forgot the problem, his mind focused on finding the jewel. He lifted each picture carefully from its hanger, searching for a hidden wall safe. Before he placed each painting back on the wall, he checked for any paper taped to the back of the canvas. Luke stopped to adjust a small frame containing a delicately stitched sampler. It read, "Look deep into the eyes of a friend, to see the real person within. Brown eyes of truth, blue eyes of mirth, but it's the eyes of green that hold a treasure of worth." Old lady Reynolds was said to have been quite good at needlework, he remembered, shrugging his shoulders while trying to contemplate the meaning of the strange verse. Luke glanced at his watch, stuffed the flashlight into his pocket, and ran quickly to the stairs. Sheriff O'Connell would soon be making his rounds. Crash! He paused, and started to turn around when he felt the pain in the back of his head. A drop of blood landed on the polished step.

O'Connell never made his rounds that morning. During the early morning hours he was called to the hospital by a very distraught Nurse Daly. "She's dead! She's dead!" she had screamed into the phone. "Help me! I can't find Doc!"

The sheriff had dressed quickly and arrived at the hospital a few minutes later. "What happened?" he asked the nurse as she ran toward the elevator.

"She's so still! No one can find Doc, so I had to call in a doctor from the emergency room!" She paused, took a breath, and continued, "When I checked on Sara around 12:30 she appeared to be in a semi-coma state. She just stared straight ahead and mumbled once in a while. Her breathing is shallow and her vitals have slowed. The emergency room doc is in there right now," she added, stopping short of Sara's room. "Oh my, oh my! What will her mother do?" she said, wringing her hands.

O'Connell ran into the room but was ordered out by the attending physician. "I'm staying," he barked back angrily. "Get Thorton!" he shouted to Nurse Daly. Daly lifted the phone and dialed, but there was no answer.

In a bar across town, Doc Thorton was escorted out the door and pushed toward the direction of his home. "Go home, Doc, and sleep it off," said the bartender.

Instead, Doc walked toward the lake. "The lake," thought Doc, "that's where all this craziness started. Trying to save this stupid lake and this pitiful town!" His eyes scanned the homes surrounding the east side of the body of water. "Maybe I should end it all right now," he muttered. "I have nothing to lose. Eventually, everything will be found out. My betrayal to Sara, the gambling, and the debt owed to the Jacobs family. Might as well end it all in the place it began." He crept closer to the water's edge. In the shadow of the trees, the stone path was uneven and dark. "That ringing sound, again," said Doc looking at his pocket, his mind in a deep fog. He swayed, took one more step, caught the toe of his shoe on an overgrown tree root, and fell into the murky darkness.

Jack's car sent a spray of gravel onto the sidewalk that led to the front door of the hospital. His face was pale and drawn, and his wide green eyes were full of alarm. What did the sheriff say on the phone about Sara? Near death? He had talked to Sara only a few hours ago. What had happened between then and now? Jack pushed through the doors and ran to the elevator. It had stopped on the fifth floor. Sara's floor. He pushed the button and waited, shifting his weight from one foot to the other. Exasperated, Jack turned and ran toward the stairwell door, shoved it open, and bounded up the stairs two at a time. Arriving at the fifth floor, he bent over and held his side. The nausea was overwhelming. Unfortunately, he had left his handkerchief lying on the bureau by his front door. When he raised his head, he saw two men wheeling Sara from room 504.

"Wait!" he yelled as he followed them to the emergency elevator. "Sara!" he whispered hoarsely. Jack had caught a glimpse of her lifeless, ghostlike face before he was grabbed from behind by a strong hand.

"Let me go! I want to see her!" he shouted to his oppressor. He turned, and saw that it was O'Connell gripping his arm. The sheriff's face was almost as white as Sara's. "Is . . . is she dead?" asked Jack.

"No," the sheriff answered. "She is still alive."

Jack leaned against the cold painted wall. "Where are they taking her? Can I see her?" O'Connell did not respond. Jack stepped closer to his friend. "What happened?"

"I was hoping you could tell me, Son," said the sheriff. "What exactly did you talk about last night?"

"I want to see Sara first. Then, we had better find a place where we can talk privately," said Jack. The sheriff looked at the young man's ashen face in anticipation, or was it fear?

Luke groaned, and weakly raised his hand to feel the sticky patch of hair on the back of his head. His eyes opened to a darkened room, the narrow beam of the dimming flashlight reflected on the ceiling above him. Every inch of his body was pounding in pain as he pushed himself into a semi-reclining position, moving his head from side to side to see if it was still attached to his neck. What had happened?

The Oriental rug at the bottom of the stairs felt soft against his aching muscles. Did he fall from the landing above? He remembered hurrying to get to his car and leave the grounds of the mansion before O'Connell made his rounds, but he did not recall falling down the flight of stairs. He groaned again as he tried to move. What was the warm sensation on the back of his shirt?

Luke pushed the silver button on his watch. The hands glowed in the Indiglo light. Eleven thirty p.m.? Have I been lying here all day? he asked himself. Surely, O'Connell had noticed his car parked in the driveway since early this morning. He grasped the stair railing and stood up, his legs shaking and quivering. Luke picked up the flashlight and directed the beam on the floor surrounding him. The weak stream of light barely illuminated the rich texture of the rug and the shiny finish of the wooden floor. The faint glow followed the thin trail of blood that lead to the top of the stairs. The top . . . he must have been on the second floor when he blacked out. Did he fall down the stairs or did someone pull him down, one at a time? Climbing the steps slowly, he flashed the light across the second story landing, and stopped to view a pool of blood. The opened duffle bag rested close to the crimson puddle.

Cool drops of sweat formed across his forehead. His breath quickened as he cautiously stepped around the slippery red spots, retrieved his bag, and descended the stairs. Luke walked to the back of the house and exited through the seldom-used wooden door. Pushing through the overgrowth surrounding the doorway, he quickened his steps, the family treasure now forgotten. A low moan spread throughout the house just as the moon was beginning to emerge from behind the clouds.

Luke sat on the barstool at Lolita's and drank his third cup of coffee, still nursing a throbbing headache.

"What are you doing here this time of day?" she asked crossly. When he didn't respond she asked, "How about a bowl of chili? I made it good and spicy," Lolita said proudly.

"Last time I ate your chili I was sick for three days."

"Jacobs, you're quite the kidder," she said laughing.

"Who's kidding?" he said gruffly. Luke picked up the cup, moved over three stools, and sat directly in front of Lolita. He watched her intently as she walked over and poured two cups of coffee for the young couple making eyes at each other in the corner booth. "What time is your shift finished, sweetie?" he asked when she returned.

"Six. Just in time to escape the breakfast crowd. Shouldn't matter to you, though. I told you I'm not seeing you again. You're not exactly the pride of Wakeegon, you know. You give my place a bad name."

Luke lifted his heavy eyes while giving her a look of distain. "You, too, Lolita? Thanks, I'll try not to darken your precious doorstep again." He threw a five dollar bill down on the coffee-stained countertop, picked it back up again, and added, "Charge me." Luke stood up, turned toward the door, swerved, and grabbed the back of the barstool.

"Hey, what's wrong?" asked Lolita, seeing his condition. "You've been drinking again, huh?" she added, disapprovingly.

He winced, rubbed the back of his head, and glared at her as he grabbed the handle of the door. Luke kicked at the parking lot stones with the toe of his boot as he walked back to his pickup. The early morning sky was dark from the approaching storm.

"Jacobs!" someone shouted behind him. Luke recognized the sheriff's surly voice.

"Sheriffff," he said mockingly.

"Where have you been?"

"Why?"

"I just came from the hospital. Your wife is in serious condition."

"I already know that, O'Connell."

"It's different now. Did you know she's in a coma?"

"How?" he asked indifferently.

"Why don't you tell me, Boy?"

"Forget it, O'Connell. You're not hanging this one on me. Lolita can testify that I was right here at the café."

"I'm not talking about today, son," O'Connell barked. "Where have you been since yesterday morning?"

Luke opened his mouth to speak.

"I'm taking you in for questioning for the injury of Sara Reynolds," he shouted over the thunder, "And, the possible involvement in the case of one missing Doctor Thorton."

CHAPTER 12

"Stevens, I told you to check last year's inventory. Didn't you hear anything I said yesterday?" Ray, the owner of the bait shop, grumbled, picked up the cracked oar, and threw it at the boy, just missing his foot. "We've got to keep the customers we already have. They won't come back renting this kind of junk," he said, giving the offending piece of wood a kick.

"Sorry," said the tall, gangly-looking teenager. "I'll try to be more careful."

"Try?" boomed Ray. "You'll do more than that if both of us want to keep our jobs. Check the other two boats and the equipment at the end of the pier before you leave today. And pick up that trash!" he added, pointing to the rubbish bobbing up and down on the water's edge.

Stevens turned toward the remaining craft, his shoulders sagging. The warm rays of the sun beat through the thin mesh material of his fishing hat. Small streams of perspiration began at his forehead, ran down to the tip of his nose, and dropped to the sand below. He wiped the sweat off his reddening face with the front of his T-shirt and grabbed the rake from the service cart. "Might as well be cool," Stevens said to the mallard watching him from the small inlet close to the pier. He passed by the dry, burned-out area close to the parking lot and walked over to the edge of the lake shaded by a huge sycamore tree.

Mud-covered cigarette butts were layered between decayed leaves and brown grass. A soggy brochure from last year's century celebration featuring the founding of Wakeegon drew a slight smile from his boyish face. He thought back to the night of the community dance and the date he had with Melinda. She sure was pretty, dressed up in a long pink gown with flowers in her hair. His mouth grew taut when he remembered the date didn't turn out quite as he had planned. Melinda ended up dancing with a new student from Groverton most of the evening. He had driven home alone and had sat on the steps in front of his house until dawn.

The grooves from his rake became deeper, his anger expelling unknown energy from his muscles. He walked around the tree and looked out at the inlet, the tranquility calming his internal frustrations. His right eye caught the reflection of a shiny rectangular object sticking out from underneath the shore remnants that had been left behind by the early morning boaters. Lying under a breakfast sandwich wrapper from a local burger joint was a silver-colored cell phone.

Stevens carefully picked it up, brushed it off and noticed it was still working. "Maybe if I call a few numbers, I'll find out who this belongs to," he mumbled. A busy signal, and then a recording followed his first dialing attempts. Stevens scrolled down to the recent dialing list, noticed a local number, and pushed the send button once again.

"Hello? Doc, is this you? Doc, where are you?" came an anxious voice over the phone.

"No. No, this is not Doc," he swallowed. "This is Andrew Stevens."

"Andrew who? Why are you calling on Doc's phone?" the woman interrupted in a high-pitched tone.

"I'm the summer help at Ray's Bait Shop. You know Ray's?"

"How did you get this phone? Why did you call this number? Who are you?" she rattled on.

"I'm Andrew Stevens, the summer help at Ray's Bait Shop! I was just cleaning up the trash down by the lake and found this phone. I called this number, hoping to find some information on the person who lost it, so I could return it to them," he informed the woman. "Who is this Doc you're talking about?"

"Doc Thorton!" she said, raising her voice. "Everyone has been looking for him. He's needed at the hospital. We thought something bad must have happened to him. He's been listed as missing. Please put him on the phone," she ended, her voice expressing her relief.

"Listen, lady! I said he's not here!" replied the boy. "I found the phone buried in the sand."

"The sand? Where are you again?"

Stevens groaned. When she heard no reply she said, "Wait! Ray's Pier, you say? I'll call the sheriff's office. They can come to you, okay?"

"I . . . I don't know," Stevens stuttered.

"You will wait, won't you?"

"Okay," said Stevens, his hands trembling. "I'll wait." He shivered slightly, wiping his hands on his shirt as he closed the phone. "I can't get into any more trouble," he whispered. "I need this job." He placed the phone in his pocket, walked to the narrow wooden pier, and sat down on the rough weathered boards.

Did the sheriff know about his dealings with another man in town? Stevens had met the man earlier in his teenage years and had done work for him before. He never intended to see him throw the camera into the lake. The five hundred dollars the man had offered him to keep quiet would help him get through the summer, since Ray had cut part of his wages when he caught him smoking on the grounds. Stevens paced up and down the waterfront until he saw the frowning bait shop owner walking toward him and the red lights of a patrol car flashing in the parking lot beyond.

O'Connell looked as if he would explode any minute, his face becoming bright crimson, as he gripped the sweaty collar of Luke's construction shirt. "Get in!" he shouted as he shoved the cursing man into the steamy backseat.

"What did I do? Can't a guy have a little breakfast?" asked Luke. "What's the matter, Sheriff? Thinking of the little woman? Oh, that's right, ex-woman!" he added, squirming on the hot material. "I'll have your hide for this, O'Connell!"

"Go ahead. Daddy's not here to get you out of this mess this time."

"Exactly what is this mess you're talking about? I've been a model citizen. I've even been visiting my sickly wife at the hospital."

"Hmpff!" answered the sheriff, looking over his shoulder. He eased the car off the road. "The Jacobs family wouldn't even know what a model citizen is," he threw back at Luke. "By the way, what exactly did you do to your sickly wife?" he paused. "Why do you want to get rid of her?" Luke opened his mouth in surprise but closed it again when O'Connell said, "Just keep your mouth shut until we arrive," as he jerked the car back onto the wet pavement.

Luke slid across the scratchy seat and glanced at the sheriff. O'Connell's face had become hardened with anger and emotion. What did he mean that

Sara was in a coma? And Doc? Missing? Could he trust Doc Thorton to keep quiet? Maybe he should have let the debt go. Luke closed his eyes until the sheriff pulled into the parking lot of the station. A small crowd had gathered at the bottom of the steps. A skinny young man with wiry orange hair ran up to him as he followed behind O'Connell.

"Mr. Jacobs! Mr. Jacobs!" said the man shoving a microphone in Luke's face. "Have you seen your wife since she's been in a coma? Did you talk to Doc Thorton before he disappeared?" he added, catching his breath before he reached the top step. Enraged, Luke surprised the man by grabbing his shoulders and pushing him up against the wet glass door. Undaunted, the eager reporter shoved the mike under his nose.

"And when . . .," he said in a rather loud voice for everyone to hear, ". . . were you planning to tell the people of Wakeegon, about the plans for the casino?"

Jack closed the door softly. His heart slowed to a steady beat. The emergency room doctors had stabilized Sara shortly after his arrival. They could not be sure of her condition when she awoke, they told Jack. She might remember nothing about the accident or the time prior to her coma or she might remember everything, even small details. "Details," said Jack, as he fingered the keys he had received that morning from the hospital administrator.

Inside the elevator, Jack withdrew the ring of keys from his pocket and looked for the one labeled Dr. Peter Thorton. Exiting, he reached into his other pocket and pulled out the handkerchief laced with cinnamon oil he had asked O'Connell to bring from his car. Placing it over his nose, Jack walked down the passage-way to the third door on the right, and inserted the key. A lamp cast a solemn hue on the well-worn desk covered with patient files, an unopened letter from Doc's sister, and a bag from Stan's Pharmacy containing chewing gum and a local betting paper. "It didn't look as if he planned to be away," Jack concluded.

Jack glanced at the picture of Doc's sister, walked over to the shelves of books, and fingered the one labeled "Addictions," lying on top of the others. Jack's eyes drifted toward the desk where a worn medical volume lay on one side. The wheels of the antique-looking chair squeaked, as Jack pulled it close to the oak desk. Jack sat down and reached for the book. Soiled pages beckoned the less familiar scholar where to start looking. Among the more frequently viewed chapters, were the ones that bore titles such as poison potions, poison plants, the effects of poison plants on the nervous system, and plants that induce comas. The last title was underlined. "Comas?" Was Doc researching the subject of comas before or after Sara fell into a coma? It couldn't have been after, thought Jack. Doc hadn't been seen since it happened.

Jack placed the book back on the desk and tried the remaining keys in the locked drawers. The top two were filled with old filing folders, paper clips, a half eaten cereal bar, and a couple of corroded AA batteries. The lock to the bottom drawer was rusted. Jack reached for the handle and the door sprang open, revealing a small flower-covered woman's journal that filled Jack's nostrils with a faint smell that reminded him of Sara. The featherlight handwriting was difficult to read until the last entry. In frail script it simply read, "I think Luke wants to kill me . . . please help me." It ended with the faded signature of Sara Jacobs.

Cramer reached for the crumbled calendar lying on the dashboard. Although the sun had faded this month's picture of a lone fisherman waiting for the morning's first catch, the black number twelve listed under the month of May stuck out like the bold lettering on an eye doctor's chart. He frowned as his eyes dropped down to the yellow highlighted number 25. Only thirteen more days left. Cramer leaned back into the car seat, flipped over the receipt from Dan's Donuts, and wrote the words, "things that need to be done," across the top. Would the town committee accept the proposal for a casino at Six Pines? He glanced out the window. This could be the Wakeegon's last chance to stay alive, or would it become like the depressing village he had driven through on vacation last year? He remembered the vacant store fronts, the row of dilapidated homes, and the forgotten playground with overgrown grass and one lone swing hanging by a single chain. It had made a lasting imprint on his mind. Dreary and desolate, the whole town looked as if a big wind would knock everything down, the final death blow of destruction.

The summer season at the lake had just begun. Cramer knew the financial woes of most of the shopkeepers would soon improve when the vacationer's returned to the lake in the month of June. As soon as the schools closed their doors, families would converge to the string of cottages lining the east side of the lake. Weekenders would spill over into the hotel, filling it to capacity. Campers would bring lawn chairs, fishing poles, and plenty of money to spend on everything from beach balls to ice cream cones.

Cramer rolled down his window, breathed in the cool air, and rubbed his eyes. He had been awake most of the night listening to the local news and radio talk shows. Murder, attempted murder, and missing people had consumed the open lines of the station. "Who in their right mind would want to vacation here?" a listener had asked.

Cramer reached over and turned the dial to WSAL. One-Eye, the colorful local newscaster, was just finishing the noon report. "And for the shocker of today, a local news reporter surprised businessman, Luke Jacobs, with questions involving the plans for a casino located at all places, Six Pines."

The lawyer sat up, turned up the volume, and rested his head against the steering wheel. "Luke Jacobs, local entrepreneur and business man, was put on the spot today when asked about plans for a casino to be located on the property of the late Mrs. Joseph Reynolds. It was stated that the reporter was shoved back against the wall by Luke Jacobs, who was placed under arrest for assault by Sheriff O'Connell. Jacobs had been taken in earlier for questioning concerning the accident and injury of his wife, Sara Jacobs, and the disappearance of Dr. Peter Thorton."

"Cripes!" said Cramer hitting the steering wheel with both hands. "Now what? This deal has to go through. I've spent most of my savings, although," he added, reaching for his phone, his voice becoming louder, "I should have inherited half the Jacobs inheritance after the old man died. Hello?" he shouted into the phone. "Pierceton? What's going on? Who found out about the papers for the licensing of the casino? What happened to your planned announcement next week?" Cramer finished, without giving him a chance to answer.

"Sorry, Cramer," was all the man said.

"Sorry? Sorry? I'll have your head!"

"I don't know what happened," stuttered the man on the other end of the phone. "Someone at the state department must have leaked the information."

"It was a local reporter!" Cramer yelled into the phone. Exhausted, he hung up and dialed Alistair Locke, who headed the legalities for the proposed casino.

"Hello," said a man with a weary voice.

"Locke? You sound funny," inquired Cramer. "Have you heard the local news?"

"Local? Local?" Locke repeated. "The whole story was on the national news, along with the murder of Hudson! He was state employed, remember? They said something about a small town with a dark secret, hitting the big time."

"I've invested most of my money on this project! It has to go through!"

"Listen, Cramer, they're looking for the man who killed Hudson. Someone will get caught and it won't be me," Locke said.

"What's that supposed to mean? Are you suggesting that I killed him?" asked Cramer. He paused then asked meekly. "You will follow through with our deal, right?"

"There is no deal, Cramer."

"If you find the papers that I need to prove that half of the Jacobs fortune is mine, you will become a rich man," reminded Cramer.

"I'm filthy rich already," laughed Locke. "The old man paid me well," he added, hanging up the phone.

"Jerk!" remarked Cramer, slamming his phone shut. "Well, at least one good thing happened. Things should go a little easier with Sara out of the way." He placed his hand over his fluttering heart. Sara's continual kindness toward him tugged on his inner self. Could it be guilt that he was feeling?

Cramer's eyes followed the tinted glass as he rolled up the car window. He continued to stare out the window and without turning his head, laid his phone on the opposite seat, and stared directly into the sheriff's eyes. O'Connell smiled, and motioned for him to roll down the window. How much of the conversation had the sheriff heard between himself and Locke? Cramer wondered.

CHAPTER 13

"Hey, could you slow down?" asked O'Connell later that day, as he limped down the corridor of the station, still nursing his knee. "Don't let your feelings for Sara override your common sense, young friend."

Jack poked his face around the worn metal door leading to the office. "I don't know what you mean?" he asked, as he began filing the interviews from yesterday. When the sheriff didn't respond Jack said, "I have a long list of questions for the infamous Mr. Jacobs. To tell you the truth, Sheriff, I'm sick and tired of people like him making life miserable for everyone and getting away with it. I'm not afraid of him," Jack added.

The sheriff knew Jack was under pressure. Twice, O'Connell had been pulled aside by the team of men hired by the state to investigate the murder of Frederick Hudson. "Why are you paying a private eye to do your work?" asked one gentleman. O'Connell explained that Jack was a good friend who was recovering from a painful past. The sheriff also knew the men investigating Hudson's murder were not any further along in their search for the killer. Mentioning the fact that Jack had more training than the entire force put together would have made them more agitated. "He's not getting paid a cent by the town," he reassured the men.

Although Jack was interested in the murder of Hudson, he had been called in to investigate the accident involving Sara. A cut brake line was no little matter. Not in a small town where almost everyone called each other by their first name. "And now," the sheriff thought, "I can add the missing Doctor Thorton to the list of investigations."

O'Connell glanced out the window, noticed the beer cans that had been deposited in the flower pots in front of the station, and sighed. He walked outside, collected the containers, and threw them in the trash bin located along the street. The Wakeegon sheriff's station looked much like the other structures in town. Cleanliness was executed to cover up the unsightly appearance of the building. The sidewalks were swept clean, and the trash was picked up daily around the parking lot and lawn. O'Connell had even asked the local garden club to plant a row of red petunias along the front entrance.

The sun was already at the imaginary mid-afternoon spot in the sky when Jack closed the door of the office. The two men walked down the hall that contained four identical cells made of thick cement walls, iron bars, and an antiquated key and lock system. The soles of their shoes echoed throughout the sterile concrete surfaces.

"O'Connell!" burst an angry voice from the last cell. "You can't keep me here overnight." Luke Jacobs stuck his face close to the metal bars, his nose protruding through the small opening. His eyes were heavy and bloodshot, and his late afternoon beard cast a faint shadow across his chin.

"Who said I was?" said O'Connell gruffly. "Just wanted to make sure I could find you. You're lucky that the reporter decided not to file a case against you, though I do admit it's nice to see you behind bars, even if for a little while," he added smiling.

"What's he doing here?" asked Luke, pointing to Jack standing behind the sheriff. "Find time to leave my wife's bedside, Wilder?"

Jack pushed past O'Connell and grabbed Luke's damp shirtsleeve that was sticking out between the bars of the cell. "Shut up, Jacobs!" said Jack. "You better keep your mouth closed! And speaking of your wife's bedside, you don't seem too overwrought over what has happened to her!"

"I tried to get one of the sheriff's footmen to make a call to the hospital for me, but they said it wasn't allowed unless the sheriff okayed it," Luke added, bowing toward O'Connell.

O'Connell ignored the gesture, unlocked the door and pointed to the right. "In that room, Jacobs, then we'll see about bail."

"Bail?" shouted Luke. "You're assuming that I'm guilty of something, but I'm not!" he said, his face close enough to O'Connell's that the sheriff could feel his breath.

"Get in the room!" yelled the sheriff. O'Connell's familiar flush was beginning to ride up his neck and had already begun to spread over his cheeks, the bright color contrasting with his white teeth. Luke, defeated for the moment, turned and walked through the doorway of room two and sat down on a folding chair that faced the table.

"Holy cow, O'Connell! Remind me never to make you angry with me," added Jack, as he stood in the alleyway. The sheriff looked slightly embarrassed as he patted Jack on the back. Jack stepped aside to allow his friend to enter the room first. He followed the sheriff, closing the door with a bang that echoed throughout the station.

Cramer held the cigarette stub tightly between his trembling lips to keep it from falling to the ground. He leaned back into the car seat, took a final puff, and tossed it out the window. A breeze was beginning to pick up. The air felt cool and comforting. "He didn't hear anything," said Cramer out loud, trying to reassure himself. "Sheriff O'Connell didn't hear one word between me and Locke. He just wanted to ask me how old man Jacobs's estate was progressing."

Alistair Locke, the Jacobs family's right-hand man, had laughed when Cramer first insisted that half of the elderly Jacobs fortune rightfully belonged to him. "You'll never get any of it," he had said.

"The old man promised my mother," Cramer had argued.

"Try to prove that," the deceased man's older, business partner laughed. "You have no documentation."

"Why have you always been against me, Locke? I practically grew up with the man's son. You never acknowledged that my mother was married to the old man."

"Samuel married your mother out of pity, boy. He had no feelings for you or her."

"Maybe not. But I'll find a way to get my share of the estate," said Cramer. "I'll search every inch of the house until I find some records or something."

"Give it up, boy. You had better watch your step around Luke. You better not let him catch you looking through his father's things," said the slightly bald-headed man. "He'll not think twice about getting rid of you."

The temperature gauge inside the police station registered 87 degrees. Luke rolled up the sleeves of his blue logoed work shirt, "Did you forget to pay the electric bill, O'Connell?"

"Shut up, Luke," replied the sheriff. O'Connell laid the folders containing the paperwork from the three investigations - Sara's accident, the death of Frederick Hudson, and the disappearance of Doc Thorton - on the table between them.

"Hey," said Luke, pointing to the newspaper clips. "This has been great for publicity. Makes people curious enough to want to see the famous site of the new casino. Good for business, you know," he added with a smile.

Jack sat across the table, his eyes boring into the flesh of Luke's face. What had happened to make Luke so hardened and cruel? Sara said that Luke had a soft side to him at one time. Did the tenderness come from the influence of his mother, before she passed away at an early age? he wondered. Jack had heard tales about Samuel Jacobs. "Beat his wife and child," said Mr. Riley, who had owned the pharmacy for more than thirty years, when he was questioned by Jack. "She came in with a black eye once and asked for pain medicine for the child. Could see his leg and arm were bruised and swollen. She swore he fell from an apple tree while playing in the orchard, and when she tried to pick him up he accidentally kicked her in the eye. Called the police station twice, I did, but nothing came of it, you know, with the local corruption of the sheriff's department at that time. Sheriff O'Connell, he sure changed that," he had added with a nod of his head.

"What are you looking at, Wilder?" asked Jacobs, returning the stare.

O'Connell pulled out the chair from the other side of the table and sat down, expelling a loud "Ompff!" from his mouth. Luke gave him a look of distain and hid his curling smile from the sheriff with a swipe of his hand across his face. Oblivious, O'Connell said, "Listen, Jacobs, I want it understood that you'll be respectful of Mr. Wilder and me while you are under questioning or you'll be spending the night right here. Do you hear me, Boy?"

"I have ears, O'Connell. I have no intention of spending a night in this dump," he replied, looking around. "But, I'm telling you, I had nothing to do with Sara's accident or," he paused, "the condition she is in now."

"What were you doing in Lolita's restaurant so early in the morning?" questioned the sheriff.

"I was out for an early breakfast. Later, I planned on doing a little fishing. This is a fishing town, Sheriff," he added.

"Why wasn't there any fishing equipment in your truck?"

"I planned on eating first, then stopping by the house to pick up my pole and gear," said Luke.

"Why didn't you just take it with you in the first place?" asked the sheriff.

"I forgot. Anyway, it wasn't really that early to eat breakfast, O'Connell. That's why there are restaurants that stay open 24 hours. Not everyone goes to bed at nine o'clock at night like you, Sheriff."

"So, where were you all day yesterday?" asked O'Connell, ignoring the man's remark. "Your wife was in a life or death situation. Her mother tried to phone you, but there was no answer."

Luke rubbed the back of head. "I do have a life, Sheriff. And someone has to earn money to pay for all of the little woman's medical bills. Is that a crime?"

"Just the fact that no one could find you. You never showed up at the job location you were scheduled for yesterday."

"Sheriff, you're looking for a lawsuit to be dropped on your lap. Who was in my office? You Wilder?" he asked turning toward Jack.

"Your crew was worried about you. They called Sara's mother first, then she called the station," said Jack, who was fidgeting on his chair, eager to question Luke. He looked over at the sheriff, who nodded at him.

"So, Jacobs," began Jack, "tell me about this casino you're planning."

"What's to tell? It's all on the up and up. Anyway, it isn't any of your business," he added smugly. "An upright man like you wouldn't be interested in a house of evil now, would you?"

Jack stood up abruptly, upsetting his chair. He leaned over, picked it up, setting it upright with such force that it banged loudly against the side of the table.

"Easy, buddy," said the sheriff.

"Does Sara know?" asked Jack.

"Know what, Wilder?" asked Luke.

Jack walked around the table and stood behind the young Jacobs. "Exactly how were you planning to get the Reynolds' property for your own use? Did you plan to get rid of her so the deal would go smoothly?"

"I had nothing to do with her accident, I tell you. She has always been sickly and whiny. I've spent half my wages trying to help her."

"So, did you cut the brake line? Or did you hire someone?"

Luke rose and faced Jack. "Sheriff, I refuse to answer this man. If you want me to answer any more of his absurd questions, he will have to ask them in front of my attorney. Besides, why would I want to kill my own wife?"

"Maybe you know something we don't," said Jack. "Is it just the casino, or is there something else you're after?"

CHAPTER 14

The short, rotund man cried out as his head came in contact with the low beam overhead. He rubbed the swollen area with the back of his dirt-caked hand as he sorted through the black trash bag one more time. The growling from his stomach grew louder as he dug deeper. He used his free hand to pinch his nose, as the stench from the rotted food was released from its holding place. Frustrated and ravenous, he turned the bag upside down, emptying the contents on the litter-covered floor. Finding nothing to appease his hunger, he leaned against the cobweb-covered wall, his heart beating faster and faster. He would have to leave the room once more.

He remembered the time when the old lady had brought him food. He wanted to go with her, out of this room to the other parts of the house, but she continually told him no. She would try to appease him by leaving two pieces of Nuville chocolate on the wooden floor. When he rose to retrieve the delicacies, she would slowly back out of the room, wearing the same slight smile that had always frightened him. One morning, when she did not arrive with his breakfast, he had gone looking for her. Cautiously, he had searched the house, listening for any signs of her presence.

He had found her slumped over the kitchen table, her mouth wide open with an expression of surprise. Even with his feeble mind, he knew something wasn't right. Throughout the day, he would return and shake her softly. Eventually, still receiving no response, he finished the leftover toast, jelly, cereal, and coffee that had been untouched. Except for the eggs. He didn't like the way they felt in his mouth. When she failed to awake he devoured everything edible in the refrigerator, grabbed the canned goods and boxes of food, and took everything to his room in the attic.

James liked to roam around the other areas of the house. At night, he had stretched out on the velvet sofas and had slept in the soft, plush beds. Once a day, and sometimes twice a day, he would fill the bathtub with water, jumping and splashing until he was covered with goosebumps. Then, one day, they came and took her away, and things were never quite the same anymore. "People come now," he thought. "They scare me." So, he stayed in his little room once more.

His soft protruding belly growled louder this time. He reached down and rubbed it gently. Sticking his feet into his mud-covered shoes, he pulled on a worn straw hat given to him by Jingles, the deceased gardener of the Reynolds homestead, and placed it over his long, matted hair. It was almost dark when he headed out into the night with a plastic bag tucked under his arm.

"You have no right to stick your nose into my business affairs, O'Connell!" shouted Luke, loud enough to be heard outside the interrogation room.

"Listen, Jacobs!" O'Connell shouted back, "I have every right to know what you've been up to!" Luke leered at the determined face of the sheriff. O'Connell looked him in the eyes and said calmly, "I'm not afraid of you."

"You come after me, now that my father's gone, huh, Sheriff?"

O'Connell reached for his coffee mug, declining to spout back another quip to the mouthy man.

Jack asked, "Luke, just tell us where you've been lately."

"Haven't you been listening, Wilder? I was working to support my family. I'm also trying to finish my boat. You know, to get it ready for the fishing season? Took it out for a spin around the lake. Never caught anything though."

"Have you learned to walk on water?" asked Jack. "Ray from the bait shop said that you haven't taken your boat out for a couple of weeks."

"Well, maybe I went with a friend. Besides, you don't need a boat to go fishing, Wilder. The shores are nice and calm in the early morning hours. Oh," he added, "I seem to forget you're a city boy. Probably never fished in your life, right? Heard you don't eat meat. Some people around here might call that strange," he said, turning his grinning face away from the men.

Jack shifted in his chair. "Since when do you have any friends, Jacobs? I mean, other than the kind that owe you money?" He leaned toward Luke. "When was the last time you visited your wife at the hospital?"

"I don't know," answered Jacobs, pushing his chair away from the table. "She has her mother. She's always there. She never leaves."

"Someone needs to care for her," said Jack.

"You're doing a good job of that, aren't you, Wilder?" shot back Luke.

Jack shifted in his chair and pretended to concentrate on the notes in the green folder he had taken from the filing cabinet that morning. He could feel the warmth creep across his cheeks. Jack knew his feelings for Sara were growing stronger than he liked.

"Jack, why don't you let me finish the interrogation?" asked the sheriff, looking concerned about his young friend.

"I'm fine," answered Jack. "I have a couple more things I want to ask." Jack stared at the man across the table. Luke was leaning back on his chair, supporting himself on its two back legs. Jack resisted an urge to give Jacobs a little shove. Instead, he asked, "Now, tell us where you were the last two days?"

"I told you twice."

"Okay. So, you were going fishing, working on your boat, and boating with a friend. Will your friend vouch for you? Are there any other witnesses?" asked Jack.

"Sure. Me and probably every other fishermen who was out in a boat that morning! How am I supposed to know who saw me?"

"What about your friend?"

"I said I might have been out with a friend."

Jack cleared his throat and stood up, "One last question. When was the last time you saw Doc Thorton?"

"That quack? Who knows where he is? He's crazy and incompetent! Ought to be put away for malpractice! He probably put Sara into that coma. Now, let me out of here, Wilder, and I'll tend to her myself."

"O'Connell, he's all yours," Jack said in exasperation.

The sheriff stood up and motioned Jack to join him in the hallway. Jack spoke first. "We have nothing to hold him on."

"Doggone!" said O'Connell, "Why does someone like him always seem to weasel out of everything? We need some really solid evidence. That kid," he added, "the one who found Doc's cell phone? He seemed really frightened when he was questioned at the scene. Ray said he had been in trouble for something a while back."

"I'll keep an eye on him," said Jack. Weary, he stuck his head around the door. "Take off, Jacobs, but stay around town."

Luke, fidgeting in his chair, stood up and smiled. "Sheriff, when will you learn you can't beat a Jacobs?"

"Get out!" yelled O'Connell. Jack looked at his friend in amazement. The sheriff straightened up, pulled his trousers from their sagging position, and walked past him with a smile.

"O'Connell, wait for me," said Jack, as he picked up the sheriff's empty coffee cup along with the bulging files.

"Sure," responded the sheriff.

Jack took long strides to catch up with his friend. "Hey," he asked. "What's happened to you?"

"What do you mean, Son?"

"Come on old friend. What's going on?"

Jack stared at his friend until O'Connell said, "I think we're after the wrong man."

Jack followed him into his office. "The wrong man? Luke doesn't have any solid alibi, but I admit that he gave all the right answers for someone under the gun."

"That's the problem. He didn't seem too nervous about the possibility of being charged for his wife's accident," said O'Connell turning from the filing cabinet, his face flushed. "A man called and gave an alibi for Jacobs. Claims he dropped Luke off at the worksite the day of Sara's accident, drunk as a skunk. The guy said he left him in the construction trailer to sleep it off and drove him home later that night. It seems Jacobs had driven his wife's car to the repair shop that day. Told everyone he wanted to get some new tires or something for it. Did you notice if the car he was driving had new tires, Jack?"

"No. Guess we should check it out. Where was his black pickup?"

"One of the guys backed into it with a dozer. It had been in the shop all week."

"He could have cut the brake cable of his own vehicle before he left for work that day."

"Doesn't fly, Son," said the sheriff. "Witnesses say Sara took Luke's vehicle out shopping all morning and returned home early afternoon. One lady swears she saw a cable repair van turn onto the road leading to Sara's cottage. Maybe Sara was waiting for an afternoon appointment with him."

"He could have gone to the old man's house."

"That old miser? He would never have cable. Old man Jacobs would never have spent money on anything that could be associated with fun."

"I'll check out those stories," answered Jack. He followed O'Connell to a large picture window, the only source of natural light in the dingy building.

"Looks like trouble this weekend," remarked the sheriff.

"Why do you say that?" asked Jack.

"Well, it's official. This confirms the notice I received this morning." O'Connell handed Jack the front page of the Wakeegon Weekender Review. "Look at this article: *Higher Lake Levels Pose Threat to Boaters*. It says here that last month the lake level was dangerously low. Now, with all this rain, it has risen to an all time high. See this? It recommends that the lake residents make sure everything is secure. It seems that a lot of things start floating away, including boats, piers, and jet skis. Any empty watercraft found floating in the lake will be considered abandoned. In that case, authorities will be looking for victims. Great!" he added. "There go my vacation days!" O'Connell wadded up the offending paper and tossed it in the trash basket.

An elderly man in a soiled white doctor's coat awoke to the shouting of the scruffy looking stranger beside him. "Hey! Hey, old man! Wake up! Are you okay?" the stranger yelled as he shook the man's shoulders. The man's bent wire glasses fell from his pointed nose onto his lap.

"Okay?" asked the man in the white coat, retrieving his spectacles. "Why wouldn't I be okay?"

"You were mumbling about someone named Sara, in your sleep. You kept repeating over and over that you were sorry."

"Sara? I don't know anyone named Sara."

"Maybe you were dreaming about a TV show you were watching last night. You were up pretty late. Me? I couldn't sleep, either." The man in the white coat scooted closer to the window. "I thought the beds were hard and the sheets smelled funny," continued the stranger. "Hey, by the way, how much do you have left?"

"Left?"

"Money, old man, money. The car doesn't run on fumes, you know," the stranger added.

The elderly man fingered the bills in his pocket before withdrawing them.

"Fifty dollars!" exclaimed the stranger. "Just enough to make it to the Keys. My uncle will help us out once we get there. He's a big wig at some research center. On the side, he has the busiest lawn care business in the Isles. He'll hire us on the spot." The stranger looked at his travel partner's hands. "Exactly what did you do to make money? Your hands look like they never saw a day of work." The tired looking man, wearing the uniform of a doctor, had the same blank look on his face that he had worn at the start of the conversation. "Do you have any identification? I know my brother will want to see something," added the stranger

"Nothing," responded the man in the white coat, his hands trembling as he emptied his pockets. He pulled out a torn piece of paper with a small picture of a hospital in the upper corner. A phone number was scribbled across the bottom, but the last three digits were smeared with spilled coffee.

"What's your name again?" asked the stranger.

The man placed the paper back in his pocket. "Jacobs," he said quietly. "Luke Jacobs."

CHAPTER 15

Jack parked his vintage car in the parking lot closest to the entrance of the hospital. The cinnamon-scented handkerchief was still in his front shirt pocket. He reached for it, placed it over his nose, took in a big breath and entered the building. He still needed to talk to Sara's mother about her daughter's accident and her current condition. How long would Sara be in a coma? Would she ever come out of it? He couldn't stand the possibility that she could die. Could her mother supply more information than the police records provided? Exiting the elevator, Jack stopped abruptly. The hallway was empty and dimly lit. Voices could be heard coming from the room.

"Hi," said a man with a faint whisper. "I . . . want you . . . get better."

As Jack neared the doorway to Sara's room, he heard her reply with a weak voice, "Thank you. What a kind thing to say. What is your name?"

"James Irwin," he replied.

"Thank you, James Irwin," she said.

Jack burst into the room. "Sara, you're awake! Why didn't they call me?" He narrowed his eyes to get a look at the pudgy man standing at the end of Sara's bed. The sudden appearance of Jack caused the man to turn around. Even in the faded light, Jack could sense the stranger's fear. The man wanted to run, but the doorway was blocked with Jack's body. Feeling trapped, the man backed into a corner and hid his face.

"Wait," said Jack. "I'm not going to hurt you. Come over here so I can see you." When the man did not respond, Jack walked over and turned on the lights. In the brightness of the room, Sara took a good look at the stout little man and screamed. The stranger squealed, pushed Jack back against the door frame, and disappeared down the corridor.

Jack turned to chase after him but succumbed to Sara's cry. He rushed toward the bed and leaned over, encasing her quivering body in his arms. "Sara! What's wrong? Why are you screaming?"

Sara stopped long enough to say, "My father! My father!" as she pointed toward the doorway.

"What about your father, Sara?"

"It's him," she said in disbelief, pointing to the disappearing figure. "But, he . . . he died two years ago." Jack reached for his phone, silently walked over to the door, and pulled it shut.

Peg ran the comb through her newly washed hair. She could hear her cell phone ringing at the bottom of her tote bag. Unable to retrieve it, she dumped the bag's entire contents on the bed.

"Hello?" Peg said out of breath.

"Mrs. Reynolds?" a man's voice asked.

"Yes?" she replied.

"This is Jack Wilder. The private detective hired by O'Connell. I'm here at the hospital with your daughter."

"What's happened?" she asked nervously. "Please don't say that . . .," she added, stifling a sob.

"No, no! Quite the contrary," said Jack. "She wants to talk to you."

"Mom?" said Sara into the phone with a weak voice.

"Sara? Tell me this is true! Is it really you?"

"Mom," Sara said with a soft laugh. "This is really me. I love you," she added.

"Mrs. Reynolds? Jack again. Could you come down to the hospital right away? We believe that Sara may be in danger. Meet me in Doc's office. I'll tell you about it there. Don't worry!" he responded, "Floor security will stay with Sara. You can see her as soon as we are finished. Mrs. Reynolds?" asked Jack into the silent phone. Peg was already backing the car out of the driveway.

Sheriff O'Connell placed the last sheet of information back into the file. Frederick Hudson, 36. Cause of death: a blow to the back of the head with a heavy object. Wood fiber found in the victim's hair. Assumed object, a tree branch with the deceased man's hair embedded in the bark, found at the site of the murder. Time of death, 6:35 a.m. Cripes, thought O'Connell, that's just a short time before Jack's appearance on the scene that morning. Footprints, not shoeprints, found at the sight, size thirteen or fourteen. Crooked toe on left foot. Victim carrying a water-testing kit in his right vest pocket, parts missing. Special note to sheriff: No camera was found at the murder site. Please fax detailed information to Jack Wilder.

"Holy cow!" said O'Connell to the receptionist, engrossed in her own work. "Thank goodness Jack didn't end up like Hudson. Now, here's the big question. Why was Hudson roaming the grounds of the mansion? And why was he carrying of all things, a water testing kit minus the vials?"

The smell of body odor and decayed food filled the small attic room in the upper level of the old house. James Irwin Reynolds rubbed the sleep from his eyes, and blinked from the brightness of the morning sun. He crawled over to the corner of the room that held his cherished treasures. Small pieces of green glass and an assortment of smooth stones were placed around a small, worn, stuffed bear, whose only attribute was one green glass eye that reflected the rays shining through the upper turret window. James reached for the stained brown bundle of fur and placed it under his chin. He climbed back under the covers, his stomach growling. Groaning, he rose and shuffled over to the small pile of clothes in the dusty corner. He shook a few dead spiders off the soiled, orange baseball cap, he had found in one of the town's dumpsters on his last visit to see Sara. He placed it on his head and looked into the cracked mirror. He liked Sara. "She's pretty," he thought.

James walked over to the makeshift bed on the floor covered with mouse hairs, and picked up a dingy looking pillow. Under the pillow was an edition of the Wakeegon News with the headlines reading: "Local Member of the Reynolds Family Hospitalized. Case is under suspicion by local authorities." James sounded out each word slowly and diligently, just like the gardener had taught him long ago. He had spent many hours with the kindly old gentleman who had watched out for him. After the man had died, James continued to keep the flourishing garden free of weeds.

James tucked the newspaper in his bag along with a slightly bruised apple, pulled on his fishermen's boots, and set out to visit his relative once more. He stopped by his treasure corner and picked up two foiled delicacies lying across a soiled ivory file cover. He was glad that the local grocer gave him a whole bag of his favorite candy when he saw the wishful eyes staring at him through the store's window. Sara would be sure to like him if he gave her two more of his prized possessions.

Outside the large Victorian home belonging to the deceased, old-man Jacobs, Cramer laid the metal pick underneath the lower branch of the shrub and covered it with mulch. He wiped the sweat from his hands on the back of his pants and removed a pair of thin vinyl gloves from his front shirt pocket. His hands shook as he pulled the gloves over his clammy skin. He gave one last backward glance at the little cottage house located on the corner of the Jacobs estate. The windows were darkened, and the driveway was vacant. "Good" he thought, "Luke is still out for the day." Cramer turned the heavy brass knob, sighed, and drew in a deep breath of stale air. "Phew!" he complained out loud. "Smells like the old man." Samuel Jacobs had always smelled of moth balls and outdated, rancid hair tonic. "Probably never threw anything away, the old miser," thought Cramer. "Well," he whispered, "I'm glad you never spent any of the family money because now I'm going to get the share of it that you promised my mother long ago."

Even in the dark he knew the layout of the house by heart. He walked cautiously from room to room, the dark shadows of the deceased man's possessions revealing the inner soul of its former owner. Cramer took a look at the painting over the mantle. "That picture alone could set me up for the rest of my life," he estimated. He walked over to the large rolled-top desk and sat down on the scratchy horse-hair stuffed sofa. Cramer could still picture the old man. Samuel Jacobs had sported a tuft of stark white hair atop a tanned head. His usual wardrobe at home was a faded blue plaid bathrobe, thread-bared at the elbows. "Got a robe, don't need a new one," he had said. "A pitiful waste of good money," he said to those who stared questionably at his apparel.

Cramer had parked his car at Ray's Bait Shop and walked the trails that led past the back of the house. The sunlight was beginning to dwindle. A flashlight beam would surely be spotted by the younger Jacobs or the town gossips. "That stupid O'Connell always has his nose in everyone's business," he said out loud. Cramer began to hurriedly search the long bookcase that encompassed an entire wall of the large study. The value of some of these books alone could fund his bank account for a long time, he mused. He was looking for anything that seemed out of place. "The old man kept meticulous order of his possessions, except for his son," Cramer thought shaking his head. He shoved the rolling ladder to the left top corner of the wall of shelving and proceeded to climb to the top.

Samuel had always valued the family book collection. It was the one possession he refused to let close friends or family members touch. When Cramer was in college, the elder Jacobs had obtained a first edition of the book, *Pride and Prejudice,* but refused to let Cramer even touch its cover. "These books are for me to read, and for you to just look at from a distance, Boy," he had said.

"This time, not only will I look at them, but I'll touch each one from cover to cover," Cramer said aloud to the empty room as though the old man was sitting at his desk. Special editions, early editions, and limited editions filled the upper glass-enclosed shelf.

Cramer opened the wood-trimmed glass door, leafed through the first few volumes, and was mesmerized by the rich textured leather fronts, gold lettering, and the fine-sheathed paper between the covers. He flipped through the pages, placed each volume back in its proper place, and reached for the next. Cramer squinted at the print type and glanced over his shoulder. It was getting late. In dismay, he saw that he had only scanned the first fifteen books or so in the last hour. "I have time for one more," he thought, noting the length of the interior shadows. Cramer reached up and grasped the next book. As he placed it on the top ledge of the ladder, it rattled. His mouth drew into a wide smile.

CHAPTER 16

Peg pulled into the hospital emergency entrance, jumped out of her car, and pointed to the upper hospital floor. "Sara's awake!" she said elatedly to the security guard, her heart pounding rapidly. Disappearing into the revolving door, she never noticed his puzzled look. The past few weeks had filled Peg with overwhelming anxiety regarding her daughter's recovery. What about Sara's coma? she wondered. How had it happened? Did Jack know? Was that why they were meeting in secret? Peg got off at the fifth floor and followed the signs to Doc's office. A fleck of light was glowing through the frosted glass. "Jack? It's me, Peg," she said quietly. She slowly pushed the door open and stared at the dark figure carrying the small flashlight. "Oh, no!" she whispered, as the figure raised his arm and plummeted her into darkness.

Jack hurried to the nurse's desk to request a security guard to stay with Sara. After everything was arranged, he called O'Connell. O'Connell answered the phone with his usual monotone. "Sheriff? Jack, here. I need you at the hospital. Sara's awake! I know! Isn't it great?" Jack paused, "Can you come here right away? I still have this feeling she is in great danger. No sirens please. Let's keep this between us, okay?" He hung up as O'Connell assured him he would leave the police station within a few minutes. Jack stood outside Sara's door until he saw the dark blue uniforms of the security guards who were rounding the corner. "In here," he pointed to Sara's room. "Don't leave until I return."

Jack ran down the corridor to Doc's office. "I wonder if Sara's mother has beaten me here." He could smell the same violet-flowered perfume that had been present in Sara's room. "She has already arrived," said Jack softly,

104

"and has probably broken every rule on the road getting here," he added. The door to Doc's office stood open. "How did she get in? I'm the only one with the key." As he cautiously entered the room, he tripped over something soft and large lying across the floor. Groping for the light switch, he covered his nose with his hand and let out a muffled moan, as the bright light of the room exposed the body of Peg Reynolds. Her petite, still figure was laying face down, a thin trail of blood running down the back of her head.

"Mrs. Reynolds! Peg!" shouted Jack, as he carefully turned her over on her back. A faint groan escaped her lips before she grew deathly still. "No!" shouted Jack. "Sara can't take anymore! Not her mother, too!" he pleaded aloud, his face turned upward. He reached for his phone to call Sheriff O'Connell. "John! Are you on your way to the hospital?"

Taken aback by Jack's use of his first name, the sheriff said, "Sure am, Son. Sorry I'm late. Had a last minute phone call. Are you with Sara?"

"I'm with Sara's mom. She's been hurt. She was hit on the back of the head when she surprised someone in Doc's office. Please don't let Sara know."

"Ok, Jack. Holy cow! This is starting to sound like those murder mysteries my ex-wife used to read! Be there soon. Fifth Floor?"

Jack called the local emergency number and bent over to talk to the unconscious woman, all the while praying that she would wake up. The emergency crew arrived a few seconds before O'Connell stepped into the room. "We thought someone was making a crank call," said the group of paramedics. "We never get a call from inside the hospital for an emergency run." Within minutes they had Mrs. Reynolds stabilized, strapped to the board, and on her way downstairs.

"Well, I'll be," said O'Connell. "This case never ceases to amaze me, Jack. You felt that Sara was in danger and now we can add her mother to the list, too."

"I don't think Peg was on a list, Sheriff. I think this was just a case of being in the wrong place at the wrong time," said Jack to O'Connell, who was standing just outside the door. Jack glanced around the room. He was reaching for the light switch when he stopped. The bottom drawer of Doc's desk stood open. Someone had taken the flowered-covered notebook.

Lolita flashed Luke a frown and brushed past him quickly, muttering something that sounded like, "Scum of the earth," through her clenched teeth.

"You too, Lolita?" he asked spinning himself around on the red-padded stool. "You'll be sorry that you didn't pay more attention to me, missy," he added. "Yep, you'll be sorry." He stepped down from the stool's platform, swayed, and caught himself on the metal railing.

"Get him out of here, Tony!" said Lolita. "I don't want my name associated with someone like him."

Tony led Luke to the side entrance without a struggle. "Get going, fellow!" he said gruffly, giving Luke a shove. "A pity and a shame," he added, as he opened the door to return to the restaurant dining room.

Luke sat down on the cement walk. His stomach churned at the sight of the strewn cigarette butts littering the pavement. Luke's heart tightened with fear like it always did around anything associated with fire. His thoughts returned to the death of his childhood dog, Baxter, his failed attempts to save him, and the loss his family suffered that tragic evening when he was just a young boy. Gone were the horses and the large red barn. He would never forget the remark his father had made as they pulled the remains of the animals from the pile of rubble. "Get over it, Boy," he had said. "It won't be the worst thing that happens to you in life," he had added over his shoulder, crushing the young boy's heart.

Luke shook his head, walked toward the black pickup truck, opened the back door, and lay across the seat. His mind wandered back to the Reynolds family treasure. "Where could it be? Sara must know more than she is letting on," he muttered, as he began to snore softly, asleep in the warmth of the sun.

Jack and O'Connell waited until the paramedics took Peg to the emergency room. Both men followed behind them, conferring with one another. "I don't know, Jack," said the sheriff. "You may be right that it was just a fluke, Peg being there at that moment. But, after all that's been happening?"

Both of the men stayed close by the room until the crew announced that Mrs. Reynolds was out of danger. "Can't question her until tomorrow, though," they added. The disgruntled sheriff and the tired detective made plans to meet early the next day.

"They have two of the best men watching over Sara tonight. Don't worry," O'Connell added, as he walked toward the squad car parked directly in front of the entrance.

"Sheriff, before you go," interrupted Jack, "do you remember that you were going to tell me what you found out about that cable company van? The one that was seen turning into the Reynolds property?"

"Couldn't find any company belonging to that name. We're checking fingerprints and footprints leading to the house. Tire treads indicate an early retired model. White, the witness said. The lettering could have been applied that morning. We're checking anything that fits that description around the area. I'll let you know everything I find out, Jack."

Jack nodded. When the sheriff was out of sight, Jack walked back into the hospital. "You're right about one thing, friend," he whispered. "There have been a lot of fishy things going on in this town lately. I don't feel secure about leaving Sara." Arriving at her floor, Jack ordered a pillow and a cot from the head nurse. Placing a call to the cafeteria, he ordered three dinners delivered to room 504, ignoring the glaring eyes of the two guards.

Cramer looked around Samuel's office and opened up the hollowed-out book. He surveyed the contents, stuffed them into his corduroy jacket, and placed the book back into its original spot. He fingered the key without removing it from his pocket and smiled. "How lucky could he get," he thought. When he was just a young boy, he remembered the old man saying that the room of books held treasures beyond belief. Old man Jacobs had winked at his bookkeeper, who was sitting beside him. The bookkeeper gave the elder Jacobs a nod, conveying that he understood the real meaning of the statement, turned toward the boy, and gave him a sinister smile.

Glancing around, Cramer checked to see that everything was back in its place before he left the room. Better to look at the contents of his pockets somewhere else, he thought. He searched for any sign of Luke's return, and hurriedly exited the back door, taking the smaller trail that led to the bait shop. "Not bad for the day," he snickered. "Now all I have to do is convince the authorities that Luke is not only the cause of Sara's accident, but also the murderer of one Frederick Hudson. And then," he added, "Find out what this little key opens."

The glaring parking lot lights awoke Luke from a deep sleep. "What am I doing here? In the parking lot of Lolita's?" he asked himself. Stretching out his body the full length of the truck's backseat, he sat up, and slipped his feet into his new brown leather cowboy boots. He stepped onto the pavement still steaming from the hot afternoon sun, and slid behind the steering wheel, closing his eyes once more. His mouth twisted into a grin. He sat up, as if he had discovered an amazing thought. "Oh, yeah!" he said loudly. "I need to visit my little lady and ask her a few questions about that emerald." A group of young girls stared at him as he spun out on the loose gravel.

Not far away, the hospital was unusually still. Sara awoke, rubbed her eyes, and glanced at the clock. She pulled the covers tightly around her neck. "Where was Jack and who were the two men standing by the door?" she wondered, drifting back to sleep.

CHAPTER 17

Jack glanced at the hallway clock. He quickly rinsed his soup bowl, grabbed his briefcase, and hurried out the door. He was planning on meeting O'Connell to correlate the information both of them had collected since Sara's accident. "And, add to that," muttered Jack, "the murder of Hudson, the disappearance of Doc Thorton, and the attack on Sara's mother, Peg. And, we've haven't even touched upon my attack at the Reynolds home."

Early this morning, before Sara awoke, Jack had searched the hospital, talked to the security guards, and had felt safe enough to return home for a shower, a quick shave, and a bite to eat. Now, before his meeting with the sheriff, he would go to Sara, and try to explain the blatant attack on her mother in Doc's office last night. When he arrived at the hospital, Sara was sitting upright in her bed, her face pale, and her eyes full of questions, as she gazed at the two sleepy men still guarding the door.

"Jack!" she said with relief at his sudden appearance. "What's going on? No one will tell me. They said I had to wait and ask the sheriff. O'Connell isn't anywhere around."

Jack sat on the side of the bed, carefully avoiding the leg with the heavy cast. "Sara," he said taking her hand, "Your mother has been hurt."

"Hurt? Where is she? How bad?" her words came tumbling out.

"She was knocked unconscious last night when she surprised an intruder in Doc's office. I had asked her to meet me there to discuss your safety. She's going to be okay. Alright?" Sara nodded, her eyes open wide. "Sara," began Jack, "I'm afraid for your life, too."

Sara looked at Jack. "Why? What's going on, Jack?" She paused to catch her breath, "Tell me now, Jack! What's been happening?"

"Unfortunately, Sara," began Jack. "There are a few people in town that could benefit from your death. The old Reynolds' home is desirable piece of property," he paused, "how much do you know about your husband's plans?"

"Plans? You mean for a hotel? He talked about it long before my dad's mother died. The property was left to me. I don't know why. I had very little contact with my grandmother. I don't know what I will do with the old mansion. I'm not sure I would want to live there with my children." She shivered, "Too many bad things have happened there in the past." Jack cringed. Sara looked at him closely. "What's the matter, Jack?" She sighed, "I'm sorry that you're involved in this mess with my family and everything."

Jack looked at the clock. "May I come back tonight? Let's say, seven o'clock?" He needed time to talk to the doctors involved in Sara's care, and to discuss a few things with O'Connell before he disclosed all the information to Sara. The sheriff would know just the right thing to say, thought Jack.

"Okay, Jack. I'll see you tonight. May I see my mother now?"

"Your mother is doing fine, Sara. She needs her rest. I will be back tonight. Bye for now," he added squeezing her hand. Sara looked perturbed and didn't return his farewell.

Jack drove to the police station. He gave the part-time receptionist a broad smile as he passed by the front desk. She smiled, nodded a hello, and watched him walk to the rear of the station. O'Connell was hunched over an old card table set up as a makeshift desk for the young detective. He kept muttering the words, "Strange. Very strange."

"Great," said Jack. "My own office," he quipped as he noticed the matching metal chair. An old desk lamp minus its green glass shade sat on the torn top of the Army-green contraption. "Am I to understand that this is my desk?"

"Sorry, buddy," said O'Connell without looking up. "You know the finances of a small town."

Everyone knew that Wakeegon had to tighten its belt since last year's drop in tourist trade. They also knew that businesses, like the "Jacobs Construction Company", kept their headquarters in run-downed buildings in neighboring towns, cheating the town of Wakeegon out of its' taxes. Jack unconsciously pulled on his own belt. He had not felt the tug of despair as much as his friend, due to the large inheritance left to him by his father. But, he had sympathy for his old comrade. O'Connell probably felt the squeeze more since his wife had filed for divorce.

"Jack, look here!" he said, as Jack pulled the chair close to the table and sat down. "I know every town has its skeletons, but I tell you, Son, never in my lifetime have I heard of so many things happening at one time in this little town. The last time Wakeegon saw this much activity ironically goes way back to the tragedy involving the Reynolds twins. You remember Sara's father and her uncle? The authorities took away the twin who became Sara's father. And the other one? What happened to him no one knows!"

"Human loss," said Jack. "Does one ever get over the pain? Tell me Sheriff. Is there any more news about Doc?"

"Still missing. No word at all from him. Seems he would be the one to talk to. He's a little scatterbrained, but I don't think he is stupid enough to think that he could run. Yep, he would be the prime suspect in Sara's case, with his knowledge of medicine and all." O'Connell's voice drifted off as he reviewed the files. He plopped down on the only other chair in the room. "The one thing that puzzles me the most is the car accident involving Sara. Who would want to hurt that girl? In that case, maybe it's the husband who is the main suspect. But, you said she knew about his desire to open up a hotel, right?"

"Yes," said Jack, "But it was not discussed any further with her. I've put out a missing person bulletin for Thorton. So far, nothing. No one has seen him since the night Sara fell into the coma, except the bartender across town that worked in the tavern where Doc stopped to have a drink. Guess Doc was kicked out of the building. The bartender said that Thorton had no car, and was last seen walking toward the lake. That's where that kid found his cell phone," he paused. "We probably need to dredge the lake. Not many tourists or the usual lake people are here yet to help spot a body, if there is one."

"The dredging will have to be done before the regatta," said O'Connell. "After that, it would be voted down by the tourist committee. Anything more?"

"Yeah. What do you know about the guy known as Cramer? Seems he meets up with Luke quite often. Is he a good friend?"

"Friend? He's the family lawyer," said O'Connell. "Those two are constantly fighting, even at the old man's funeral. Someone said Cramer was the mastermind behind the plans for the hotel. Have you seen the plans? I heard there were some environmental concerns." The word "environmental" caught Jack's attention. "It's also rumored," O'Connell continued, "that the Reynolds house was built over an area of Indian mounds. Maybe the state environmental agency was contacted about the plans and kept the identity of Mr. Hudson a secret. Maybe the prospective owners found out the reason why Hudson was here and had him killed. That branch almost went clean through his head!" Jack grimaced at the thought.

"Sorry, old boy. I always forget, don't I?" O'Connell finished, watching Jack's face go from a pasty gray to a ghostly white.

Jack swallowed. "I believe Hudson came here on his own will. Remember he was on a month's sabbatical for a special research project involving Indiana lakes, or so he told everyone. He was staying at the Willows for an undetermined amount of time. At least, that's what the person at the front desk remembered. Seems Hudson knew where to find the planning committee. Went straight to Willie's without any directions. By the way, the hotel owner made sure that I knew Hudson still owed him money. And, he also commented that Hudson had bragged about the new hotel that is being built. The owner was as mad as a hornet on a rainy day. 'Didn't need any more competition,' he said." Jack sat quietly, in deep concentration, then, asked, "Sheriff, did you talk to Willie, yet?"

"You mean Willard? He wouldn't even let me past the lobby! Said I needed a search warrant to step on the premises. I told him I just wanted to ask him a few questions. He said I would have to take him to the station. Didn't want to start anything. There were quite a few old-timers there, giving me dirty looks. I had the warrant drawn up today, though." O'Connell took a deep breath. "Who is this Goodman fellow, Jack?"

"They say he is the architect and planner for the hotel. Not from around here. He's been staying at the same hotel where Hudson was camped out, arrived at about the same time, too."

O'Connell reached for the felt marker and drew a line across a name on the paper in front of him. "This fellow, Pierceton, looks pretty innocent. He's been in business here for quite a few years. You know? On Main Street? I've never crossed paths with him. Looked at his background. Never been in trouble or anything." Both pairs of eyes came to rest on the last name on the list. Grayson Locke.

Jack looked up. "He's the legal comrade of old Mr. Jacobs. I heard he was sent away to work with the lawyer who was planning to set up the casino in West River. Locke is prepared to fight for whatever the casino needs." Jack paused, "That's all I have for now."

"How's Sara? And, her mother?" O'Connell asked. "Pretty scary time for the both of them, huh?"

"They're doing all right. Sara asked to see her mother today. She's," he paused, "still in the dark about her children."

"What are you going to tell her?"

"Everything, if her doctor is present. Why don't you come with me, Sheriff? I could use some help."

Knowing that he would be facing an empty house again, the sheriff agreed. "Sure. What time?"

"Seven," replied Jack. "And don't be late. I don't want to face her alone."

CHAPTER 18

Sara pressed the button by her bedside and requested the nurse's help in showering. Her clumsy leg was still encased in the heavy cast. "Jack said he would have it removed and then order further testing," she excitedly told the nurse. "When I'm finished with my shower I'd like to visit my mother."

"The sheriff said that no one was to visit you or your mother today."

"What about me?" asked Luke, standing just inside the doorway. "Surely that does not include her husband? Nurse Daly, isn't it?" Luke continued, "Who's your supervisor, Miss Daly?"

The broad-shouldered woman looked at Sara. "I'll be back dear," said Nurse Daly, gently tucking a blanket around Sara. As she was leaving the room, Luke laughed, "Doesn't take much to scare her, does it?"

"Luke, why do you always do that?" asked Sara.

"Do what?"

"Intimidate people wherever you go?"

"Shows who's in charge, my dear," replied Luke, sitting on the edge of the bed.

Sara shifted under the covers. "So, why are you here?"

"I'm your husband," Luke retorted. "Why wouldn't I be here?"

"Oh, I don't know. Maybe it's the fact that you've only visited me a couple of times since the accident."

Luke looked at his wife. "I need to talk to you."

"What about?" asked Sara.

"Old lady Reynolds. Was there really a family treasure? Have you seen it?"

"That's the reason you came to visit me? Gee, thanks, I'm so honored," said Sara. She sighed. "You've heard the family speak about the emerald many times. Why are you so interested in it now?"

"I've just walked through the house again. Just wondering where the old hag kept it."

"Luke! You're not supposed to be in the house! Remember what O'Connell said? Only the immediate family is allowed. That means my mother and me."

"Thanks for including me in the family, Sara," he added snidely. He stood up. "Come on. I'm just curious about the place."

Sara paused and stared at him intently. "So, how's the planning for the hotel and casino coming along?"

"Great!" he said absentmindedly. "The county and the state approval, is set for . . . ." He stopped and looked angrily at her. "How much do you know?"

"Enough to know you have been planning this for awhile, Luke. Just how were you going to get me to sign the property over to you?"

Luke leaned over the bed and placed his face against her cheek. "Sara, you know you are not capable of thinking straight since the accident. This project will provide us with money for all of our needs for the rest of our lives."

"I don't want my needs supplied by money from a gambling institution, Luke! I just want a simple life with my husband and my children."

Luke closed his eyes and sighed. "Sara, answer my question. Did you ever see a family treasure?"

Sara lay flat on the crumpled sheets. "Only in the family ancestry book at the town library. A large, flawless emerald brought over from Ireland. It has been missing since the death of my grandfather, shortly after my father was born. They say either he had it hidden somewhere where it would never be found, or, my grandma sold it to provide for herself and her son," Sara said solemnly, rolling over on her side, facing the wall. "I've told you what you wanted. Now, please leave!"

Luke was taken aback by her outspokenness. "You really are slipping old girl. I'm sure the new docs don't know the change in you since the accident. The coma really did you in! You really are not capable of caring for yourself."

"I'm more than capable, Luke. Besides, I have friends to help me."

"Who, may I ask? Not the infamous Jack Wilder?"

"I have my mother and Sheriff O'Connell, and yes," she added, "I have Jack."

"Just wait, Sara! I'll get what I want! I always have!" he spouted as he stormed out of the room.

Sara looked at the vacant doorway, "Not this time, Luke. Not this time."

Jack changed his clothes, picked up his phone, and dialed his mother's number. "Mom," he said rather loudly, "how are you?"

"Quite well, dear. We must think a lot alike, son. I was planning on calling you tonight."

Jack cleared his throat. "I need to discuss something with you. Is it okay to come home this weekend?"

"Sure, dear. Is everything all right?"

"Just a minor problem. Besides visiting you, I need to see my old supervisor about a couple of suspects we're investigating. They're under suspicion in a case that involves a local girl," said Jack. "Someone tried to kill her," he added.

"Oh, dear! Poor thing!"

"The girl's beautiful, smart, and one of the kindest people I've ever met! Her husband is the chief suspect. A scum if I ever saw one!"

"Oh, how sad," replied Jack's mother. "What time will you be here, Jack?"

"It will be in the evening. Probably late."

"I'll see you then, dear. Drive carefully."

"Goodnight, Mom."

"What? Oh, goodnight, dear," said his mother preoccupied with her thoughts. "Drive carefully," she added as she hung up the phone. Could it be that Jack's interested in this girl? If so, would he be careful around her unpredictable husband?

Jack paused in the front hallway, picked up the picture of Beth, and kissed it gently. He grabbed his cinnamon-scented handkerchief just before he closed the door.

O'Connell was waiting for him in the hospital lobby. "A cup of coffee to get our heads together?" he asked.

"Sure," said Jack, motionless.

"Are you prepared son? I know it's a big weight on your shoulders," he said as they walked into the coffee shop and gave the waitress their order. Both were quiet, as they sat their cups down on a corner table. "Well," said O'Connell, interrupting the silence. "What would you like me to do? Break the news? Are the doctors ready?"

"They'll be there. They have a sedative ready to ease the pain, though I don't think that's possible. I remember when Beth died. Nothing took the pain away. Only the passing of time. Then, you are so weary you can't think anymore," he paused. "Sara. She'll be mad at me," he added. "I'm the bearer of bad tidings."

"You want me to tell her, Jack?"

"No. She sort of trusts me now, although she might not want to see me ever again. By the way, O'Connell, after I talk to Sara I'm driving to Chicago. I want to visit my mother. I'll also be searching for information on a few of the suspects."

O'Connell knew Jack would have access to better data in Chicago. "Sure. Hope you find what you're looking for." Jack nodded, drew the handkerchief, heavily laden with cinnamon oil, out of his pocket and stopped in the hallway to take a deep breath before he entered Sara's room.

CHAPTER 19

Jack knew Sara would be waiting for him, unaware of their future conversation. Confident that he could handle the difficult task before him, he put on a smile and walked into her room. She was sitting up in bed, her upswept hair resting against a pile of fluffy pillows. A new application of primrose-colored lipstick had been added to her plump contoured lips, softening the harsh background of the pallid walls. She sat up and adjusted the dingy blanket.

"Jack! How nice of you to come!"

Jack took her hand and pressed it to his lips. "Madame," he said, bowing from his waist.

"Oh, Jack," she laughed, "You are so gallant."

Jack pulled the hard, uncomfortable chair closer to her bedside and nodded to O'Connell who was hovering in the doorway. Two doctors, present at the nurse's station, stood quietly, prepared for anything that could happen.

"So, Jack, what is the big mystery that brings you here, tonight?"

Jack cleared his throat. "Sara, tell me again. The night of your accident. What do you remember?"

Sara looked confused. "Jack, I've told you everything I know."

"Tell me again, about your children that night," he requested.

"My children? I told you they were sleeping. When I put them in the SUV, I didn't know how long I would be at my mother's. I thought maybe I could stay overnight, until I saw his car. You know, my mom's friend?"

"How are your children doing today, Sara?" asked Jack.

"Jack, you know that Doc won't let me see them! My mother follows his every word! She refuses to bring them to the hospital."

"Have you talked to them on the phone?"

"Jack, why are you asking all of these questions?" she asked, twisting the corner of the blanket into a tight knot.

"No one has seen your children since the accident. They're gone, Sara."

"What do you mean?" Sara asked, her voice rising. "Did Luke take them somewhere? Where's the sheriff? I want to talk to him!"

"Sara, they're gone. To Heaven."

"To Heaven?" she paused, her voice becoming soft as a whisper. She sat up straight and stared at Jack. "You're wrong, Jack! My mother has them. Ask her! Ask her!" she blurted. Her face paled as Jack motioned to O'Connell to bring the two new doctors into the room.

"You're wrong! Get out, Jack! Get out!" she screamed, as one of the doctors held her down. "Don't come back!" she added.

Jack backed out of the room. He waved off the sheriff as he approached. "Monday," he said solemnly. "I'll be back on Monday." He turned quickly so O'Connell wouldn't see the tears in his eyes.

Jack drove to his house in silence. He kept the car windows closed, and turned off his favorite Jazz station that was playing on the radio. He walked to his bedroom, grabbed a worn, tattered-looking duffle bag from his college days, and jerked the antique bedroom dresser drawer open. A couple of T-shirts and a pair of new jeans were hastily folded and stuffed into the bag. He passed by the bathroom, knowing that everything he needed was already at his destination. Jack grabbed a few twenty dollar bills from an empty coffee can in his refrigerator, added them to his bag, and threw the duffle into the back seat of his old blue Thunderbird.

Pulling away from the curb, Jack glanced at the home he and Sara had shared to see if he had turned off the lights. The house stood dark and quiet, seeming to have forgotten the joy and happiness it once held. Jack twisted the radio knob until he heard a familiar tune. He took a deep breath of cinnamon and leaned back into the seat.

Jack's mom untied her apron and looked at the clock on the mantle for the third time. Eleven thirty. Jack should be here in half an hour. He sounded troubled, she thought. Had he gotten himself entangled in a difficult criminal case? She leaned against the picture window and looked for the approaching headlights.

She had always worried about Jack. Even as a young boy, he was always involved in other people's affairs. Not in a bad way, she thought. It was because Jack was so deeply concerned about their welfare. His desire to help others, and his interest in a career as a law-enforcement detective, began shortly after the death of his favorite schoolmaster, Isaac Zielinski.

The morning Zielinski's body was discovered started out very routinely for Jack. Because of Jack's small stature, she had made sure her son was accompanied each morning to school by the tall brawny teenage son of the family next door. At least, that's the excuse she gave to everyone why she wouldn't let Jack walk to school alone.

In actuality, she and her husband were both lawyers whose commitment to injustice extended into the immigrant community. Soon after accepting an invitation from Professor Zielinski to visit the neighborhood Polish Community Center, they both began devoting their spare time there, helping the needy. While working at the center they became close friends with the Sawicki family, members of the Polish community, who were also involved in the operations of the center. Both families agreed to join ranks, striving to build a bridge between the two neighborhoods.

Jack Wilder and Luis Sawicki, were both born into their families as an only child. The boys quickly became as close as brothers. Some of the parents at Jack's private school felt the Wilder's had gone a bit too far this time, overstepping the neighborhood boundaries. Jack's mother could not stop worrying about his safety, so the teenage boy next door continued to walk Jack to school each day.

Although the two families were bonded by their mutual devotion to community integration, the similarities ended. Jack's parents had met and fallen in love their second year of college. Because they were both environmental lawyer students by trade, they became interested in the preservation of the local lakes. While their friends marched at campus peace rallies, they spent their weekends at the dunes working alongside the park rangers. Their friendship continued throughout college and eventually culminated with a wedding proposal graduation night. Once married, they continued to fight for the preservation of the environment in the huge metropolis of Chicago.

The Wilder family home, a Victorian brownstone, stood out from the ordinary ones. Ornate trim and painted ironwork beckoned those who passed by to take another look. Fragrant flowers overflowed the compact front yard, designed by Jack's mother after her training as a master gardener.

Luis's parents, on the other hand, led quite a different life. The Sawicki family fought hard to put food on the family table. Few families in the neighborhood could afford to have their homes repaired. So, the decaying houses in the Polish neighborhood would remain that way until they fell into complete ruin. Luis's father, a private contractor and carpenter, had to look outside the community for jobs. Because of a tight family budget, even the Sawicki home was driven to disrepair.

Following the same pattern of the Polish neighborhood homes, the local school was extremely rundown, struggling to provide the necessary education for the young students. It didn't take long for Jack's parents to offer their help to the Sawicki family. Registering Luis at the same school Jack attended seemed the right thing to do. The Wilder family signed an agreement for payment and Luis became the newest pupil of Jack's favorite schoolmaster.

Shortly after Luis's appearance, Professor Zielinski became the target for a group of parents whose children attended the private school. Over the past few months the professor had received several written threats, which were investigated by the district police. One letter referred to him as "a traitor to his own school by blemishing the rich lineage of quality students." The other one simply read, "Take him {Luis} back where his kind belong or else," the "or else" printed in red, with inked-in droplets resembling blood. Zielinski convinced the authorities that the threats were "just a lot of hot air." He added, "This school hasn't seen any violence since it began 30 years ago." Two days later, the same police removed his body from the musty smelling blood-stained office. A tap on the door brought Jack's mother back to the present.

"Mom," said Jack giving his mother a peck on the cheek. "Why didn't you go to bed? You didn't have to stay up for me."

"I wanted to give you a hug," she said cheerfully. "Come, I'll make some cocoa. It will go well with the cookies I made this afternoon."

"Chocolate chip with macadamias?" asked Jack, sniffing the air.

"Your sense of smell never does you wrong, son," she laughed as she prepared Jack's favorite hot drink. Both were quiet as she poured the cocoa and placed a plate of cookies in front of Jack. "I was just finishing up the laundry before you came home, Jack. Do you mind if I put a load in the dryer? Then we can have a nice chat, okay?" Jack smiled and nodded his head. His mother started walking from the room, stopped, and turned toward Jack. "Before you arrived I was reminiscing about you and Luis. Do you still remember the day Zielinski's body was found?

"Sure, like it was yesterday," replied Jack, as she continued down the hallway. He could still remember the sights and smells that morning. Luis had spent the night with the Wilder family. Dressed for school the boys waited on the front porch.

"Listen boys, you will have to walk alone today," said Jack's mom. "Charlie's mom called. He's very ill. He won't be able to walk the two of you to school. It's too late for me to change my plans, so, we'll have to make an exception today." She grabbed them both by their shirtsleeves. "Watch out for each other. Go straight to school. Okay?" Both boys nodded their heads and took off with lightning speed.

Jack remembered that he and Luis were in high spirits as they ran toward the schoolhouse. Their favorite major league team had upset their opponent the previous evening.

"Hey, tell your parents thanks again for taking me along," Luis spoke excitedly.

"Wasn't it great? That was the best game ever!" replied Jack. "Let's go see Zielinski! He'll be interested in all the details," stated Jack. "Too bad he had to miss the game last night."

They raced to see who could get to the school first before the bell rang. The school building looked insignificant next to the mammoth century-old stone church. The Precious Church of the Angels got its name from the bigger than life statues that guarded its rooftop. Visitors would exclaim that the inside held a beauty that could contend with any church in Italy.

As they approached, the boys saw the line of police cars at the same time. "Holy cow!" remarked Luis. "I wonder what happened!"

"Maybe old Mrs. Davis finally blew up the kitchen with one of her weird concoctions," stated Jack. "Remember her brownie surprise?" Both boys laughed as they recalled the horrible tasting mess.

"Just a minute, boys," said an officer, putting his arm out to stop them from entering the building. "You can't go in there. School is closed for the day." The officer gently turned Jack around. "Go home and listen to the news for further instruction."

"Yippee!" shouted Luis as he jumped down the concrete steps two at a time.

"Wait!" said Jack, grabbing his shirt sleeve. "I want to see what's going on. Let's go through the secret door." Jack and Luis walked quietly to the right side of the school building, glancing back over their shoulders. Behind a giant Rose of Sharon bush stood a faded wooden door the boys had discovered long ago when they had skipped one of their classes. Jack turned the handle slowly. The door opened, emitting a faint squeak. Tiptoeing toward the steps that led to the first floor, Jack grabbed Luis's sleeve to prevent him from going any further. "Listen," whispered Jack, raising his finger close to his lips. Both boys stood as quiet as a fawn awaiting her death in the still morning mist.

"Yep. Dead as a doornail," chirped the District 12 sergeant, loudly. "Everyone said he was asking for it."

"What are they talking about?" asked Luis.

"Shhhh!" Jack replied, out of breath.

"Time of death, somewhere around eleven o'clock," stated the sergeant. "Wonder what the old codger was doing here at that time?" Luis was still oblivious to the conversation that was taking place, but Jack could sense the smell of blood and death. "Tag him, boys," said the sergeant to the men in uniforms. "Take him to the morgue," he finished, his loud voice echoing down the stairwell. Backing down the stairs, the boys turned toward the door that led them outside, and ran as fast as they could without looking back.

"Stop! Stop!" shouted Jack, holding his side. "Let's get a bottle of soda, Luis. My treat!" Jack and Luis slowed down as they approached old man Cooper's drug store.

Mr. Cooper was standing outside surrounded by a group of men, including a few from Jack's neighborhood. "Too bad about Zielinski, huh?" said one. Curious, Jack stuck his head closer to the circle of men, listening in on their conversation.

"Yep," replied another. "All because of that Polish kid! What a waste," he added. Jack backed away, unsure of what he had heard. Running inside he grabbed two colas and placed the money next to the cash register.

"Mr. Cooper! The money for the sodas is on the counter," he shouted as he ran from the store.

"Thanks, Jack," said Mr. Cooper absentmindedly. "Jack?" Mr. Cooper called out after the two disappearing boys. The men stopped their conversation and looked in the direction of Jack and Luis who were scurrying down the street.

"Too involved," said one man. "Look what it has done." Mr. Cooper silently said a prayer for the two boys.

Jack's mother, hearing the news about Zielinski, had returned home immediately. Dressed in her gardening clothes, she was waiting on the front steps.

"Hey, Mom! You're back! Is the man from the plant center coming over again today? Is that why you're home?" asked Jack. Jack sounded worried, thought Mrs. Wilder. Did he already know what had happened?

"Come on inside, boys. I need to talk to you," she said as she turned toward the house. Two anxious-looking faces looked at the kind woman and followed after her.

Jack's school was closed the following week. No other student took the death of Zielinski as hard as Jack. In the privacy of his room, he had vowed to fight against those who took life so casually. Jack and Luis met several times in the following days to plan out their fight against crime. *Dragnet*, and reruns of *Perry Mason*, began to show up frequently on the living room television screen.

Each morning before school, the boys sealed their union with a secret handshake. Later, that very same handshake marked the end of school at the police academy for both of the boys. Luis began working for the police force in Chicago. Jack left two days later to begin training as a detective. The two still met several times a year to exchange birthday gifts and to argue over who had cracked the most dangerous case.

Jack never noticed when his mother returned to the table with a cup of cocoa for herself. She looked at him questionably. Jack sighed. Zielinski's killer was never found. Neither he nor Luis ever talked about the murder again.

CHAPTER 20

The wooden screen door banged loudly as the spring coiled back into its position. "So, Jack. Why are you up so early this morning?" inquired his mother, as Jack bent over to give her a kiss on her forehead. Quietly, he just smiled and headed for the kitchen.

"I took a nice walk around the block. It's good to be home," he called over his shoulder. "Anything good in the fridge?"

"You know I always have your favorites."

Jack noticed a pile of colorful beads, sorted into small groups on the table. "Hey, what are you working on?" he asked his mother.

"Rosaries," she said excitedly. "I have to find something to do with my spare time." She paused briefly before she resumed sorting the tiny pieces of glass. "It's been two years this month."

"It's hard to believe, Mom." Jack absentmindedly glanced at his father's favorite chair. Jack's father, EJ Wilder, had died unexpectedly on a business trip to Michigan, investigating pollutants found in a local stream.

"Jack, dear," said his mother in a soft voice. "Have you gotten into the habit of going back to church?"

"Sure, Mom. I sing in the choir, occasionally. Apparently, the choir members say that I have the voice of an angel, at least according to the sheriff. Although, O'Connell does have a little bit of a hearing problem," said Jack.

Jack's mother laughed, rose from her chair, and peered into the refrigerator. "A full breakfast, dear, minus the bacon?" she asked. Jack smiled and nodded yes. "So, Jack, why are you really here?" asked his mother, not willing to wait any more for the reason for this spontaneous visit.

"Work and pleasure. Mostly, just to see you and Luis, if I can catch him at the station," he answered, then paused sniffing the air, "You made oatmeal and raisin cookies, too?"

"Your sense of smell was always one of your best features," responded his mother.

"Or worse! Depending on the smell!" said Jack still wearing a smile. He grabbed two oatmeal and raisin cookies from the earthenware jar on the kitchen counter, walked into the adjoining sitting area, and plopped down on the comfortable sofa. Staring at the wall he said, "It's Beth, Mom. I still miss her."

"Well, that's pretty normal, Jack. You loved her. She was your wife." She paused and waited for Jack to continue.

Jack walked over and stood directly in front of his mother. "I'm working on a case involving a young woman. Not only did someone try to kill her, she also lost her two children in the mishap." Jack's mother gasped. Jack buried his head in his hands. "It's the first time I've felt anything for another woman since Beth died. I feel like a traitor." Jack stopped talking, and became very quiet. He raised his eyes and searched his mother's face. She stopped what she was doing, and gathered him in her arms.

"Don't feel guilty. Beth's gone. You were the best husband any girl could ever ask for. The problem isn't that you care for this girl, Jack, it's the fact she's still married. It sounds to me that she needs some time to recover, whatever that involves. Promise me, Jack. Guard your heart," she added as Jack sighed and leaned his head against her small frame.

After searching the elder Jacobs' home, Cramer closed his eyes and leaned back into the seat of his car. He knew Samuel didn't trust the local banks. In fact, the old man had recently started to keep many of his valuables at home, a practice highly disapproved of by his friend and advisor, Grayson Locke. "Just an open door to every rotten man around," he remembered Locke telling the elder Jacobs.

Samuel had laughed. "Am I to add your name to that list, my friend? When I'm gone, who will stop you from stealing everything I own?"

Locke stared at the man whom he had befriended his entire life. "Surely, you don't feel that way about me, sir? Not only have we been business partners, but I hope friends for all of these years."

"The only friend I have and trust is the greenback, boy. You could stick a knife in my back tomorrow," the elder man had replied.

Cramer shuddered, his thoughts returning to the present. Opening his eyes, he turned on the interior lights of the car and reached into his pocket. He pulled out the odd assortment of items that he had taken from the hollowed-out book in old Jacobs' office, and laid them on the seat beside him. A stained newspaper clipping read, "Jessie and Nathaniel Cramer announce the arrival of their son, Richard, on this day, December 20, 1971." He turned the yellowed clipping over. Nothing of significance was on the other side, he thought, except for the numbers 4391447, written in pencil. Why would Samuel keep a newspaper clipping about Cramer's family hidden in an old hallowed out book? he contemplated.

Cramer wished he could remember more about his father. He was only a lad of seven when Mrs. Smith, a neighbor, came to his school. She had talked quietly to the young teacher, reached for his hand and walked him slowly to his house explaining as best as she could about the accident.

"Local man electrocuted," headlined the paper the following morning. His father had been replacing the engine of the old blue Plymouth when the crane of the small lift he was using grazed the live electrical lines leading to the house. The surge of energy caught the house on fire. The black acrid smoke alerted the next door neighbor to the dead man lying on the gravel drive toward the back of the home.

Returning from school, young Cramer remembered that his mother's face was filled with a combination of emotions. Sadness. Fear. Perhaps an expression of guilt? Her reaction had puzzled the lad mourning over the loss of his father. The Reverend Johnson came later that day to console the young mother. Cramer was sent to his room, but he opened the door a crack attempting to hear the conversation. The Reverend had listened intently to the dead man's wife, then, reared back in surprise when she spoke, her tears and feelings beyond control. Cramer never knew exactly what his mother had said to the clergyman, but he did remember overhearing the Reverend say that he needed time to respond to her confessions, as he was leaving. The man reassured his mother that he would be back the following morning. Cramer never saw him again.

The following day an elderly gentlemen known to him as Uncle Jacobs came to the house. He continued to come every day for two weeks. The next weekend Uncle Jacobs brought a justice of the peace to the house and his mother became the man's wife. One morning, soon after the marriage, his mother and the older man had a huge argument. Uncle Jacobs left in a huff. Young Cramer and his mother continued to live in the tenant house until his mother's death.

The day after her funeral, Cramer was given a notice to vacate the premises and report to a college up north. The old man would pay for his schooling, followed by law school, with the stipulation that Cramer would become the sole family lawyer. Even if the relationship between Samuel and Cramer had always been strained, Cramer agreed, hoping to make a small fortune from the man who had ignored him most of his life. Little did he know his services would be limited only to the businesses owned by the elder Jacobs, and his shady comrades. "The money that financed your schooling, will have to be paid back immediately if you try to step outside the family's dealings," said the old man. The debt remained forever, binding him to the Jacobs family. That is, until the old man died.

Cramer took the key from his pocket and turned it over in his hand. The tiny crafted piece of metal had lost its shininess long ago. What treasure did it unlock? he wondered. He had decided to search the house again tonight. But first, he would question the man that probably held the answer to the key. Samuel Jacobs's confidante and business partner, Grayson Locke.

Cramer frowned and picked up his thinning wallet. He had reassured himself that the new casino would solve all of his money problems. But now, construction would surely be delayed with the murder of Hudson. He remembered old man Jacobs telling his mother that half of his fortune would go to her and her son, upon his death. She had frowned and locked herself in the bedroom for the rest of the day. Did Luke know of his father's plans? Cramer wondered.

He shoved the key back into his pocket and looked once more at the number written on the back of the old clipping. Whose handwriting was it? Could it have been his mother's or father's? So long ago, he thought. He placed the small folded slip of paper into the worn journal that had belonged to his mother. Cramer had read the scribbled entries, spanning a total of six months, over and over. The inside-cover was inscribed, "The property of Jessie Cramer, the year 1978." The final entry was dated June nineteenth. "What have I done?" it read, "I think he knows. The similarities. How will we survive?" The next day his father was dead. The remaining pages were white and empty.

"What similarities?" he asked himself, as he started the car, and steered it back on the road. He reached for his cell phone and noticed that the battery was almost dead. Sighting a public phone at the gas station, Cramer pulled over and searched the directory for the number of the local phone company.

"Yes, sir, I understand your inquiry," said the man from the phone company. "I wouldn't know that, sir. Couldn't tell you anyway, privacy, you know? The first three digits suggest an old discontinued number. Try to find an old directory. Advertise if you have to, and offer a reward. Drives people mad looking for things if you offer a reward." Cramer thanked him, hung up, and dialed Fred's Antiques.

"Don't carry anything like that," said Fred. "Have a friend that's a packrat, you know? He might have one. Give me your number and I'll call him. That it then?"

"Yeah," muttered Cramer. "No wait!" he paused, "I want to offer a thousand dollar reward."

The old man coughed. "Did I hear you right, son?"

"Yes," answered Cramer.

"For an old phone book? Say, maybe I'll hunt for it myself."

Cramer returned to the car. He reached for the journal again, reading the last entries one more time. "Called him. Needed money. Don't know what to do. Told him husband would be home tomorrow fixing vehicles all day, not a good time for me to talk. Said he would call later in the week."

He placed the journal close to his nose, smelling the combination of musty leather and his mother's perfume. Gently, his hands caressed the cover. What was his mother thinking the day she wrote her final entry? Who was the man she needed so desperately to talk to?

Cramer sat back in his seat and yawned. "I need to get some rest," he concluded. "Those eyes I saw looking back at me from the old house! I must be more exhausted than I realized."

Not only was Cramer physically tired, he couldn't seem to escape the talk filtering through the town concerning Hudson, either. "I thought I saw you with that man that ended up dead. Known him long?" the local druggist had asked him.

What bothered Cramer the most was the fact that the sheriff had not said a word to him yet. Did he know of his relationship with the environmentalist? Surely, he did. Everyone's business was loudly broadcasted throughout the town.

"Hudson! What an idiot!" said Cramer out loud, recalling his last conversation with the now deceased man. Hudson, dressed in outback clothes, had yelped with pain from Cramer's harsh grip. "Listen, buddy," shouted Cramer. "You already agreed to our deal, remember?"

"What deal? No papers, no signatures," Hudson had said. "Doesn't mean a thing. I've been putting on a good act in front of the other men, don't you agree?"

Cramer frowned, "Not good enough, Hudson!"

"I've done everything you wanted up to this point," Hudson added as Cramer increased the tension around the man's throat. "I'll do the water test in the morning, okay? I placed the bacteria in the stream two days ago. Should be good and ripe by now." When Cramer lessened his grip, Hudson continued, "The artifacts have been put into place. All genuine for this area of the country. Cost a little to borrow them, though," he rattled on, "Don't you think it's funny that Luke paid me to keep quiet about the very thing we started? I'll show you where I placed them, tomorrow. Meet you there at six in the morning, at the waterway behind the house, okay? Park down the road, and walk."

He was there, exactly at six a.m. the following day. "Remember, Cramer, since you insist I follow through on our deal," said the slim, bug-eyed environmentalist, "I get 60 percent, or I'll throw the test kit into the trash. You'll find no one better connected to the environmental department than me. They actually trust me," he had laughed, bending over to fill the vials with water from the stream. Cramer had paced back and forth. He stopped and stood behind the laughing Hudson, bent down to reach for a thick branch lying on the ground beside him, and swung with all his might. Hudson fell into the water. Cramer turned him over to see if he was dead. The smile that was frozen on the surprised face still haunted him.

"Fool!" Cramer had muttered, placing the caps on the newly-filled test tubes, and picking up the blood-soaked branch. He took a deep breath and noticed the footprints from his old fishing boots. Leaning against the nearest tree, he removed one boot and stopped. Was that the sound of a car door? He wondered. He walked to the edge of the woods with his foot still unclad. He kicked off the other boot. "Wilder? What is he doing here?" he grumbled. Cramer grabbed both boots, hid behind the large sycamore tree, and waited.

CHAPTER 21

Cramer placed his mother's journal in the car's glovebox, put on the spare pair of shoes from the trunk of his car, drove to the Barbecue Pit, and ordered two zesty shredded beef sandwiches at the drive-up. After filling his stomach, he pulled into the graveled parking lot under a shade tree, placed the vials from his pocket in the trunk and fell asleep.

It was dark when he awoke. Grumbling, Cramer stuffed the sandwich wrappers into the greasy take-out bag. He drove toward Samuel's house, and parked along the lane under a large sycamore. Flashlight in hand, Cramer walked the familiar trail to the back of the house, quietly stepped up to the entrance, and turned the knob. To his surprise, the door swung open. The old wooden floor gave a loud squeak as he stepped into the grand foyer. He quietly removed both shoes, rubbed his blistered toe, and walked cautiously toward the faintly lit office. The mumbling voice of Samuel's partner could be heard echoing throughout the small corridor. What was Locke doing here at this time of night? Cramer wondered. Pressing his body against the door, it accidentally bumped against the back wall, startling the bent-over man who was shuffling through a stack of old papers.

"Locke! What are you doing here?" asked Cramer.

"I worked for the man, what's your excuse?" answered Locke, as he stuffed the pile of papers into a file folder. Grabbing his hat, he ran toward the door.

"Wait! I need to talk to you!"

"Forget it, Cramer! We're done talking!" replied Locke, as he ran toward his car.

"Why are you running? What do you have?" yelled Cramer chasing after him. Locke jumped into his car, and sped away. Cramer winched as he stuck his feet into his shoes, ran down the trail, jumped into his vehicle, and followed the trail of dust.

The bumpy road stopped at the fork where both directions were paved. One of the paved roads led into town. The other paved road began along the lake and ended abruptly into a layer of finely-oiled gravel and sand, and continued around the body of water. Cramer slowed his car and chose the lake route. The road went past the old Mitchell place and Ray's Bait Shop. Locke's familiar rust-covered station wagon was parked in Ray's lot. "What is he doing?" complained Cramer, loudly. Everyone knew that Ray's opened at six each morning and closed each evening at exactly six, with all boats accounted for, regardless of the complaints by summer vacationers. Cramer pulled his car close to the entrance and walked in on the sleepy-eyed shopkeeper, dressed in his nightclothes, arguing with Locke.

"Listen, buddy! Are you crazy? I don't rent boats out at night! In fact, I'm not renting any motor boats at all right now. Don't you know about the water level danger that's out there?" exclaimed Ray.

"Fine!" Locke said, pushing the man aside and grabbing the keys. "Bill me," he added, as he hurried out the door leaving behind the shocked business owner. Locke ran down the partially lit, uneven trail to the pier. He turned to see Cramer following him.

"Locke, wait! I have to speak to you!" said Cramer.

"Not the money issue again, Cramer. I can't do anything for you now that the old man's gone," replied Locke.

Locke was holding a folder and a small painted black tin box with a tiny keyhole, encrusted with dirt, close to his chest. Cramer could see that the man was griping both articles so tightly that his knuckles were beginning to turn white. Locke turned and tripped over a broken oar, lying in the pathway.

"What's in that box? Why are you running away? What do you have in that folder?" Cramer rattled on. He grabbed one corner of the file, spilling the contents. Locke, still kneeling on the ground, reached for the oar and hit Cramer square in the face. When the man doubled up in pain, Locke frantically retrieved the box and blindly gathered up the papers that had fallen from the folder. He looked over at Cramer writhing on the ground.

"Surely, you've known all along? Known that you and Luke are half brothers?" Locke blurted out. He continued speaking, spewing out information about the Jacobs family.

Shaken, Cramer turned away, leaned close to the ground, and expelled the contents of the hasty meal of pork and grease that he had consumed that day. Drops of sweat dripped from his forehead and landed on his lip, leaving a salty taste to mingle with the contents of his stomach. As a young boy he had always marveled at the facial similarities between himself and the son of the wealthy Samuel Jacobs. "Makes you seem more like brothers," he remembered his mother saying. Cramer took a big breath before he turned to the man who had worked side by side with Samuel Jacobs. He stared at Locke's face without speaking.

"Got all the information in a safe place," said Locke, patting the files and tapping the top of the tin box. His lips curled in a partial smile. "The old man wanted his 'real son' to have his wealth when he passed away. No one will ever know. The inheritance will pass directly to Luke."

"Does Luke know . . . anything?" asked Cramer in a hoarse voice.

"Everything was kept from him. Samuel didn't want Luke to be more reckless with his money than he already was. He also didn't want him to know that his dad fathered a child with another woman. Your mother was never allowed to tell you. He would have sent her packing, leaving her, and I guess you," he added smugly, "without any support. Too bad your father died in that 'little accident' when you were a kid. Your 'daddy' never found out about his wife's disloyalty." He coughed and gave Cramer a smile.

Cramer, struggling to rise, lurched toward Locke, and grabbed his arm. "Give me those papers!" he demanded. Locke drew back his fist and punched Cramer in his stomach. The young lawyer fell to the ground moaning. Locke raced toward the line of boats, and jumped into the nearest one. He started the motor and backed out into the darkness, his laughter echoing in the foggy night.

Cramer rose and ran to the nearest boat. "No keys!" he exclaimed as he grabbed the oars. Defeated, he threw them into the water, and watched Locke disappear into the darkness.

Locke turned the throttle higher and switched on the large floodlight, directing the beam ahead of the boat. Trying to get comfortable, he glanced down and removed a lifejacket lying on the seat next to him. Looking up, he saw something white bobbing up and down in the water ahead. "What on earth?" he whispered, as the floating pier loomed in front of him. He tried to swerve, but it was too late to stop. The townspeople were awakened from their slumber by the explosion that filled the quietness of the lake. A puff of black smoke hung over the water.

"Local man loses his life in boat explosion," the news story in the local paper read the following morning. "Police say Grayson Locke, local attorney, was boating late last night, and failed to see a floating pier that had broken from its anchor. At approximately twelve-thirty a.m. the resulting explosion shook residents awake more than a mile away."

Jack was glad to be back. He rose from his chair and walked over and opened the window. Wrinkling his nose, he closed it again except for a small crack at the bottom. The faint cool breeze smelled of rotted grass and fish. The lake was quiet and still. No motorboats were heard, not even the sound of children's laughter was in the air. The town was still in shock from the early morning's event.

"Two tragic deaths in such a short span of time gives the town an eerie atmosphere not likely to attract vacationers," whispered Jack. "The regatta might as well be cancelled." He yawned and stretched his arms.

The sheriff had awakened him at one-fifteen that morning to tell him the news. "Hey, Jack," Sheriff O'Connell had said in a voice too loud for that time in the morning, "How did the trip to Chicago go, Son? Did you see Luis? What did you find out about the men you were investigating?" Before Jack could respond O'Connell continued, "Did you hear the news?" he asked. The sheriff spent the next few minutes relaying the details of Locke's accident. Jack had dressed quickly and met O'Connell at the bait shop's parking lot. Rubbing his eyes, Ray, the owner, attempted to answer their questions.

"Cramer and Locke were fighting over something. Couldn't make it out. Cramer looked really mad. And that stupid Locke ignored everything I said, grabbed the boat keys and," he yawned, "you know the rest. Sounded like he hit something out there. That's all I know."

Jack, Sheriff O'Connell, and two emergency appointed deputies, climbed into the wooden row boats. "Don't want to disturb any evidence, or bodies," said O'Connell, shining the hand-held search light out over the moonlight surface of the water. Pieces of charred-wood boat decking and a badly burned body were hauled into the vessels by the sullen men. A bulletin was sent to the local newsroom naming Locke as the boating victim, along with the statement that the lake was being closed down for the following day.

After a breakfast at Lolita's, O'Connell and Jack took a short nap on the police station office cots. The sound of a ringing phone, and the smell of burning coffee, shook them awake. "Sorry, Sheriff," whispered the receptionist, cupping her hand over the phone's mouthpiece. "You need to take this. The caller sounds really mad."

O'Connell answered with an annoyed, "Hello?" and muttered, "Sorry, I'll see what I can do," several times before he hung up. "Can you believe it?" he spat out angrily. "That was the mayor of Hyattsville. He acted like everything that has happened is my fault! Called me an incompetent old fool!"

"Easy, Sheriff," said Jack. "We both know Locke has been using his influence, casting rumors around town. I didn't tell you, yet, that we've found evidence that a hefty donation from the Jacobs family was given to the campaign of Hyattsville's esteemed leader. No ties to the mayor before this year. So why now?"

"Hopefully, everything will come to the surface," O'Connell had replied. "Anyway, I wanted to tell you the search and dredging of the lake has been approved for eight a.m. tomorrow morning. But right now, I want to check the lake one more time. Want to come along?"

At exactly one minute to eight the next morning, two semis loaded with equipment and a group of muscular-looking men pulled into the bait shop parking lot. They jumped out and asked, "Is this the right place?" and proceeded to pull diving suits from one of the two large tackle boxes. They quickly emptied the other box containing oxygen tanks and large underwater lights for searching the murky water.

"Lot of rain here, lately?" asked one, gazing out at the green scum floating on the water's edge.

"Sure is quiet," said another. Slowly, the beach filled up with onlookers who had read the news of the accident and the scheduled dredging in the morning paper. Some spectators brought their breakfast and ate while sitting on the lawn chairs they had placed in the parking lot of Ray's. They spoke among themselves about the series of crimes that had taken place in their town.

"A shame, a shame," said one gray-haired man. "Never in my day," he had said loudly to the younger man taking pictures.

The coroner, who had just arrived from Hyattsville, spat on the ground and nodded to the new arrivals. "Jack, I've lived here all my life. I've never seen anything like this! At least, not since the Reynolds family tragedy. I was just a boy then."

They both watched the team of scuba divers search the shallow shores by the pier. The soft splash of the disturbed water disrupted the silence between the spoken words of the onlookers. A shout from one of the divers brought the sheriff closer to the shoreline. Another member of the team lifted two green slimy boots from the water and placed them on the wooden deck.

"Jack!" yelled O'Connell. "Could you bring a couple of those large plastic bags from the patrol car?" Jack retrieved the bags and held them open while O'Connell placed one boot in the bag, and then the other, and sealed them with tape. "Boots!" said O'Connell, "Just boots?

Another shout was heard, and this time a mud-caked camera was brought to the surface. "My dad's camera!" shouted Jack, reaching for the newly found evidence. He turned it over and over in his hand.

"Whoa, Jack," said O'Connell, "Don't handle it too much."

"Not likely to find anything, Sheriff," answered Jack. "Although, it was one of the first commercially produced waterproof cameras made. I don't know if the waterproof part worked after all these years," he added, as he placed the camera in one of the smaller bags.

"Waterproof, huh? Bet the crook didn't count on that when he lifted it," said O'Connell. "Think it was the same person who conked you on the head, Son?"

The boots and camera were taken to the sheriff's car and locked away in a large wooden box kept in the trunk, labeled "Weapons." "Can't remember the last time I opened this thing," he stated as he turned the key.

The old man who had followed them to the car asked loudly, "Must be somethin' important, huh?"

"Smart observation!" replied the sheriff loud enough for the elderly man to hear. The man satisfied, nodded and spat out a stream of fluid through the space where his front tooth was missing in his weathered smile.

O'Connell walked over to the pier with his red-haired companion. "Need to keep this under wrap as much as possible, Jack. Don't know how though, with all the publicity and stuff. I admit I'm a little puzzled. We've started this day searching for Doc. Now, we've found your camera instead and a pair of old boots. I tell you, Jack, I'm worried about Doc. I was silently hoping that we wouldn't find him, you know? But the other part of me wonders where the heck he could be."

"You're right, Sheriff. It seems very strange that all of these things are happening at the same time." Jack paused. "We still need to question that boy who worked for Ray." The sheriff nodded. Jack continued, "This Cramer fellow, he's the one who scares me the most, Sheriff. I've heard a lot about him, and none of it is good." The two men said a few more words quietly to each other and walked over to the water's edge.

The diving team finished searching the area around the pier and the silent dredge, and rounded up Jack and O'Connell. The group of men rowed one of the boats out to the sight of Locke's death, once more. After a couple of hours, they ended their investigation and returned to the pier.

"I think we need to close the lake one more day, Jack. Just to fine-tune the area, you know? I know the regatta teams will be madder than a wet hen, but I keep having these visions of Doc's body floating to the surface during the race. After tomorrow, we'll have to open it no matter what," he paused. "Probably should inform the homeowners on the lake shores to look for any washed up evidence. Got the number for the local TV and radio station handy, Son?"

Jack sat in his car while O'Connell gave the stations a commentary on the status of the lake and the death of Locke. The sheriff kept his ideas to himself about the murder of Hudson and the disappearance of Doc Thorton. "No, nothing yet. We'll give a news conference tonight for the six o'clock news. Five-thirty on the steps of the police station? Right." Jack lifted his eyes toward the sheriff who was giving him a pleading look.

"I'll do it," said Jack, reluctantly. O'Connell nodded and walked over to the diving team members who were storing their gear.

Jack sat on the stone retaining wall and opened the small leather notebook that had been given to him by his late father on the day of his police academy graduation. Every case he had investigated was written up in neatly penned script. Evidence, smells, sights, interviews with local people and crime victims, even the dialogue of the suspects and convicted criminals. Everything was there.

He found a blank page and began to put together what he knew about Doc. Jack had recorded Doc's drinking binge the night he disappeared, his walk past the pier, the discovery of his cell phone in the sand, and his last communication with his sister. He had discovered the middle-aged woman's phone number written across the top of the calendar on Doc's desk. She had seemed reluctant to talk to Jack about Doc until she let escape the fact that he was a compulsive gambler. She cried and admitted she had tried to keep the secret life of her brother quiet.

"I thought he would lose all his patients. He was hard up for money for months," she sobbed for a while, and then continued, "And then, all of a sudden, he was able to pay his debts the week before he disappeared. He said a patient owed him a lot of money and finally paid up. He seemed really happy after that, although, I don't think it stopped his habit. He usually told his friends that he was coming to see me on the weekends. But the truth is that he really only stopped by on Friday nights to sleep here, then would 'go exploring.' At least that's what he called his gambling adventures. He usually didn't stop on the way back. He was planning on spending the whole weekend with me, before he was reported missing. He never showed up," she added sadly.

Jack knew that Doc had specialized in mental and emotional health. Although their paths never crossed when his own wife was fading away from leukemia, he had heard a lot about the great Doc Thorton. What had happened to change him? Townsfolk, and even his friend O'Connell, had said that Doc had become absentminded and jittery lately. "Missed an important meeting," said his hospital supervisor. Betting papers had been discovered on his desk and a disturbing notice appeared in his hospital mailbox, notifying him that he checked out two bottles of drugs without the qualifying signature of the head pharmacist.

There were signs of two new meds in Sara's body, the night she fell into a coma, Jack recorded. The drugs had interacted with the medicine Sara was taking for her depression, the head nurse had said. Sara had been under Doc's care for some time. Why would he mess up now? thought Jack. Did someone else administer the meds who knew of her past history?

Doc. No one had seen him since Sara's coma and the night he was seen stumbling from the bar. The boy who found his cell phone had said that he never knew a Dr. Thorton and was only doing his job cleaning the beach for his boss, Ray. "What had happened to Doc that night?" thought Jack. Did he drown somewhere in the lake? If so, where was his body? Did someone follow him and kill him for the money in his billfold? His sister had said that Doc had come out of his hard times. There was no blood at the scene where the cell phone was found and no evidence. "It could have been washed away by all of the rain," whispered Jack.

Doc's cell phone had contained normal entries, the last a voicemail to his sister telling her he would be at her house on Friday, as usual.

And what about the owner of the Flying Fish Bar? thought Jack. The man had heard Doc mumble, "So sorry, so sorry," the night he came up missing. "He was walking, so I thought he would head home to his condo a couple of blocks over," reported the solemn bartender. "I never would have pushed him out that door if I knew he was going to get himself killed." It was the same night Sara had fallen into a deep coma. Did Doc's feelings of sorrow involve Sara?

Jack closed his book and joined the sheriff in the patrol car.

CHAPTER 22

The news conference would take place in one hour. Jack would stand at the podium and inform the lake residents of the grim news involving Grayson Locke. Jack knew that there would be a few of the townspeople who would ask questions about Doc Thorton. But, there was no body. No bones. No sign of Doctor Peter Lyle Thorton, anywhere. Funny, thought Jack, he had never heard Doc's full name. Only his sister had addressed him by the name of Lyle. What happened to Doc after he left the bar? He had walked by the lake, and then disappeared the night of Sara's coma. Or, could Doc be hiding from a crime he had just committed?

Sheriff O'Connell met Jack the following morning in the parking lot of Ray's Bait Shop. A bag of powered donuts and a cup of strong brewed coffee were waiting for him. O'Connell sighed as he slid into the passenger seat of Jack's car. He eagerly grabbed the insulated cup from Jack's hand. "Heavy cream?" asked the middle-aged sheriff, looking tired and drained. The thin skin under his eyes had turned a blackish tint.

"I know I'm not the best looking thing in the morning, but really," said Jack with a smile, "why the big sigh?" O'Connell bit into his second donut, the previous one leaving a thin dusty layer on the front of his brown shirt and pants.

"Son, this thing with Doc I don't understand. I don't think that it's possible that he could have hurt someone like Sara. Cripes, he's been a friend of the Reynolds family forever, even before the death of Sara's father, Jedidiah."

"Unless," said Jack, "Doc was in a bad situation that led him to turn from his normal behavior. Let's assume that he owed someone money, lots of money. Or, he needed to return a favor. Perhaps, someone was blackmailing him." Jack paused, "By the way, the crowd at the news conference yesterday about ate me alive! I told them what I could, but they wanted facts about the crimes and everything else that's going on. I couldn't give them a thing! I even got booed by a man in the back row! And to top it off, a woman stopped me as I left the podium and asked why I even bothered holding a news conference when there was nothing new to tell."

"Sorry, Jack," said O'Connell, his face turning the familiar red that Jack had grown to know.

"I know you love this town, Sheriff. The fact that I never grew up here enables me to look at everyone objectively with no relatives or ties. I'm not as attached to the fact that no one from this little community could possibly be a cold-hearted killer. Listen, first, there was Sara's accident, the murder of Hudson, and then the attack on me at the homestead. Then, add Sara's coma and the attack on Sara's mom. Finish that off with the disappearance of Doc and now the death of Locke. Not a normal couple of weeks in your average town, my friend."

"You're right," said O'Connell. He sighed again and finished downing the last donut from the box. "Ready to question Ray? Seems his hired boy is too sick to talk to us today, so says his mother. She seemed a little frightened. Spoke real quiet. Voice quivered a little."

"Sounds as if he's trying to avoid us. By the way, how close are you to Ray?" Jack asked, pointing to the bait shop sign.

"Not very," said the sheriff. "I'm the only one around here that hates hunting and fishing. Get kidded a lot. Never heard anything bad said about Ray. He's pretty staunch and seems to be a rule setter. Follows the laws. You know, runs a legitimate business and all. Not like a lot of others in this town."

Jack and the sheriff entered the bait building that smelled of fish skin and earthworms. The two men, along with Ray, walked to the deck at the back of the shop. Jack held the cinnamon-scented handkerchief tightly across his nasal passages, while Ray paced up and down the steps retelling the verbal argument that began in the shop a few minutes before the fiery explosion on the lake.

The shop owner admitted he vaguely remembered the details of what had followed that night. "Woke me up by pounding on the door! Could see who it was through the peephole, otherwise I wouldn't have opened it. About knocked me down," he said, "the crazy nuts! Don't know what they were fighting about but they were sure mad!"

"Can you remember anything else? Anything peculiar?" asked O'Connell.

"Well, them being here at midnight. I'd say that was pretty peculiar!" said Ray. "Wait!" he suddenly called out. "Seems to me Locke was carrying something in his arms. A box? Maybe there were some papers? Can't remember. Too darn late!" he said in exasperation.

When O'Connell asked him about the boy, the shopkeeper replied, "Goin' to fire him. He's been in trouble before he moved here. Thought I'd give him a chance but he's been nothing but a darn nuisance. Know anyone I can hire?" he asked as they were leaving. Jack walked the sheriff to the police car and sat in the passenger seat.

"What's next, Jack?" asked O'Connell.

"Cramer," Jack said bluntly. The sheriff grabbed his coffee as it slipped from the dashboard, leaving a small stream of the liquid dribbling onto the floorboard. Jack grabbed a handful of napkins, got out of the car, and ran over to his friend's side. "Okay, Sheriff?"

"Sure. I'm a little tired. Can't sleep with all this going on in the town I'm supposed to protect. People are giving me a hard time."

"Who?" asked Jack.

"Town Council, the committee for tourism, and Willie. He threw me out the other day! Said I needed a warrant to enter. Only wanted a fish dinner. And Luke," he added. "That doggone Jacobs family has been badmouthing me ever since I won the election over the last sheriff, who, like you discovered, Jack, was paid off by the family to overlook a few sins. I'll admit Luke scares me, Jack. I suppose it is possible that he and his men would resort to almost anything to get what they want. But murder?"

"Town's changed, old friend," corrected Jack. "Follow you to Cramer's house?"

"No house, Jack. A condo on the west side of town, overlooking the lake. High-end area. Lawyer business must be on the upswing in order to live there."

"Or something else is funding his bank account," said Jack, thinking of the fight between Cramer and Locke before the accident.

"Okay, Cramer, open up!" yelled the sheriff standing before the wood-paneled door. The loud knock awoke the sleeping man lying across the bed. He sat up and rubbed his eyes. Why were there people yelling and pounding on his door? Cramer glanced down at his pants, stained from scrounging in the garbage bin behind his condo complex earlier that morning. After a restless night, Cramer had walked to the corner newstand to pick up his daily newspaper and had overheard an old man say to his companion that an antique camera and a pair of boots were discovered in the water beside the pier close to Ray's Bait Shop. "A waterproof camera at that! Could be evidence of foul play on the film," the old man had added.

Cramer stretched his body the full length of the bed and looked over at the clothes rack beside the entrance hall. He had thrown the damaged, green algae-stained clothes away the morning of his scuffle with Hudson, but he couldn't locate the orange hat from Joe's Smoke Shack. His pants and torn shirt were easily located, but that hat! Joe said he only gave a few away to his favorite customers. Cramer even went back to the site of Hudson's death, but again no hat. Could it possibly be seen in the pictures the naïve young private eye had taken that morning?"

"Cramer! One more minute and the door's coming down!" shouted the sheriff.

The disheveled lawyer rose and yelled back, "I was sleeping! Just hold on!" Why didn't he leave town last night? he thought. I just need to face them. Give them all the information they need. Maybe they won't watch me so closely. "Stupid Locke!" he whispered as he unlocked the door. "Where were you running to and to whom, when you met your untimely death?"

Two haggard faces greeted him. "Sleeping in a little late, aren't you, Boy?" asked O'Connell.

"You should try it, by the looks of you, Sheriff," replied Cramer. "Got in late, that's all. You do remember what happened?"

O'Connell glanced at Cramer's clothes. "Don't need to be rude, Son. Heard you had a problem with Locke. You two should be on the same side, right? Working for old Jacobs and such?" he added, answering his own question.

"What do you need, Sheriff?" Cramer asked stiffly, as he nodded to Jack standing outside the door.

"Have to take you in, Boy, for a little questioning, since you were the last one to see Locke before the explosion."

"Listen, Sheriff, you can't possibly blame his accident on me! He hit a floating pier in the dark going thirty miles an hour!"

"Did I say that I'm blaming you? Just come. We'll have you back for an afternoon nap. Jack will drive your car."

Cramer grabbed his jacket and anxiously glanced once again at the empty hat rack. He walked to the sheriff's car, slid down in the back seat, closed his eyes, and thought back to that day at the Reynolds property. Cramer had just heard from the mining company before his struggle with the environmentalist, Frederick Hudson. "Listen Hudson," he had said, "The mining company will be here next week to perform the necessary tests. How will we keep it from Luke?"

"Tell him I'm doing a test for the drainage system. He'll never know the difference. I guess you convinced me to look out for myself. Who cares about this stupid town, anyway? Right?" he laughed. "You know, Cramer, I plan on becoming very rich. I always knew there could be a possibility of hitting limestone in this area," Hudson continued. "The computer survey indicated that it could be a deep vein. A literal gold mine or limestone mine," Hudson laughed. "Much more money than Luke could ever make with a casino. We'll have to give a cut of the money though."

Cramer looked at him quizzically. "What are you talking about?"

"Not to Luke! His wife! She owns the place, remember?" continued Hudson. "Though, with all of her health problems, maybe we'll get lucky." He stared at Cramer. "You'll have to eliminate Luke."

"What are you saying?" exclaimed Cramer.

"Well, maybe we won't have to get rid of Luke. He'll probably pull out of the casino deal, due to financial problems, once his old man is exposed, you know," he added, clamping his hand over his mouth.

"What do you mean, Hudson? Tell me what you know!" demanded Cramer.

"Just overheard them talking one night. You know at Willie's. They thought everyone had left."

"Who was talking?" asked Cramer.

"Locke and old Jacobs."

"Why would Luke have financial problems? He's one of the wealthiest men in the group. Especially, since he'll inherit everything from his father."

"Not everything," said Hudson with a sneer on his face. "The old man ruined it for Luke, you know? The time he spent with your mother?"

Cramer still looked dumbfounded. "What do you mean ruined it? Tell me, Hudson, or I'll . . . ."

"You'll do what?"

"You're not making sense! What about my mother?" exclaimed Cramer.

"If you want to know anything more, talk to Locke. He's the one who's kept everything quiet," exclaimed Hudson. "Better look out, though! No one wants to cross him. He even scares me."

"Hey, Cramer, wake up! We're at the police station! You must be really tired to fall asleep on such a short trip. Get out, and follow Jack!" said the sheriff.

"Do you have a warrant to search my house?"

"No. Why? Is there something you'd like to show me?"

"I've nothing to hide," said Cramer.

"Great! Then you won't have any trouble answering our questions. Go in my office. Second room on the right, please."

Cramer sat down across from O'Connell. "Please, make this quick. I have a case this afternoon."

"Fine. Jack, you first."

"Mr. Cramer," Jack began, as he shut the door. "Tell me what took place prior to your argument with Locke."

"I saw him at the old man's house just before he took off in a huff and ended up at Ray's."

"What were you doing at the Jacobs place?"

"Just driving home from reviewing the case I have today. I saw the lights on at the house and his car parked out front. I knew Luke wouldn't like him being there without his permission."

"Isn't that a little bit out of your way?" asked Jack.

"Not really. I sometimes drive around the lake to get home. It helps to calm me."

"Do you need to be calmed?" asked Jack, seating himself on one of the uncomfortable chairs.

"What kind of a dumb question is that?" Cramer asked Jack as he glanced over at O'Connell.

"Seems Locke handled all the affairs for the Jacobs family for a long time. So, why did it bother you so much that he was at the old man's house? And tell me? How was your relationship with Locke?"

"He kept things inside. The family's been trying to tie up loose strings since the old man died. Locke acted like he was co-owner with the guy! I was the one who took care of the family's business problems. The old man paid for my schooling, you know," said Cramer, rattling on from one subject to another.

"Did you have any idea what Locke was trying to do the night he was killed?"

"He took some papers from the old man's office. I questioned him, but he ran out. When I followed him to the pier, he hit me in the face with the oar."

"Then what?" asked Jack.

"That's it," said Cramer. "He jumped into the boat and took off. I wanted to follow, but I had no key. A few seconds later, I heard the explosion."

O'Connell stood up and reached over and touched the swollen bruise on Cramer's face. "You should see a doctor about that, Boy."

"Is that it, Sheriff? I really need to be going."

Jack stood up, and walked around the table. "Tell me Mr. Cramer. How long have you smoked?"

Cramer shifted in his chair, "Half the town smokes, Wilder! Why do you need to know?"

"What brand?"

"Do I have to answer that, Sheriff?"

"I guess we've all had enough. You're free to go, Cramer."

Cramer stood and looked out the window toward the lake. "Too bad the old man's dead," he said, "and now, Locke." He added. "I'm sure Locke knew more about the Jacobs estate than anyone else. I don't know how long it will take to be settled now." Cramer paused, "If you're finished, Sheriff, I need to go before I'm late."

Cramer walked toward his car. Shakily, he climbed in and rested his head on the steering wheel. What should he do now? he wondered. He couldn't seem to concentrate on the conversation between himself and the two men. He was still in shock over the news that Locke had spewed out before his death.

"Half-brothers," Locke had said. "Your father told me the dirty little secret when you almost died trying to help save Luke's dog from the fire. I guess he was a little nervous about losing you, though I don't know why. He never spent much time with you. By the way, I helped him draw up the papers."

"What do you mean half-brothers? Me and Luke? What papers are you talking about?" Cramer had asked.

"Everything is in this folder," said Locke, running toward the boats. "Mr. Jacobs gave the information to me when I took over the handling of the business. Luke and your father hit the bottle quite frequently in those days. They would've lost everything if it wasn't for me. You, his illegitimate child, deserve nothing!" he added. Locke had jumped into the tiny boat, and backed away from the slip. "By the way, your dad paid me quite well to keep his little secret," he shouted as he disappeared into the darkness.

Cramer had knelt down on the pier. Was this the secret Hudson had overheard? Why didn't his mother tell him that he was a Jacobs? He suddenly felt nauseous and leaned over the edge. He knew he had better watch his step. Luke could easily have him eliminated and receive the whole inheritance. But maybe, Luke didn't know, like Locke had said. In that case, he himself was holding the reins, he thought as he rubbed the sore spot on his face. Hurrying to his car, he drove toward town. No matter what his feelings were at that moment, he still had to find that hat!

"Well, what did you think, Jack?" asked O'Connell after Cramer had pulled out of the parking lot following his interrogation.

"He's lying. I could tell by the way he never met my eyes. Squirmed a little. Seemed preoccupied with his thoughts. I had the receptionist call the courthouse. No cases with Cramer today."

"He could have had a misdemeanor case. I'll check when I get back there this afternoon," said O'Connell.

"He definitely didn't want to talk about his smoking habits," said Jack. "He uses filter tips from a company called Old John Smokes. A few other people in town use them, too. Matches up with the cigarette butts down by the pier where the fire took place."

"Can't throw the book on him for littering, Jack, but it does place him close to the brush fire at the pier. Though, he may have thrown his smoke on the ground before he went fishing. Ray said he took his boat out prior to the date when the restrictions on the lake started."

"I'll ask him when I search his home. Hope to get the warrant this afternoon. Don't want him to throw any evidence away."

"What happened to the warrant for Willie's?"

"They said it got tied up in paperwork! Some of his friends work at the courthouse. But, I've got it now."

"How close were Willie's ties with the old man?"

"Close. Knew each other since they were boys. Could be in for trouble with him. We still need to search the old man's house and Luke's." The sheriff sighed. "This case gets more confusing every day."

"You mean cases," corrected Jack. "But, they all seem to intertwine with each other. And remember? We still have the regatta to deal with next weekend. Do you think we need to postpone it?"

"Are you kidding, Jack? The townspeople will take our hides and staple them to the 'welcome to the lake' signs! Besides, this town can't afford to lose any more money. The tourists will soon be pouring in for the ceremonies and the boat race. I'll request extra help. Maybe the culprits will slip up when they're not expecting someone's watching over them. Hey, by the way, when are you going to tell me about your trip home?"

"How about right now?" said Jack. "Let's eat first before you serve Willard the warrant." Jack's stomach growled loudly. "I just hope he lets me finish my cheese sandwich before he throws us out," he added.

CHAPTER 23

The town library had a majestic entrance, thanks to a large financial gift from old Jedidiah Reynolds. Two stone Corinthian columns were flanked by two large shelves of marble, each holding a kneeling lion carved of stone. Luke Jacobs took the steps two at a time, pulled on the heavy wooden door, and stepped inside. A stiff looking older man sat at the front desk.

"Where is the family history section?" Luke demanded.

"Left stairway to the basement, then first door on the right," the man answered gruffly. Luke walked slowly down the darkened stairwell, and opened the door to a cool musty room. An attractive young girl at the desk smiled and asked what records he needed.

"The Reynolds family records?" she repeated, her eyes twinkling. "It seems those are pretty popular this week."

"Who else has been looking at them?" inquired Luke.

"Some older guy. Seems he's interested in a family treasure, or something like that," she replied.

"Rachel!" said an older lady working on the files behind her. "You're not to disclose the list of people who sign out the books! Remember the privacy law?"

"Oh! Right! Sorry!" she said to her co-worker. "I forgot." Frowning, the young girl looked at Luke. "Sign in and have a seat, please." She walked over to a narrow archway and disappeared. A few minutes later, she reappeared with a large, cold, black-bound book that smelled of mold and damp cement.

"Where do you keep this at?" asked Luke. "The freezer?"

"Here," replied the girl, ignoring the young man's question. "You must wear these gloves to protect the pages."

"What is that awful smell?" asked Luke, wrinkling his nose.

"Before the storage room was built, these books were stacked in a leaky basement room for years," the young girl replied.

Luke reached for the book, and started to place it in his briefcase. "Oh no, sir!" said the girl. "You must view family history books in this room. And don't forget to put on these!" she added sternly, pointing to the box of transparent gloves on the large table. Luke groaned, and placed the slippery gloves on his hands. Carefully, he opened the book to the first page that read, "The Family History of Jedidiah Reynolds of Hyattsville and Wakeegon Lake." Uninterested in frivolous facts, Luke quickly flipped through the pages until the title at the top of a page caught his attention. "Reynolds Family Treasure: Fact or Fiction?" The rest of the page had been torn out.

"Hey!" he said loudly.

"Quiet," whispered the older lady, coming to the table.

"The page is missing," he pointed out. He turned the next page. It was gone too! The whole story about the family emerald was ripped from the bindings. "What are you going to do about this?" asked Luke, shoving the book in the woman's face.

"Why, this has never happened before!" she exclaimed. The younger woman walked over to see what the commotion was all about.

"Holy cow!" she said in a surprised voice. "Must have been the man that looked at it last week." She searched the signature list from the following week, "Thorton. Lyle Thorton."

"Rachel! What did I just say?" interjected the older woman.

"Sorry again, Miss Edgars. This is so exciting!" Rachel added, hugging her shoulders. Miss Edgars gave the girl a threatening glance, producing a loud sniffle from the younger woman who ran from the room.

"Now look at what you've done!" said Miss Edgars, looking at Luke. "I'm going to have to ask you to leave."

"What did I do?" asked Luke. "You're the one that messed up," he added pointing a finger at her. "How did Thorton tear pages from this book right under your nose?" When she pointed to the door he said, "I'll send the sheriff over to see about this!"

Grumbling, Luke walked up the steps and exited through the main entrance. Thorton. Why was he looking up information about the Reynolds family? Did he know where the emerald was? He had been the family doctor since Sara was a little girl. Did she disclose the jewel's location? Is that why he suddenly disappeared?

On the outskirts of town, Luke drove past the old homestead, stopped abruptly, and backed into the drive. He personally had the electricity turned off last week to save money. So, why was there a faint light on the third floor? Luke got out of his car, turned on his flashlight, and walked quietly around to the back door.

"So, Son," said the sheriff, taking a big bite from his fish sandwich. "What's new about Sara?" Jack wrinkled his nose at the sight of seafood on the sheriff's plate and pulled his own sandwich closer. O'Connell looked up and saw Willie staring at them from behind the bar. "Better talk quietly," he said nodding toward the back of the room as Willie retreated.

"I need to talk to you about that, Sheriff," said Jack. He hesitated, then said, "She's staying with my Mom in Chicago."

"What?" The sheriff asked between coughs. "Why didn't you tell me sooner?"

Jack blushed. "Right after her mother was attacked I felt she was in danger. I had Luis sign her out of the hospital and deliver her to my mother's house. She'll be there until I figure out what's going on."

"You don't have to convince me. I'm scared for her, too."

Jack nodded. "Luis will watch over her, there, so I can be more productive, here. I'll be able to concentrate on other things, like who attacked her mother." Jack paused, "Before I left for Chicago, I drove over to interview that woman who owns the restaurant Luke and Cramer frequent. Lolita. Do you know her?" he paused, "I imagine you've heard the talk about her and Luke?"

"I've heard the gossip," said O'Connell.

"Well, I overheard a conversation between her and Cramer. You know, Sheriff, I feel he's quickly becoming the main suspect."

"Cramer? I know he's a conniving cuss," said the sheriff, "but murder?"

"Let me finish," said Jack. "The conversation between the two of them convinced me to move Sara immediately."

O'Connell looked at his friend's serious face. Jack continued, "Like I said, I went to see Lolita. Cramer was sitting on a stool at the counter. He kept staring at her. You could tell by her facial expressions that she was scared, but she pretended not to be bothered by him." Jack remembered that Lolita had flipped over the two eggs Cramer had ordered, taking extra care not to break the yolks. She prepared the rest of the food, and then placed the buttered toast and a couple of slices of bacon beside the eggs on a white dinner plate with Lolita's logo on the rim. She sat the plate in front of Cramer and turned around toward the grill.

Jack stopped talking. "Just a minute, Sheriff," he said, pulling his journal from his pocket. He began reading the following conversation to O'Connell:

"Wait, Sweetheart. We need to talk," said Cramer.

Lolita replied, "I've told you all I know about Luke, Cramer. Please leave me alone. I don't want to be associated with you, anymore."

"You know more than you're letting on, Lolita. Surely, Luke has had a loose tongue when he's been around you after one of his drinking binges. I've got my eye on you." He paused, then said, "Is Luke paying you to keep quiet?"

"Quiet about what?" she asked. "What are you talking about?"

"I'll pay you more. I plan on becoming very rich, very soon," said Cramer.

"Lolita turned from the coffeemaker and plopped the cup in front of him," said Jack, "spilling the contents on the counter and spraying droplets onto his shirt front."

"Cripes, Lolita," said Cramer. "Take it easy. You get so upset over little things."

"Little things? Little things? You have my future in your greasy hands, along with that Jacobs creep. This," she added spreading her arms and looking around the room, "doesn't belong to me anymore."

Jack paused, "This is the part that stumped me the most, Sheriff. Cramer leaned over and whispered something in her ear. 'How could you possibly think about doing that to that nice girl, especially since she just lost her children?' Lolita asked him. Not only was she angry but I could see the fear in her eyes. She placed her hands over her ears, moved to the back of the kitchen, and watched from a distance as he finished his food. He winked at her, rose from his stool, and left without paying his bill."

"What happened next?" asked O'Connell, who had finished his sandwich and was peering over Jack's shoulder at the journal entries.

"Well, after he left," continued Jack, "she started choking. 'Get a drink of water, dear,' said the other waitress. Instead, Lolita walked over to the phone booth. 'Lolita!' yelled the woman wearing an apron, 'there are customers waiting to be seated!' Lolita placed the phone back on the hook. When the cafe quieted down, she walked over to the phone again. I heard her whisper into the phone, 'I know you didn't expect a phone call from me. Well, I'm sorry if I'm causing a problem for you!' She proceeded to tell the person on the other end of the line what Cramer had said to her."

"I'm pretty sure she was talking to Luke. She said, 'I supposed you were involved with it, too. If you give me a little more money to make it through the week I won't go to the authorities.' She spewed out a couple of obscenities at the person on the other end of the line and listened to the caller a little while longer, then yelled, 'Stop calling me your girl!' and hung up. Sheriff," Jack paused, "she skirted out of there before I could reach the door. I think Cramer was talking about getting rid of Sara. I called my mom and arranged to have Sara moved that very afternoon."

"How long do you plan to keep her there?" asked O'Connell.

"As long as I can. She's determined to return home. Sara's convinced it was Doc who put her into that coma. When I mentioned the possibility that it could've been her husband, she flew into a rage. She's still mad at me for keeping the death of her children from her, Sheriff. I've arranged for Luis to talk to her about the time leading up to the accident and also what she remembers up to the day of her coma. I don't know if I can protect her if she returns home. I've talked to her about staying at my house, but she said she doesn't need any more negative talk around town about herself. I can't let her stay at her mom's either. I don't want anyone else at risk right now."

"She's right, Jack. Say . . . ?" paused O'Connell. "What about my old RV? It's in pretty good shape and can be parked about anywhere. My wife, I mean ex-wife, doesn't seem to want it from the divorce settlement. I'll bring it around tonight. By the way, it looks a little outdoorsy," said O'Connell apologetically. "Took it to the lake on weekends to escape the house."

"Thanks, O'Connell. Park it in the back of the station. Brady can help us watch over Sara. Great!" exclaimed Jack. "It's settled then. That is, if she agrees to come. Anyway, I'll have my housekeeper clean it this weekend."

"I'll call Peg and let her know," said the sheriff. "Keep me informed."

"I will," said Jack, sheepishly. "Sorry I didn't let you know about moving Sara."

"It's okay. Sometimes our hearts don't always connect with our head."

Jack nodded to his friend and called Luis. Would Sara open up to his longtime friend? Would she mention how she felt about Jack?

CHAPTER 24

Peg took a deep breath and called the Chicago number given to her by O'Connell. She had spoken to Sara only once since she was whisked away to the stranger's house. "Just a moment," the woman responded softly.

"Mom!" replied Sara, sounding relaxed and assured.

"Sara, are you all right?" asked her mother.

"I'm getting lots of rest and a lot of attention from Jack's mom. I'm afraid I'm not very good company for her, though. I've been sleeping a lot."

"But that's a good thing, dear. You sound great." Peg hesitated, "Sara, I'm . . . ."

"You don't have to say anything, Mom. Sorry I came down on you so hard," interrupted Sara. "I realize that you just wanted the best for me. Doc should never have withheld any information from me about the children. I can imagine the pain you also went through."

"Some things will never become easier. You just have to keep going."

"Just like after dad's death?"

"I wanted the world to stop and cry over his passing, but it went on as any other day."

"I didn't get to talk to him," Sara interrupted. She paused and sighed. "I remember that the day was beautiful. Dad had left a message to say he wanted to take a walk with me and the kids. I was going through my own problems with Luke. I told Dad I would see him on Sunday as usual." Sara sat down on her bed. The fall that year had crept in silently, and left abruptly leaving a trail of shocking colors. Life is often that way, she thought to herself. She hated how quickly the seasons passed, often, without a thought.

"So many things and too late," Sara said somberly to Peg. "My children. I'll never hold them again." She began to sob.

"I'll be here, Sara, always," said Peg, softly into the phone.

"Sara!" yelled Mrs. Wilder from downstairs. "The doctor will be here at 1:30 with Jack's friend, Luis!"

"I'll let you go now," said her mother. She paused, "Have you made up with Jack, Sara?"

"Not yet. Got to go, Mom. Call you later," she added as she hung up.

Sara walked to the kitchen in search of Jack's mom, grabbed a couple of oatmeal cookies, and found her in the laundry room sorting the clothes into small piles. "Hello, dear," said Jack's mom. "I'll do your laundry as soon as these loads are done." She looked at Sara's face, "You seem distraught." Sara knelt down on the floor, carefully folding her stiff leg beneath her. "It will take time to get some strength back in that leg," said Mrs. Wilder observing her struggle.

Sara sighed. "I'm nervous about talking to Jack's friend, Luis. What does he want from me? Is it about Luke? Jack said that Luis needs to ask me some serious questions. Has Luke done something wrong? Something illegal? How did he handle the death of the children alone? And the death of his father?" she finished as she stretched out her legs and leaned against the dryer. "I've not been there for him," she said. "Why didn't he tell me about the children?" She began to cry uncontrollably.

Jack's mom knelt on the floor beside Sara. "Don't worry, dear. We can't explain or change the past. You have a lot of people that want to help you." Sara laid her head against her shoulder, as tears dropped down onto her shirt. "Let's make some tea to go with those cookies," Jack's mom added, standing up and pulling up Sara. Sara wiped her eyes with the back of her hand, and followed her to the kitchen.

Jack groaned, turned over, and picked up the ringing phone. "Hello?" he asked sleepily.

"Jack! Get in here! Two big things have happened this morning!" said an excited O'Connell. "The warrants for Luke's and old man's residence have come in. And listen to this! A man from the Midwest Regional Mining company called today about a permit being issued to, you won't believe this, a Frederick Hudson! I told him the guy was dead, but he insisted I see him.

Said it could've affected the whole town if it went through. What do you think of that?"

"I think the list of suspects will grow. Listen, Sheriff, I'm leaving tonight to travel to my old precinct office in Chicago," said Jack.

"Again? So soon?" asked O'Connell.

"They found a list of local men who are involved in the building of the proposed casino," said Jack, "and, I want to see Sara," he added. "What time will the mining company representative arrive tomorrow?"

"Noon. Thought I'd take him to lunch at Willie's and see if I get a reaction from old Willard."

"Good idea. I'll head back in the morning. Will you wait to do the searches until tomorrow?"

"Wouldn't want you to miss it, Son. No warrant for Cramer's yet. Friends in the court system, you know."

"Then, I'll see you at noon tomorrow, Sheriff."

Jack received a second phone call within the hour. "Hey, Jack, this is Ben from the police photo lab in Chicago. I've got those pictures developed from the underwater camera that was pulled out during the dredging of your lake. I'll e-mail them to you if you like."

"Thanks, Ben," said Jack. "But, I plan on arriving in Chicago tonight. I'll pick them up personally. How long are you working this evening?"

He laughed. "I never have set hours, Jack. But, I do have a lot of work that just came in today. I'll probably be here until the wee hours of morning. See you tonight."

Jack hung up the phone, showered, dressed, and packed his clothes for a quick departure for Chicago later that afternoon. He would need to get the pictures and return immediately if he was going to make the midday meeting with the man from the mining company. What was Hudson doing the last few days of his life? Did the other men involved with the casino plans know of Hudson's association with the mining company? What did they plan to mine and where? Jack sighed. Were the casino plans just a ploy to cover up the mining venture?

After seeing the unexpected light in the Reynolds' mansion, Luke hesitated, his head still throbbing from the memory of his first search of the upper rooms. Should he investigate alone? Sheriff O'Connell would . . . ? he laughed. What would O'Connell say about his visit to the house? Luke removed the letter opener from the desk on the second floor landing and proceeded up the final flight of stairs. Light flickered through the crack of the partially opened door. A flame in the old mansion? He really didn't care about the house, but the artifacts could bring in extra cash to bolster the building account. And, what about the mystical family emerald? he shivered. The possibility of a fire could bring all kinds of investigations.

Luke hung his jacket over the stairway rail and slowly placed his keys on the carpeted step. He leaned over and rubbed his left knee, aching from an old football injury. As he stepped on the top step of the servant's flight of stairs, it gave a loud creak. The flame went out just as he switched on his flashlight.

Luke walked into the room, holding his sleeve over his nose. Litter was strewn about the wooden floor, and the smell of rotten food and body odor made his stomach lurch. "Who's there?" he asked. He heard a shuffling of feet and a noise that sounded like a foot hitting a tin can. The can rolled until it bumped up against his shoe. Luke brought his foot back and kicked it so hard that it went spinning toward the door. He heard a thud and the muffled sound of someone crying. Luke crept closer and saw a shadow retreat into the farthest recess. His flashlight revealed the exposed beams as the ceiling grew lower. Luke continued to move forward.

"Don't hurt me!" said a voice from the darkened corner.

Luke turned the flashlight on the figure. Two grimy hands covered the face of a childlike man who was shaking and weeping. Holding the flashlight in one hand and using the other hand to dislodge the man's fingers from his face, Luke asked sternly, "Who are you?"

The man hung his head and repeated the same words as before, "Don't hurt me!"

"What are you doing in my house?" asked Luke, peering at the stout, dirty man through the sparse light. The man looked oddly familiar.

"It your house? James always live here," said the little man. "They took my momma away. She was very still. James was very bad. I didn't stay beyond the second door like momma told Jamesy to do. Are you going to hit me? I give you Jamesy's favorite chocolates. Do you like chocolate? My bear likes chocolates. See?" he rattled on, placing the chocolates next to the old stuffed bear's nose. "Sara likes chocolates, too."

Luke stiffened, "How do you know Sara?"

"Jamesy visit her at hospital. She very sick. Jamesy take care of her. Protect her from bad man."

"What bad man?" Luke asked abruptly.

"The one who tried to hurt her."

"Was he wearing a doctor's coat?"

"What is a doctor's coat?" asked James.

"A white coat. Was he wearing a white coat?"

"Doctor bad. Took away my mamma," said James.

"Yes, yes. You said that already," sighed Luke. Who was this child-man, and what was he doing here? He said he had always lived here. Luke swallowed. Could he be the long lost Reynolds twin? He did resemble Sara's father. If so, his mother must have hid him all these years. How would Sara feel about meeting her long lost uncle? If he was her uncle, then the old Reynolds house belonged to him, not Sara. "Listen James," said Luke. "How about we play a game?'

"Okay."

"If you promise not to leave the house or visit Sara again, I'll bring you food every day."

"Hamburgers and pie?" asked James.

"Sure, anything you want."

"Chocolates, for Jamesy and bear?"

"Sure, just don't leave this house."

"Don't need chocolates for Sara," he said sadly, hanging his head. "She's gone."

"Gone? What do you mean gone?"

"Not at hospital any more. Jamesy not see Sara."

"I'll be back later and bring you food," said Luke, frowning. "Use this flashlight. No fire, James. Do you understand?" James nodded and sat down on the dirty mattress pad.

Luke handed James the flashlight and picked up the candles and matches lying on the floor. "Remember, stay inside!" commanded Luke as he left the room. What should he do now? The casino deadline was nearing and construction would begin soon. Could he draw up papers for James to deed the property over to him without Sara finding out? And speaking of Sara, if she wasn't at the hospital, then where was she? "With that Wilder character," he said aloud. He debated driving to Jack's house and confronting him. Instead, he did a u-turn in the road, and drove toward Cramer's condo. Could the lawyer have the papers drawn up right away to sign over the property? Luke knew the real question would be . . . how much would Cramer want for his contribution to quickly seal the deal?

CHAPTER 25

Cramer placed his hand over his heart and pulled his car over to the side of the road to catch his breath. "Half of the Jacobs money is mine!" he exclaimed with a tone of disbelief. Luke had bragged to the rest of the committee members that approximately five million of the Jacobs family fortune would be spent on the casino and house renovation, with the rest being backed by various sponsors. For most of his life, Cramer had worked exclusively for the Jacobs family until recently, when the old man died. Except for his soured real estate deals, Cramer had lived well. But now, he was filthy rich. If he invested his part of the inheritance in the casino, too, he would be in equal partnership with Luke.

Perhaps now, his money problems would be solved. He would demand that Luke sell all of his father's assets. Locke and the old man were dead. There was no one to stop him from getting everything he wanted. Excited, he began to think of how his life would change, until he remembered the missing orange hat. Could the sheriff order a warrant to search his residence?

Before he returned to his home he would stop by and pick up the old phone book that Mr. Higgins had located for him. Cramer pulled his checkbook from his briefcase and wrote out a check for a thousand dollars. He pulled back on the road and drove down the dirt lane toward the man's house. An old shriveled up man who looked about ready to die was waiting on the porch steps when he arrived.

"Here ye be," he said in a proud voice. "Didn't take long. Sorry it smells funny." Cramer gave him the check. The old man handed him a book that smelled of mildew and mice. Cramer got into his car. "Looked it up already for ya," the old man shouted. "Belonged to a Doc Andrews. Practiced right here in town. He's still alive, you know? Lives at the Lakeside Nursing Home. He be about 97 years old, if'n I recall."

Cramer stared at him. "Tell no one, and I'll double your money," he said getting back out of the car.

"No need," said the old man. "I was just curious."

Cramer grabbed his checkbook, wrote out another check for a thousand dollars, and said, "Here! Keep quiet, okay?

"Whatever ye say," said the old man with the yellowed teeth. "Never seen this much money for a long time. Thank ye."

Cramer returned to his car and drove toward home. The contracts between the mining company and himself and Hudson had to be destroyed. He caught his breath when he saw Luke's truck parked in front of his house. Luke got out of his truck when he saw Cramer approaching.

"I need to discuss some business with you, Cramer," said Luke. "Looks like a wrench is being thrown into the plans." Cramer backed up, his face showing the fear he felt inside. "Why are you so scared? A big boy like you?" He laughed. "Found something in the Reynolds house I thought you would want to know about," said Luke. "You knew Sara's father had a twin brother, right? There seems to be a man who looks like Sara's father living in the attic rooms of the old mansion! I thought," he said gruffly, "that you had an exterminator go over that place a month ago?"

"He cancelled," said Cramer. "I forgot to get another one. I'll get him first thing tomorrow."

"Don't you understand, Cramer?" asked Luke. "If he is Sara's long-lost uncle, like he says, he is the rightful owner of the house, not Sara! If it is him, we need draw up papers immediately for him to sign over the old mansion to us before anyone else finds out he is still alive. By the way, he's been to see Sara. I don't know if she has seen him. Seems she has disappeared from the hospital. Probably with that Wilder fellow," he added. "Figure something out, Cramer!" he yelled out the window as he climbed back into his truck and spun the vehicle around the graveled parking area.

Cramer ran up the stairs to his unit and placed the old phonebook on the table. He had to find old Doc Andrews and ask him if he remembered his mother. But first, he needed to destroy everything that linked him to the mining venture and look for the missing orange hat.

Jack pulled into the parking lot of Willie's and saw O'Connell and the mining representative entering the restaurant. "Sheriff!" yelled Jack.

O'Connell turned around, walked the man over to Jack's car, and introduced him. "Great to meet you," said Jack, smiling. "I'm interested in what you have to say about our little town."

The man shook his hand and frowned. "I hope you weren't counting on the mining venture to make this town's financial woes disappear?"

"This is the first we've heard of this 'venture' as you call it, Sir. Exactly where was this mining boom supposed to take place?"

"Why, the 20 acres surrounding the west end of the lake property."

"The old Reynolds property?" asked the sheriff. "I'm afraid you've been had. That's the location of the controversial casino. It's been in the works for some time now."

"According to the map, that's the place. Quite a large vein of limestone. This deceased man, Hudson? He had a partner." The three men began to walk toward Willie's when the man from the mining company turned around and asked, "Wouldn't know a man by the name of Richard Cramer would you?" The two friends looked at each other in surprise.

"Why?" asked Jack.

"He's going to be surprised when I tell him he's not going to be a rich man."

Cramer opened the closet and started throwing things on the ground until he retrieved a small cardboard filing box from the upper shelf. "Easy enough to burn," he thought. He laid a newspaper and kindling on the brick floor of the fireplace, threw the box on top of it all, and lit a match. Once the fire burned out, he scooped the ash into a metal bin. Cramer knelt on the floor to see if every scrap of paper had been destroyed, and reached for his flashlight. He would search for the orange hat, but first, he would stop by the nursing home to visit the elderly doc. Would he remember his mother, and why she called him that day, long ago?

A few patients were sitting on the porch of the Lakeside Nursing Home, rocking back and forth on the white wooden chairs. Some were engaging in conversation with each other, and some were staring straight ahead, oblivious to the happenings of the town except for a few feet ahead of them. "I need to see a Doctor Andrews," said Cramer to the girl at the front desk.

"He's sleeping. Are you a relative?" she asked.

"No. But he may have some information about my family."

"Okay. Let me see if I can wake him up." She returned a few minutes later. "Follow me, Mr. . . . ? He gave her a weak smile, but didn't offer his name.

"Doc. Doc Andrews!" she repeated. The thin wrinkled man opened his eyes. He stared at the stranger, and then, at the woman.

"Is this the man who wants to talk to me?" She nodded, helped him into a sitting position, and left the two of them alone. "And you are?" he asked in a frail voice.

"I think my mother may have known you. A Mrs. Jessie Cramer? She had me rather late in life. Her husband, my father, died in a tragic electrocution accident when I was seven." The old man's eyes widened with recognition.

"Yes, I remember her," he said in a dry raspy voice. "A beautiful quiet lady. Seemed scared when she called me. Didn't know what to do."

"You mean about my father's death?"

"No, son. She didn't know what to do when she found out she was carrying you."

"Was she disappointed? Scared?" Cramer asked.

"Too long ago," said the old man, lying down and turning toward the wall.

"Listen, my future depends on what you know. Was the dad that I knew my real father?"

"No, son," he said, still facing the wall. "She was ashamed to tell anyone and wanted to know what she could do. Didn't want to give you away or end her marriage. I told her I would fix the birth certificate. No one would know," he said quietly.

"Is Samuel Jacobs my real father?"

"He is," said the old man tiredly.

"Will you sign a paper admitting it? I'm having serious medical problems," he lied, "and I need to have the records of the family's medical history."

"I will sign. Now go. I'm tired," he replied, still facing the wall.

Cramer walked slowly back to the car. He turned off the small recorder in his pocket. What shame and embarrassment his mother must have suffered! Richard Cramer should have been Richard Jacobs! What would Luke say now?

Cramer drove by his favorite restaurant and ordered two of his favorite barbecue sandwiches, topped with coleslaw, before looking for the intruder Luke had seen in the Reynolds' house. Cramer had heard many things about the infamous mansion. In its glory days, the third floor was mainly dominated by a large ballroom for dancing, flanked with servant rooms on either end. Later, when the family went into seclusion after the unfortunate birth of the disabled son, it became a secluded playroom large enough to ride scooters and tricycles. When the youngest boy, Sara's father, was taken away, it fell into ruin like the rest of the home.

"James Reynolds? Could it be possible?" Cramer whispered. "No one has seen him for ages." He drove to the haunted looking house. The sunlight was almost gone. He retrieved his flashlight from his trunk and climbed the stairs in silence hoping to surprise the man. The top floor was dark and still.

"James?" he asked in a soft voice. A shadow crossed the room and disappeared. "James, come out! Now!" The short man crept from the corner slowly. Cramer directed the light toward the figure. "I won't hurt you," he said as he shined the light on his own face.

The short man screamed and ran toward the door.

"Wait!" shouted Cramer, shining the flashlight around the room. Food wrappers, old newspapers, and a soiled orange baseball hat from Joe's Smoke Shack lay on the floor in a pile. Orange hat? He reached down and picked up the grime-covered cap. The size was correct. He walked slowly toward the door, "James, I have a surprise for you." He reached in his pocket for a packet of gum. "Do you like gum, James?" The slight figure crept closer. He reached out his hand. Cramer suddenly grabbed it and held it tightly.

"No! No hurt!"

"James, I'll give you the gum. Just tell me where you got this hat," he said shoving it in his face.

"I look for food."

"Where? Do you remember where?"

"Big brick building."

"Was it by a grove of trees?"

"Big trees, pine trees."

"Will you show me, James?"

"James never go out in sunshine. Promised. Bad man might take me away."

"Bad man? Who?" asked Cramer. After a few moments of silence, Cramer said, "I'll bring you lots of gum, if you show me where you got your hat."

"James show you. I walk now," he said as he led the way down the servant's stairs to the kitchen door.

Jack, O'Connell, and the mining expert sat together on a wooden picnic table in the farthest corner of the restaurant, away from Willard. When they entered, Jack saw no recognition of the out-of-town man from Willard. The waitress looked at them warily, took their orders and returned to the counter. "Okay," said Jack, "What does Richard Cramer have to do with the mining plans for the mansion property?"

"Would anyone mind telling me who this Cramer is?"

"He was part of the lawyer team that took care of the Jacobs family business along with Grayson Locke."

"Who also is deceased," added the sheriff.

"He died in an accident recently," said Jack.

"Which also looked fishy," added the sheriff.

"What do you mean also, Sheriff?" asked the mining representative.

"You knew Hudson was murdered?"

"Murdered!" replied the man. "I just spoke to him a couple of weeks ago. That's why I'm here. I couldn't get him on the phone. Now, I know why. Cramer was supposed to be a partner with him. He wouldn't answer my calls either."

"How did they plan to get the Reynolds' property switched over to their names?" asked O'Connell.

"They said they had discussed it with the owners and were planning on sharing the profit three ways."

"That's funny. Luke just announced in the local paper that the casino plans would be revealed at the opening of the regatta. Any questions and concerns would be answered at that time. It doesn't seem to me that he's heard of the limestone venture."

"Well, it's a good thing he didn't switch his plans to mining. The presumed million dollar vein turns out to be Harrodsburg Limestone. Not very durable or valuable. Anyway, I still have to tell you the big news. A couple of my men have been doing some small digs up on the mounds on the other side of the hill. Seems to be a few Indian artifacts located there. I wanted to talk to you about it first, Sheriff."

"Wow!" replied O'Connell, "You sure put a lot of things on my plate at once. Have the artifacts been appraised?"

"Just found them yesterday. Now get this! One of the men heard that there were a few items taken from a museum last week. The curator thought it was an inside job, so they haven't leaked the information to the public yet."

"Holy cow!" said the sheriff. "Jack, do you think Luis can head down here and help? I think you've told me once that he's interested in old artifacts."

"I could have Luis here by morning."

"Great, Son," said the sheriff. "Now," he said looking at the man, "Let's get someone in here to work with Luis, gather up the possible museum pieces, and give an opinion on them. And then, on the way to the station, tell me everything you know about this deal involving Hudson and Cramer. By the way, Jack," said O'Connell, as the three men walked toward the parking lot, "bring Cramer back in for questioning in the morning, will you?"

"I'll take Luis with me. That will give him a scare," said Jack. Jack left for Chicago at exactly three-thirty that afternoon. He phoned Luis on the way and told him the news. Luis promised to be at Jack's mother's house when he arrived. "By the way Luis, how was your interview with Sara?" asked Jack. The two men spent the next few minutes discussing Sara.

"Definitely foul play going on," said Luis. "I thought you were moving to a quiet, peaceful town, Jack?"

Jack laughed, "Wait until I tell you the latest news when I arrive. By the way," Jack asked hesitantly, "is Sara willing to see me?"

"She's very angry, Jack. Mostly, because you withheld the information about her children. Try to imagine how she feels! The loss of two children must be unbearable. Add to that a disloyal husband! She feels pretty alone, except for her mother. Sara said they talk every day, now."

"Maybe, if she forgave her mother, she'll forgive me, too," said Jack hopefully.

"That's family, Jack. She feels differently about you. She said she was just beginning to trust you. I don't know, buddy," said Luis. "She's getting along alright, otherwise. One of the local doctors came in to remove the cast. You were right. He couldn't find anything wrong. No fracture. No nerve damage.

Doc evidently didn't want her to move from that bed. I don't know why, Jack. She thought Doc was her friend. She feels pretty low about that, too."

"Thanks, Luis. I'll see you tonight."

Jack called his mother next and told her he and Luis would arrive very late that evening. "Sara wants to talk to you, Jack," said his mother.

Jack swallowed, "I was hoping she would."

"Hello, Jack," said Sara shyly.

"Sara! Luis said you were doing well."

"Luis is a very kind man," responded Sara. "At least, he is being honest with me."

"I'm sorry, Sara. I didn't tell you about the children because I care for you."

"Care for me? That's how you show you care for me?" she asked.

"Again, all I can say is that I'm sorry. I did what I thought was best, Sara," replied Jack.

She hesitated, "I want to talk to you alone, face to face, when you arrive. No Luis. No mother."

"Okay," he said softly, "I want to talk to you, too. There has been some new information uncovered about the things that have been happening in this town. I have to bring Luis back with me."

"Okay, Jack," she said quietly, her anger dying down. "I'll see you tonight."

Jack called the police station next. "Jack! I was just going to call you," said Luis. "After you hung up, some information about the 'Casino Seven' came through the wire, you know, the men involved with the plans to build the casino? And, the photos you wanted just arrived here, too. I haven't had a chance to view them yet," he added. "By the way, what were you looking for in those pictures?"

"There could be some clues about Hudson's murderer and my attacker in the background surrounding the crime scene," said Jack, "Or else, why did the suspect knock me down and steal my camera? Whoever it was must have really panicked. They could have just taken the film and left us without any evidence. I hope the quality of the pictures was good enough. Is Cap going to be there, too?" Jack asked hopefully.

"Everyone's interested in the happenings of your little town, Jack," he laughed. "It even scares me. And I've lived in Chicago my entire life!"

Jack sighed. "Scares me, too. I'd like to see it return to the quiet sleepy little town it was when I arrived here. Talk to you later." Jack removed his earphone and punched the CD button to blast his latest purchase throughout the interior of the car. He hoped the answers he was looking for would be revealed tonight.

Cramer pushed James, knocking him down face first in the dirt path. "You're going too slow!" James got up, brushed off his shirt and began to run. "I didn't mean for you to run," Cramer yelled. James slowed his pace and eventually arrived at the destination point. "Is this the place where this hat came from?" asked Cramer holding the hat in front of James. He nodded. Cramer sighed in relief. The dumpster was behind his condo complex. "Okay, James. Let's go back to the house."

"You not mad at Jamesy now?" asked the funny little man, puffing from the long walk.

"If you do something else for me, I won't be mad anymore."

"What you want Jamesy to do?" he asked.

"Something I think you'll like James. How would you like to visit Sara?"

"James happy! Sara make Jamesy happy!" he replied. James jumped up and down, stopped, and hung his head. "I don't know where Sara is at. She not at hospital now."

Cramer raised his eyebrows. "Really? Well, I'll find out for you, James. I want you to look special for Sara. I'll bring some new clothes for you to wear when you visit her, okay?"

"Okay," said James. "And some chocolates, too. James all out of chocolates. Have one left for Sara."

"Show me what kind of chocolates you like when we get back to the house, okay? By the way, will you show me your room again?"

"James give you present from room."

"Good, James. Now be very quiet on our way back."

"James scared out here. James like home better."

Cramer nodded. He wondered what else James had seen in his outings. Perhaps a murder . . . or two?

CHAPTER 26

Luke picked up the phone and called Alistair Goodman.

"Luke, how are things going? Moving along okay?" asked Mr. Goodman.

"Got a new wrench thrown in, sir. I'll tell you about it later. Right now, I need to ask you a question. Do you know why Hudson filed a stop order petition?"

"Yep. Polluted water." said Goodman. "Seems some chemical element has been leaking from the old basement into the stream. Has a bit of mineral deposits too, from the hills that surround the back property. I should know more within the week." He paused, "I never knew Hudson had such a vendetta against us, Luke. What did you do to the man?"

"He ticked me off most of the time, but I didn't do a thing to him," replied Luke.

"Maybe, we should have offered him more money. Usually that's enough to keep the wolves away and the dunces happy," Goodman laughed. "If nothing else happens, the construction company should be here at the beginning of next week. So, what is this 'new wrench' you were talking about?"

"Nothing to worry about, Sir. I'll take care of it. So, the construction company will be here right after the regatta?"

"Yep," he replied. "We don't want to give the townspeople too much time to reject it, do we?"

Luke thought about James. "Right, Sir. Call you tomorrow?"

O'Connell hung up the phone. He had just informed Jack that one of his deputy's had found a yellowed cardboard file under an old overturned boat at Ray's Bait Shop. "Just put the boat there last week," said Ray. "The boy was supposed to have it repaired. Shouldn't have expected him to follow through," he added.

Stunned, O'Connell laid the file on his desk. The file's enclosed papers contained valuable information about the Jacobs family, along with details pertaining to the estate planning of Samuel Jacobs. One important item had stood out. The carefully scripted papers drawn up by Grayson Locke had listed that one third of the fortune went to himself, a third to Samuel's son Luke, and a third to someone listed as R. Cramer. The title of "son" was placed after the name.

"Cramer? A son of Samuel Jacobs?" O'Connell said out loud. Did Luke, or Cramer, know they were brothers? he wondered. Did anyone beside the old man and Locke know this information?

How would this news affect the construction of the casino? O'Connell knew that rumors had been flying around town for weeks about the proposed opening of the new structure, but the actual date for the groundbreaking had emerged only three days ago. He had received several calls at the station. Some people were thrilled about the prospect of new jobs that would be coming to the little town. Others were outraged that the information was not shared until it was close to the actual building time of the new structure.

Yesterday, O'Connell had read the front page article of the local paper with mixed emotional. The reporter from the local paper had asked the townspeople if they felt that the new casino would affect the charm of the lakeside town. The old folks made comments such as, "Not worried about charm. There will be no town if something's not done soon. Don't like the idea, but it'll provide a few jobs and put food on the table." The younger residents had offered their own opinions, "No jobs no people. Eventually, they'll move away, especially the young."

O'Connell sighed. Jack was right. The town had changed and would be changing again, soon. The sheriff drove into the parking lot of the town hall. The finalization of the regatta plans would be made tonight, but, would anyone want to come to a town whose local newspaper headlines read, "Who will be next?"

Cramer drove toward his office. Richard Cramer. Richard Jacobs. The names kept repeating themselves over and over in his mind. Once inside, he methodically put together the papers for James Reynolds to sign over the property and the mansion, but his mind was elsewhere, his thoughts random and confused. Unable to sleep the night before, Cramer had pulled out an old photo of Sara's father and had stayed up most of the night scrounging around for clothes that looked similar to what Jedidiah Reynolds, Jr. was wearing in the picture. Early the next morning he had driven to the mansion. "Put them on, James. I'll be back and take you to see Sara. Don't leave the house," he said as James dug into the cooler full of food he had left behind.

Cramer still didn't know where Sara had disappeared. No one in town had seen her. He had even called the hospital. All they could say was that she was signed out a few days ago. Evidently, Luke didn't know either. "Her husband came around yesterday looking for her," said the floor nurse. "Cursed, and pounded his fist on the counter. I told him I would call security if he didn't leave!"

Collecting his thoughts, Cramer knew that all he had to do was to finish drawing up the papers, and then take James to see Sara. Maybe she'll finally crack when she sees her lookalike deceased father making an appearance at her bedside. It wouldn't take too much to get her declared incompetent. I'll have no problem getting James to sign over everything, if I bait him with food and chocolates. "If he won't sign, I'll banish him from the house," he said aloud. He paused, "I just hope James is able to write his own name."

Jack took a while to soak in the news that Cramer was a half-brother to Luke. Evidently, the two didn't know they were more than just partners in the casino ownership. What would happen now? he thought, as he pulled into the parking lot of the old Chicago precinct building. His car barely missed the trash that had blown out of the large over-flowing bin, sitting behind the station. Luis pulled into the space beside him and laid his hand on the horn. Jack smiled and nodded. Suddenly, the back door of the station opened and five men poured out, shoving each other down the steps. "Wilder! About time you came back!" one of them yelled. The group of uniformed young men came alongside Jack's car, yanked him out of his seat, and patted him on the back and head with five pairs of hands.

Jack laughed. "Hey! When are you guys going to pick up this mess?" he asked motioning to the trash.

"We were just waiting on you," one of them said, picking up the trash, while the other four men pulled him inside.

"Cap's here, Jack. You want to see him? He's on the phone."

Jack opened the door to see the District 12 captain leaning over his desk, reaching for a broken pencil. He nodded as Jack placed an ink pen in his hand.

"Okay, Mrs. Anderson," answered the chief, writing furiously. "Right. I'll see what I can do. I know. The youth are not what they were in your time. Sure. Okay, I'll call tomorrow." He winked at Jack and hung up the phone. "Some kids stole the pink flamingos from her front yard. You know? Hard crime stuff," he laughed. "Need to stop them now, though," he said seriously, "before they get into real trouble. So, Jack," he said slapping him on his sore back, "how long are you staying?"

"Only a few hours. Luis has been doing some investigating for me. And, I guess some photos I've been waiting for are ready. Did Luis have time to tell you anything about the Casino Seven?"

"Sure did. What kind of crazy town are you mixed up with, Jack? The news of your town has reached the big city papers. And the regatta? Is it this weekend?"

"In three days. The town council members are meeting tonight to plan their strategy for crowd control and security measures. They're afraid people will show up just to see a town where a murderer is on the loose and an important doctor is on the missing person list," he frowned. "The regatta teams are already mad that the lake has been closed down for a few days. The town committee members wanted to reschedule, but the teams argued that this was the traditional weekend. They also made sure to emphasize that the weather was going to be perfect."

A tall, skinny, bespectacled man knocked on the doorframe. "Are you Jack?"

A deputy standing beside him butted in. "Jack, this is Ben. He's been working on those pictures you sent him."

Jack rose and followed the man to a side room reeking of photo chemicals. Jack grabbed his hankie. "I left them hanging over here so you could see them better," said Ben. Jack saw a line of photos hanging from a steel wire. "See here," said Ben. "Unfortunately, the majority of the pictures were in pretty bad shape. Most of them were pictures of trees, flowers, and a couple of squirrels chasing each other. The only one that held any human form was this one," he said, pointing to the enlarged photo at the end. Jack gasped when he saw the tall silhouette of a man peering out from behind a large tree. An orange hat lay on the ground close to the man's feet.

"Can you enlarge the logo on the hat for me, Ben?" asked Jack.

"Sure, Mr. Wilder."

Jack walked to the fountain located in the hallway in front of the captain's office. "You look a little pale, Jack," he said, rising from his desk. "Need help?"

"Could you call O'Connell?"

"Sure," he said looking up the number on his desk file. He handed the phone to Jack.

"Sheriff?" said Jack. "I think I've found something very interesting."

He talked quietly to the sheriff until Ben called out, "Jack, come in here." Jack took one look at the photo and wondered how many hats were given out for Old John Smokes.

"Cramer!" yelled Willard, as Cramer stepped inside the restaurant to order a sandwich to go. "What on earth's been going on? I heard a rumor today that a stop order permit will be issued for the casino. Why?"

"Don't know exactly why, Sir," said Cramer, puzzled.

"Don't Sir me! I've invested most of my retirement in the casino, Cramer! I want my investment protected! You're our official attorney now, since that stupid Locke got himself killed. You should know everything that's going on! Luke's nowhere to be seen, and he doesn't answer my calls."

Cramer was still standing in front of him in the same frozen position. "What's wrong with you, Cramer?" asked Willard. "Are you listening to me?" He paused, and then added, "Did you know that the model for the casino is already in the backroom? Care to see it before we meet tonight to finalize our speech? I know I need to soften a few things for the public. That stupid media bunch has been calling me everyday to see if I'll give them an exclusive pre-announcement. Can you believe that?" Willard continued, "I told them, just let the townsfolk know that the casino will provide employment for many people in this town. That'll shut them up."

Cramer stood silently. He was thinking about James, the rightful owner of the house and how he needed to get the papers signed before the meeting tonight. Willard continued to babble, "Cramer! Are you listening to me? Do you want to see the model, or not?"

"No, not now," Cramer responded, walking toward the door. Willard stared at him as he walked out and got into his car.

"Luis," said one of the older men at the precinct station. "Good to see you again."

"How are you, Nick?" asked Luis.

"Well, my body's getting a little too old and a little too fat for chasing down criminals. So, I've been doing a little of the investigating work." He smiled and smoothed his graying hair.

"Thanks for helping," said Luis. "What did you discover?"

The man walked over to his desk, sat down, pulled up a screen on the computer, and pointed. "Is that the group?" he asked, as a large black and white photo appeared on the screen.

"Yep! There's old man Jacobs, his son Luke, Grayson Locke, Frederick Hudson, Alistair Goodman, and Daniel Pierceton. . . ."

"Do you know the last man in the photo?" asked Josh.

"That's Richard Cramer. According to Jack, he's the scary one."

Nick pulled up a new screen, containing a list of the casinos in Indiana. "The owners, for two of the three casinos, are officially listed as 'Seven Men Investments,'" he said. "The one they didn't own just got their license cancelled. Makes me wonder if those men caused it, you know? They promised to reopen the casino within the next month if it was under their ownership. And listen to this!" he went on. "All seven are being investigated by the internal revenue and are listed as forging construction licenses and permits. The state's in a panic. Can you imagine the loss of money?" he added. "Listen, Luis. Do you know Luke Jacobs?"

"Unfortunately, Jack does," said Luis, as Jack walked into the room.

"It seems that he will be signing the permit next Monday. The construction starts the same day."

"The house is still standing," said Jack. "The property officially belongs to Sara. I'm afraid for her life, Nick. That's why she's here in Chicago with my mother."

"Better be careful, Jack. Sounds like another murder wouldn't slow this group down."

Jack nodded. He scribbled down the info and was getting up from his chair when Nick asked, "Do you know a Doc Thorton?"

Jack jerked his head toward the screen, swallowed, and sat back down.

Luis grabbed the glass of milk, spilling some on the tile floor. "Sorry, Mrs. Wilder. Guess I've been spilling stuff on your floor for over 20 years."

She laughed. "Sit down, Luis. I guess it's just you and me. Sara and Jack won't be back for another hour. I'm glad you talked him into staying the night and returning home early tomorrow morning."

"I know Jack's anxious to serve Luke the warrant, Mrs. Wilder, but I'm glad he'll have a chance to talk with Sara alone. He's taking her to his old haunt, you know? The fifties diner on Lincoln Avenue? It's open all night." Luis looked at her anxious face. "Don't worry. I'll drive in the morning." He added, "I know he'll get Sara to understand the seriousness of her situation."

"I hope so, Luis. It's been hard on the both of them. Sara's beginning to feel like a daughter to me. I like her mom, too. She sounds really nice on the phone."

Jack entered the fifties-styled diner with Sara. They sat in the booth in front of the large window. Sara smiled. "You and Luis sat here, right? When you were little boys?"

"Right," said Jack, liking the smile on her face.

"Nice place," she said to the waitress.

"Thanks, dear. What will you have?"

"Order the hamburger with pickles and French fries," suggested Jack. He ordered a tripled breaded deep fried cheese sandwich with cheese fries. "They're the best! I'm only making an exception because you're here," he said. "I promised O'Connell I'd lose a few pounds along with him. You know, misery loves company?" Jack had worn his old suit to the office a few days ago. "Fits like it did when I bought it," he had said to the sheriff, patting his taut stomach. O'Connell groaned, said he needed the donuts to relieve his stress, and had changed the subject.

"How do you like Luis, Sara?" asked Jack, returning to the present.

"I like him very much. You and Luis are very similar. Both of you remind me of my father."

"Tell me about your dad, Sara."

"You have a lot of the same qualities as my dad. A strong, confident, quiet leader. Gave of himself, and his finances, until he was almost broke.

He always gave solid advice. Unfortunately, I rejected it, and him, when it came to Luke. Look where it's gotten me now," she added.

"Where has it gotten you, Sara?"

"Jack, don't start again." She frowned, "You know what I mean. He's my husband like it or not. Luke and my father were as far apart in character as they could possibly be. Maybe it was his charm," she said wistfully, looking out into space.

"Charm?" asked Jack. Sara sighed. She looked lost in her own world, thought Jack.

"Our families were rivals from the beginning," she began again. "My father tried to patch things up between the Reynolds and the Jacobs families, but old Samuel would have nothing to do with him. My poor father," she said with sadness, "never really got over the fact that I married Luke. My relationship with my dad was never the same." She continued to speak rapidly without stopping. "It got to the point where I couldn't take the marriage anymore. The lies. The affairs. I started to take a drive every day. First, to the local drive-in to get a burger and a coke, and then to the lake and back. When Luke's drinking became worse, I couldn't trust him to watch the little ones while I was gone, so I asked my mother and father to watch them for me when I went out. My mother finally found out what was going on. My father was furious. And then," she paused, her eyes misty, "he died unexpectedly. Things really got bad between Luke and me after dad's death. My relationship with my mother was very strained, but she stood by me nevertheless. I've talked to her a couple of times since I've been here. I know she's been hurting, too." Sara looked at Jack. "I had to keep everything together. My children, they deserved a home like I had when I was a little girl . . .," she trailed off in a whisper.

Jack got up and sat beside her in the opposite bench. Sara leaned her head against his shoulder. "Isn't it time to finally give it up, Sara? Are you going to wait on him to die so you can start living?"

She turned her head. A small stream of tears fell from her green eyes. "Please don't say that anymore, Jack."

Jack was silent for a while then said, "Sara, I think we may have a lead on your case."

"I'm not sure I really want to know," she said sadly. "What I do want to know is how long do I have to stay here, Jack? I've appreciated your mother's hospitality, but I want to go home."

"Not much longer," he replied. "I'm going back with Luis early in the morning."

"I miss you already," she said, her soft hair lightly brushing his shoulder. Jack said nothing.

Jack dropped Sara off and kissed his mother. "Come on Luis, I'll drive you home. Sara, I'll take you to a little café down the street sometime. Another favorite of mine." She smiled and walked upstairs.

Jack drove Luis home. He would mention the old RV to Sara when he returned. O'Connell said it could be ready in a couple of days. Jack knew he was treading on thin ice. Lately, he had thought about Sara all the time. Would she agree to come back knowing that she was a target for murder?

Chapter 27

Richard Cramer pulled the tie tighter around the chubby man's neck. Black with wide red stripes, just like the one Sara's father wore in the photo Cramer had taken from the wall at Willie's. "Wore it to church, too," said Willard. "That should jar a few memories." Cramer had given the restaurant proprietor the news about Jedidiah's twin, still living in the upper floor of the Reynolds mansion. "Hard to believe he kept to the house all these years," said Willard. "Sure he's smart enough to follow through with your plan?"

"He's sane enough," replied Cramer. "He's really fond of Sara. He takes her candy and stuff."

"He knows Sara?"

"That's what I've heard. Hospital employees have witnessed him visiting her, ever since the accident." Willard looked at Cramer with a quizzical glance. "Must have overheard someone talking about Sara, or he has seen the news about the accident in the newspaper. Maybe someone taught him how to read when he was young."

"Who's to say that he won't tell the authorities?" asked Willard.

"I don't think so. I've discovered he has a weakness. He loves chocolate! I'll just tell him either he visits Sara and pretends he is her father or he's out of the house and no more handouts. I finally found out today that Sara is in Chicago with that Wilder fellow. When she returns we'll pay her a visit. Then, we'll have the new doc declare Sara crazy. She won't be considered well enough to contest the casino permit."

A loud complaint brought Cramer back to the present. "No like," said James, pulling at the tie.

"You can take off the nice clothes and put on your dirty ones. These are just to visit Sara."

"Sara like this?" asked James, pointing to the suit of clothes and the loud striped tie.

"Sara will love you dressed in these clothes. She will be home soon. Then, we'll show her how handsome you look in the new suit."

"Sara think James handsome?"

"Sure, James. By the way we'll play a little game with Sara, too."

"Game?" asked James. "I like games."

"Let's practice, James. First, try to imitate what I do. If you do well, you'll get a snack."

"Goody!" said James clapping his hands, following the man to the upper floor.

"Jack, are you on your way home?" asked the sheriff, answering the phone in a slurred voice.

"No. We decided to stay the night. Just wanted to call you so you wouldn't worry. You sound like you need some sleep."

"Need to push on with this case, Son. Bringing those photos back with you?"

"Sure thing. Listen, I need to talk to the owner of the Smoke Shack, Sheriff. Find out who got the orange hats he ordered. Get him out of bed in the morning, if you have to."

"Sure. See you around eight a.m.?"

"Okay. And bring some donuts if you have time. Luis loves them."

Early the next morning, Jack closed his eyes while Luis drove. "How was your time with Sara, Jack? Has she forgiven you?" asked Luis.

"We never even talked about that. She talked about her dad and . . . Luke."

"Seems you have forgotten she's married, friend."

Jack looked out the window. "I haven't forgotten," he paused, "I told her about the RV this morning. She's not too keen about the idea."

"Maybe you need to find a different place to park that thing, Jack. What about O'Connell's? He has a barn around the back and an electrical outlet. I'm sure Luke has found out about Sara's disappearance by now."

"I guess we're going to keep the RV behind the station. It'll be safer for everyone. You're right, though. I'm afraid to bring her back, but she insists." He hesitated. "Luke might harm her because of me. I guess I need to keep some distance from her until all of this gets figured out."

Luis looked at his old friend. "Hey! How about a strong cup of brew at our favorite coffee stop?" Jack sat up and put on his hat.

"I guess that's a yes," said Luis sleepily.

"Brady!" said O'Connell to the deputy. "Let's lay out everything we have. Starting with the Sara Reynolds accident and ending with the death of Grayson Locke." The two men drank the strong coffee, with a shot of espresso, a famous mixture O'Connell used in his younger days to keep him awake while on night duty. He carefully laid out the Indian artifacts, still in the plastic bags collected by a university researcher, on the large table used for the interrogation of criminals.

"What's this, Sheriff?" asked Brady, pointing to the relics.

"They were discovered by the mining company when they collected samples of limestone on the Reynolds property." The bags containing the pair of boots were also laid on the wooden table.

"Whoever wore these had huge feet. They're worn a little around the outside toe," said Brady.

"The boots have been stored in a locked room at the station, ever since they were found. Never noticed that," said O'Connell thoughtfully. He sighed. In the past three weeks it had seemed that all the town's hardships and struggles were coming to a head. He knew that the hardest part was still to come. The town members did not want to cancel the upcoming regatta that would take place in two days. Anticipating the worse, he had deputized ten outstanding citizens for the event. But, would it be enough?

Nervously, Cramer rechecked every part of his condo. Willard had called earlier and said the mining company representative was eating lunch with O'Connell and Wilder at his restaurant. "I wish you hadn't asked me to be your partner after Hudson was eliminated. Now we have no deal and I'll probably be on the list of suspects. Don't call me anymore." Cramer phoned Luke.

"I fixed it with that funny little Reynolds man."

"I don't need your help, Cramer. He knows I mean business. Keep out of it."

"I guess you don't want to know that Sara will be staying in an old RV in the back parking lot of the police station, arranged by your competition."

"Wilder? How did you find out?"

"I've got a few friends. She's been in Chicago staying with Jack's mom." He paused, waiting for a response. When there was none, he said, "By the way, her health problems have been wiped clean by some big city doc. They know someone was keeping her in the hospital under false pretences. They also know that you okayed everything Doc Thorton did." Luke didn't respond. "Well?" asked Cramer. "Do you still want my partnership or not? I'm the only lawyer you or the casino has now."

Luke grunted. "Meet me at the big house tonight at seven and we'll decide what to do with Jamesy."

Jack and Luis pulled into the station parking lot at exactly 5:45 a.m. "What! Didn't you stop for a break?" boomed O'Connell. "Do you know how dangerous it is to drive on the highway in the wee, morning hours?"

"I know. How many times have you reminded me, friend?" said Jack, slapping the sheriff on the back. "Anyway, Luis drove. He's a better driver than I am."

Luis laughed. Both men had no trouble remembering Luis's driving record as a teenager. After having a license for only six months, Luis ran into the side of the neighborhood ice cream stand. His punishment was painting the repaired siding while withstanding considerable teasing and gawking from his school chums. O'Connell looked at Jack, who said, "I'll tell you about it later."

"So, you're here really early, Sheriff," said Luis. "What's up?"

"Well, I'd like you to take a look at these artifacts removed from the proposed mining sight, located on the Reynolds property. We think they were taken from the museum in Hyattsville. Maybe, look for fingerprints and matching fibers and such? I also have a letter from the local environmental agency that reports a chemically polluted stream located on the same property."

Jack grabbed the letter. "What else can possibly be happening at the mansion?" he paused then looked at Sheriff O'Connell. "Did you talk to Joe from the Smoke Shack?"

"His wife said he'd be back from a fishing trip this afternoon. We could go together."

"I might be picking up Sara. I told her I'd pick her up in a couple of days, but she wants to come home, now. Said she'd take a bus home if I didn't want to return to my mother's so soon."

"So, is the RV going to be okay with her?" asked O'Connell. Jack shrugged. "Well, can I see those pics? I've waited up all night," O'Connell added.

Jack retrieved the photos from his backpack. "Luis's department blew this one up into an 8x10. Look at the hat," said Jack.

"Not just that," said Luis, pointing to an object in the photo. Stocking feet protruded from behind the tree. "A good size 14 or larger." The men looked at each other in wonderment. "I'll look at everything, take a break for lunch, and tell you what I find."

"Great!" said O'Connell. "Jack and I will be searching old Samuel's house and the infamous residence of Luke Jacobs."

"Sara's house?" asked Luis. "Does she know?"

"I'll tell her on the way home tomorrow. We may find nothing."

"Or," butted in O'Connell, "We may find everything to put her husband in jail for a long time."

CHAPTER 28

Sheriff O'Connell grabbed Luke by his collar and turned him around. "What?" said Luke, struggling, to keep himself from falling.

"Hope you had a nice meal, Jacobs. That sandwich is my favorite, too." said O'Connell, nodding toward the wrapper in Luke's hand. "Care to come along, Boy? Got this little warrant to serve to you. Sorry, you don't have time to spiffy up the house. Have to leave your car here in the restaurant's parking lot for now, okay?"

Luke opened his mouth, closed it again, and stared at Jack. Did he clean out everything that could incriminate him in the two houses? He had removed the most valuable items from the house and had them placed in a vaulted room in town. What did Locke take with him the night he died? Cramer said he was in the Jacobs house sorting through files from the locked cabinet. Why did Locke run from Cramer? What information did he know?

"Out, Boy!" said O'Connell, after he had parked in the Jacobs driveway, and headed toward the front door of Samuel's house. "You have a key?" Luke opened the door and a rush of stale air hit the men in the face. "Open a couple of windows, Son," O'Connell said to Jack. "Get a little fresh breeze in here. Jacobs, you just sit on the couch while we do our job."

Luke sat down. He thought about the last conversation he had with his deceased father. Samuel was on one of usual ranting and raving sprees and had chided Luke about his lack of care for his wife. Luke spit out, "I must have learned it from you, Father."

Samuel had laughed, "Right, boy. Good response."

"Hey, Jacobs! How long did your father take this medicine?" asked O'Connell, holding up the two empty bottles. Luke leaned forward to take a look.

"I don't know. Call Doc Thorton."

"Your dad was a patient of Doc's, too? You know that Doc's missing?" remarked O'Connell, placing the bottles in a plastic bag. "Looks like the office has been searched. Know who's been in here beside you?" he added, picking up a few papers from the floor. "Most of the files have been emptied. Have something to hide, Luke?"

"I'm not answering anything without my lawyer present."

"So, would that be Cramer, now that Locke's dead? Did you know that Cramer's also a prime suspect? Seems he was seen with Hudson a few times. Add to that, his connection with Locke. Had an argument with him right before his boat exploded."

Why had Cramer failed to tell him that he was the last to see Locke before he died? thought Luke. What were they arguing about? What was Locke trying to hide? Luke felt that Cramer had been acting stranger than normal around him lately, wanting to be reassured that he was taking Locke's place as the family's official attorney. Luke needed Cramer to draw up the papers for James to sign over the house. At least now, with James present he could bypass the conflict with Sara.

He and Cramer were the only two people that knew James still existed. Had anyone else in town seen the heir to the Reynolds' estate? Didn't Cramer say James had been visiting Sara? Did she know James was her long lost uncle?

"Okay!" bellowed the sheriff. "Let's go visit your little abode." Luke rose, followed him to the door, and turned toward Jack.

"Where is my wife, Wilder? It seems its being spread around town that she's been living with you!"

"Then, you've heard wrong, Jacobs," said Jack.

O'Connell squeezed himself between the two men, as they walked up the path to the tiny cottage house. "She hasn't been home since the accident," said Luke. "She'll probably end up in the hospital nut ward again when she faces the empty house. But luckily, I'll be here to hold her hand," he added, smugly.

"How can you say such a thing about your wife? What kind of a monster are you, Jacobs? She's just lost her family! You've just lost your family!" shouted Jack, stopping in front of Luke. "As far as I'm concerned you won't be present with her when she returns to the house. I'll make sure she has a restraining order against you!" he paused. "You'll probably be in jail, anyway."

Luke grabbed Jack and flung him to the ground. "Why would I want to kill my own children, Wilder? Maybe, I'll get a restraining order against you. Stay away from my wife and our home!"

O'Connell stood between the two men, "Okay, boys! Get up and act like adults? Let's get this over with," he added as they walked toward the house. Luke opened the door and stood aside. "Have a seat, Jacobs and don't move!" said O'Connell. "Jack, l want to get back to the station as soon as possible. I'm sure Luis will have a few things to tell us." Jack brushed off his clothes, and nodded to his friend. Both men hurriedly searched for the specific items listed on the warrants. "Jack, check the kitchen, will you!" yelled O'Connell from the bathroom.

Jack stepped into the kitchen and stopped. Toys were laying about the floor, and piles of newly washed and folded children's clothes were stacked beside the laundry basket. Jack shivered. How could Sara ever come back here? If Luke cut the brake line, would he try to kill Sara again? Jack wondered. If he didn't do it, then who hated Sara enough to want to kill her and her family? Sara had driven her husband's car to her mother's house that evening. Was the killer really planning to kill Sara, or was it Luke they were after?

"Don't leave town, Jacobs," warned the sheriff, when the two men had finished their search.

"I plan on being here for the regatta, and the announcement of the casino. I have nothing to hide, Sheriff."

"We'll see," said O'Connell. "The meds from your father's house might put you right back on the interrogation chair."

After the search was over, Luke yelled a few colorful words at O'Connell and got into his car. Monday morning the remainder of the furnishings in the mansion would be packed up and held in storage until it was auctioned off. He had planned one last search for the infamous emerald tonight, right after he had a talk with Cramer. Could Cramer be trusted? What would they do with James? He would have to be removed before the wrecking crew arrived on Monday morning. Could they have him placed in an out-of-state institution, away from everyone who knew the family?

Jack answered the phone with a growl, "This is Wilder."

"Holy cow, Jack! Did Luke throw a punch at you again?" asked Luis.

"As a matter of fact, he did," said Jack. "Knocked me right on my bottom."

"Great! Well, I've got some info I think you'll like to see. Are you on your way back?"

"Be there in ten minutes. Put some coffee on, will you Luis? I have a splitting headache."

"Sure enough, friend."

O'Connell drove his usual snail pace back to the station. "Jack, I'm still worried about the regatta. I don't feel we've covered all the bases."

"Everything will be alright, Sheriff. The extra deputies can watch over the ceremonies while we work on the cases. Luis is planning on staying. I'm going to Chicago this afternoon to retrieve Sara, and will be back by nine. My mom is a little upset that I won't be staying as planned, but she knows the next few days are crucial."

Jack remembered Sara's disappointment at not being able to see another of Jack's favorite spots in his hometown of Chicago. She had sounded anxious to return to Wakeegon. "I need to have some closure, Jack," she had said.

Jack had promised to accompany her to the graves of her family and children. He had emphasized the need for her to stay at the RV and not her family house. "There are too many uncertainties," he had told her. "We still don't know for sure who made those attempts on your life, Sara. This weekend will be chaotic enough." She agreed to follow the orders for her safety.

"Jack, sit down," said Luis, sitting at Jack's makeshift office at the station. Sheriff O'Connell was summoned to the front desk and had promised to return. "I had Brady pay a visit to Joe today and found that only two hats were given out to his favorite customers. The hats were an advertisement for Old John Smokes. One was sent to his brother in Michigan and the other was given to one Richard Cramer."

Jack shook his head. "He's a hard one to figure out, Luis. Smart. Cunning. Not a man to trust. Remember, he's the attorney for the Jacobs family businesses. He shared the job with Grayson Locke."

"By the way, did you know the Cramer family was taken on by old Jacobs when the boy's father was electrocuted? Old Samuel sent him to school, and paid for his bills until his mother died," remarked Luis.

"That's only part of the story, Luis," interrupted O'Connell, entering the room. "We've found evidence that Cramer is really Samuel Jacobs' illegitimate son."

"What?" Luis paused, "Well, Cramer's on top of my list of suspects, along with Doc Thorton. Still, no one has seen Thorton the past couple of weeks. I pulled up a listing for Doc while I was in Chicago. Seems he is behind on his housing payments and owes money to almost everyone in town. Owes a few back taxes, too. The nurses at the hospital said that he had been under a lot of strain since the Reynolds girl's accident and that he hadn't seemed the same the last few weeks before he disappeared. The hospital administrator said he hadn't been to the required meetings, and was put on probation."

"His behavior has been under suspicion for some time by the hospital officials," said Jack. "Two medications were not accounted for in the hospital pharmacy, and there was evidence of label remnants in the basket under the paper shredder. Doc could have changed the labels and used the medications to put Sara into that coma. The fact that there was no nerve damage in Sara's leg tells me that he's not afraid to lie, and is capable of hurting someone," he paused. "People in town have said that Doc had changed," added Jack. "The fact that he disappeared so soon after Sara's coma tells me, maybe he had a hand in it. By the way, Luis, what size feet does Cramer have?"

Luis laughed. "You're serious?"

"Definitely!" replied Jack. "The imprints on the insoles of the boots are a good size fourteen. They match the plaster casts of the stocking prints set in the mud at the scene of the Hudson murder. Unfortunately, the boots were in the water too long to match prints. There is something that could help us, though. Brady noticed that the outer portion of the insoles in the left boot had a slight indentation. It could be that the little toe on the left foot is slightly crooked. Maybe, from an accident or something? Probably causes him some pain."

"You're saying," said Luis, "that the suspect would have a sore toe on his left foot? How are we supposed to find that out?"

"Just get a pair of Cramer's shoes, a pair of Luke's, and a pair from Doc Thortons' closet. Doc's sister will get us a pair of Doc's shoes, if she thinks we'll find him. She's been calling every day."

O'Connell stood up. "Need a couple of warrants, then. I've got an inside track with the court system now. It's someone who has been taken financially by the Jacobs family," he added whistling as he walked from the room.

"So, Luis, what else did you find?" asked Jack.

"Well, the fingerprints were undetectable on the Indian artifacts. They definitely came from the museum. The fibers that were stuck to the bottoms of the relics match the fibers from the exhibit material lining. One of the museum guides remembers a man asking a lot of questions about the security of the building. He finally told him to talk to the man in the front office. The guy got rude with him, then left. Jack, I think the stolen artifacts were hidden at the property just to get us off track. The main thing Cramer and Hudson wanted was to retrieve the limestone. How they were going to do it without that Jacobs fellow is a puzzle. They also needed to get rid of Sara to pull that off. She still has full ownership of the property. When I questioned Luke he seemed unaware of any other plans. I think he was pretty confident that Sara would sign the estate over to him. Unfortunately, I think she would do almost anything to keep their marriage together," he added.

"Let's pay a visit to Cramer. Should be at the courthouse about now," said the sheriff, solemnly.

"I'll stay here, Jack," said Luis. "See you for lunch?"

"Make it a little later than usual. Let's meet at Lolita's. Just ask anyone here for directions. I still need to question her about the discussion she had with Cramer the other day at the restaurant."

"Great! About 1:00?"

Jack knocked on the door of Cramer's office. The lawyer was deep in concentration. "Come in," he said grouchily, without looking up. "What do you need?"

"We have a search warrant for your home," said O'Connell.

Cramer looked up in surprise. "I'm busy! Can't you see?"

"I can see. But you're coming with us right now."

"I can't let my colleagues see you walking me to the patrol car, Sheriff."

"Well," said O'Connell. "I guess you'll have a lot of explaining to do when you return." Cramer walked quietly to the car, climbed into the back seat, and slammed the door.

"Watch it Cramer! I'll send you the bill if there's damage!" exclaimed O'Connell. Cramer pulled his sports jacket tighter around his chest and buried his face. The car drove down the country roads for about ten minutes and pulled into the parking lot of the condo unit. "Swell place, Cramer," said the sheriff. "Now open up the door and sit down somewhere." Feeling confident that he had destroyed the papers linking him to the mining company, Cramer chose a comfortable chair, leaned back into the cushions, and closed his eyes.

O'Connell bent over the fireplace. "Been burning a fire, Mr. Cramer? On these nice warm evenings we've been having?"

"I was cold."

"See bits of paper," said O'Connell. "Don't you burn wood?"

"I burned a little bit of trash," he said. "The trash man left before I got it to the dumpster."

"I can smell garbage. Been to the lake, Cramer?" asked Jack, sniffing the air.

"Huh? What?" asked Cramer. "We live in a lake town, Wilder!"

"Hmm," said O'Connell, staring at Cramer, who had removed his shoes and was now rubbing his toes. "Those big feet get real tired, boy?" asked the sheriff.

"I'm not going to answer a stupid question like that, O'Connell," said Cramer. O'Connell took the pair of shoes and placed them in a plastic bag.

"Hey! What are you doing? Those are my most comfortable pair of shoes."

"I'll give them back," said the sheriff, with a hint of sadness in his voice. He still didn't want to accept the fact that someone in his town could commit such a crime. Jack helped O'Connell finish the search and told Cramer to stay in town.

"Why would I leave? The casino breaks ground on Monday," he replied. "You act like I'm guilty of something," he added as the two men were leaving. Cramer groaned when he remembered that his car was still in town. He was supposed to meet Luke at the mansion at seven o'clock. He could walk, he told himself. He went to his closet to get another pair of shoes. What on earth did the two men want with his shoes? Glancing at his watch, he rubbed his foot again, put on his sneakers, and walked toward the mansion. Could he have forgotten something other than the orange hat at the scene of Hudson's murder? Could it be possible the film survived the time it was under water in that old relic of a camera?

CHAPTER 29

"Hello, Lolita. I'm Jack Wilder. I'm here to meet a friend of mine from the police department in Chicago. We're investigating the recent incidences involving two local residents of Wakeegon. Sara Jacobs and a Dr. Peter LyleThorton. Do you know them?" Lolita smiled nervously. "I also want to ask you a few questions about a man I saw you talking with the other day. Richard Cramer?"

"Rotten scum!" she said vehemently scraping the remains from a customer's abandoned plate. "He's a worse scab than that friend of his."

"You mean Luke?"

"Those two have made my life miserable. I should never have borrowed money from that creep to keep my business going. I'll always owe him something. Everybody does, including poor Doc. Probably did away with him for not paying up," she ended.

"I overheard you talking to Jacobs the other day," he added. She bit her lip and sat down.

"How much did you hear?" she asked Jack, just as Luis walked in the side door.

"Holy cow!" said Luis as he and Jack walked into the station. "Talk about hearing a first-class confession. Should we have booked her for being an accomplice?"

"Not yet," said Jack, walking over to the makeshift crime lab.

"Look, Jack," said Luis. "The same pattern as the insoles of the boots! He must have walked on the inside of his foot to minimize the pain from that little toe." Luis looked at Jack. The circles under Jack's eyes appeared darker than normal. "Tough times, huh?"

"This is the first time since Professor Lewinski was murdered that a man has threatened someone I deeply care about," said Jack. He paused in deep concentration. "There is plenty of evidence pointing to Cramer. I feel he's capable of doing almost anything. The smell of his brand of cigarettes has permeated everything he touches and wherever he goes. Don't you smell it, Luis?" he asked, as his friend shook his head no. "Anyway, my friend, do you think you can finish up your investigation by tomorrow evening? We can arrest Cramer for the murder of Hudson and the attack on me. And Luke? I don't know the extent of his involvement yet, but I'm close. Just in time for the regatta, huh?"

"I'll try Jack, but I'll have to pull a few strings."

"Pull away, friend," said Jack. "Sheriff, is the RV ready? Sara will be coming back with me tonight."

"Sure, Son. I'll be attending the final security meeting for the regatta tonight at the community building. Luis will be here off and on, and Brady's on duty here at the station tonight. Should be okay."

"Thanks, Sheriff. I'll be leaving within the hour. See you tonight after the meeting."

"Be careful!" yelled the sheriff from his office.

Jack's foot was heavy on the gas pedal, until he turned down the street that led to the house he grew up in as a young boy. He had experienced an exceptional childhood. A loving mother, a hand's on father who enjoyed spending his free time with his only child, and a childhood friend who was still his best friend today. Except for viewing the tragic demise of his favorite school teacher, his life as a young boy was pretty good. Reality had set in when he unexpectedly lost his father and then his wife.

Jack pulled up to the curb beside the house and leaned back against the seat. Were his feelings for Sara love, or did he just hate to see someone overpowered and victimized? Last night he had a dream about Sara. He was meeting her at the café on the corner. He had planned to tell her how much he cared for her and would be by her side if she decided to leave Luke. The sky was dark and stormy.

Sara had dressed in her favorite summer skirt and had driven her tiny car to the town square. She looked up at the threatening sky. The wind carried along the black clouds that would delay her plans. Sara had just ducked under a large awning when a sudden torrential rainstorm burst from a passing cloud. She rushed toward the small corner building and paused for a moment, her clothes drenched with moisture. Was it confusion, or was it excitement that overtook Sara's usual sensible manner, in his dream? When she reached her destination, she smoothed her hair with a hand that trembled slightly. Unconsciously, she moistened her lips with her tongue and shook off the beads of water that clung to her clothes.

The day was fading quickly, and the time of Jack's appearance drew nearer. Suddenly embarrassed, her cheeks became the color of soft faded rose petals as the wind swirled around her ankles, blowing her long-flowing garment around her knees. Quickly, she wrapped her thin sweater tighter and glanced at the church tower clock. She turned abruptly and with eyes cast downward, she ran from the square toward her car. The wind blew fiercely and rushed through the buildings with a roar. She never heard the anguished cries of "Sara" coming from behind her. Running, she disappeared out of sight as the rain pelted the street. Furious with himself for arriving late, Jack kicked a stone so hard it ricocheted off a nearby car. Angry questioning eyes from a passing couple made him feel like a scolded schoolboy. Why did she run? Did she still not trust him? What else could he do to make her feel his sincerity?

"Jack, are you alright?" yelled his mother from the front porch.

Jack sat up and opened his car door. "Just resting. I'll be right in," he added as he grabbed his duffle bag from the back seat. I guess I am in love with Sara, he thought. What does she think of me? Should I tell her how I feel?

Sara watched Jack approach the door of his childhood home. She had spent a lot of time thinking about Jack and how she felt about him. Had she given him the wrong message? She cared about him, but still wanted her marriage to last. The last time they were together, Jack seemed hurt that she wanted to stay with Luke. Sara had spent last evening writing a letter to Jack, expressing her gratitude and feelings for him. She felt she had leaned on him too hard, and he had probably mistaken her neediness for affection toward him. If she were single she wouldn't hesitate to grab the kind and gentle detective. She backed from the door and allowed Jack's mother to shower him with hugs and kisses.

"Hello, Sara. Are you ready to go home? If not, you can stay with mom for awhile."

"Thanks Jack. I'm scared to face the emptiness of the house and the memories," she added, "but, I'm ready to go home. Is the RV ready?"

"It's clean. Just remember it belongs to O'Connell," replied Jack. She laughed.

"Let's have some cookies before you leave, Jack," said his mother. "Then, I'll help you carry Sara's belongings to the car." They talked and laughed for a few more minutes. Later, Sara went to her room to retrieve the rest of her things. She picked up the letter, placed it in her purse, and prayed that Jack would understand.

"Alright, calm down!" said O'Connell as the townsfolk crowded into the meeting room of the town hall. "I'll hear all of your complaints in a civil manner. Marie, open up the storage closet so people can grab a folding chair."

"That's good," he said. "Find a seat and raise your hand if you have a question or want to voice an opinion. Okay, Mr. Anderson."

The man rose. "Sheriff, how do these highfalutin people get away with something this big? You're in charge of this town, right? Why don't you stop this from happening?"

"First off, Mr. Anderson, I'm not in charge of this town. I'm hired to uphold the law."

"Well," he said, "this casino thing is as big a crime as you can get!"

"Yeah!" said the crowd of people in unison.

"What can we do to stop it?" asked one woman.

"I'm sorry this has taken everyone by surprise. I'll do whatever I can to answer your questions, but I'm as uninformed as you. I know the plans will be revealed, and your questions answered at the opening of the temporary office of the casino. There will be a model of the facilities, and the prominent investors will be able to answer your questions. I've also heard applications will be taken for working positions that will be available."

"Whoever applies for a position will answer to me!" said Anderson in an angry voice, standing up and sneering at the crowd.

"Sit down, Mr. Anderson. If that happens," said O'Connell, "I'll uphold the law and take you in, Sir. I know there is concern about losing the charm of our little community, but financially it may turn our ghost town into a boomtown."

"Charm?" said Mr. Harmon, who owned the only grocery in town. "Who finds charm in rundown buildings and abandoned businesses? There's nothing charming about not being able to eat." He sat down and shrugged as the others booed him.

"He's right!" said a middle-aged woman with scraggly hair. "The young keep moving away because there are no jobs."

"Sinful!" said an older gentlemen who had been listening quietly. "That's the main issue. People ruining their lives, driving their families broke, the suicide rate climbing... they say it's going to be a family place! Family place? Can you believe it? What will this town come to? And the people that the casino will bring to our community? You better increase your police force Sheriff, that's all I'm gonna say!" he ended, pounding his cane on the wooden floor.

"We will end this discussion and move on to the plans for the regatta," said the sheriff. "My hands are tied. Call your town board and voice your opinion."

"The town board is made up of the very scoundrels who are trying to pull the wool over our eyes!" said the old man. "And what about this crime wave that has taken over this town? Probably related to those fellows, too."

"This is not an informative meeting about the investigations that have been ongoing," interrupted O'Connell. "Read your local paper and listen to the news. We will keep you posted."

The man grumbled something, stood up and left the room. "Good riddance!" said one woman. "Let's move on, Sheriff. I've got a cake to bake for my boy's school carnival tomorrow."

"Sure thing, Katie. The school carnival is the first kickoff of the regatta weekend. Let's begin with that. Then we'll move on to the parking situation."

"Will there be enough security, Sheriff? I'm getting a little scared about what's been happening here."

"All of you know this kind of crime is not common for our town. I plan to deputize ten local men to aid in supervising parking and to handle petty incidences. We also have one area detective and a police investigator from

Chicago who will be staying with us the entire weekend. Unfortunately, it sounds like more people will be visiting our town to see what a community looks like that has had murder and missing people in its newspaper headlines the last couple of weeks, than watching a few boats sail around the lake."

A few of the people groaned at his statement and began settling down to hear the agenda of the evening. Although the sheriff had answered the best he could, they eyed each other warily, each wondering if the murderer was sitting beside them.

CHAPTER 30

Sara leaned back in the seat and closed her eyes. She was too tired to get into another discussion of why she should leave Luke.

Jack looked at her, opened his mouth, and closed it again. Should he tell Sara about his dream? She looked tired. Was that the reason she wasn't talking?

Sara opened her eyes, glanced at him, and asked, "How long have you been interested in the Catholic faith Jack?"

"Since I was a little boy. I really accepted the faith when I attended parochial school. I was taught by the spiritual giants at our church. They made a lasting impression on me. The only negative part of my education was the death of my favorite teacher. I told you about that, right?" Sara nodded. "My parents were true to their faith. They taught me how to be faithful, honest, and especially the importance of showing love to others. When they took Luis in and treated him like their own son, I saw how believers are really supposed to live their lives here on earth. I know I've fallen short the last couple of years. The deaths of my father and my wife were hard to take. I questioned God about everything after that. My mother, bless her, stayed solid and sure. I guess that's what happens to you after believing so long."

"It's not time, Jack, that makes us stronger. It's the relationship between you and God that makes it bearable to survive hardships and to carry on. You sound like you've lost some of that closeness with the sorrow you've experienced. Do you blame God for the deaths of your dad and Beth?"

He sat silent. "You don't know what it's like to lose your best friend."

Sara hung her head, "No, but I've lost the two sweetest things that ever lived and my life is so empty without them."

Jack looked at her. "Sara, I'm sorry . . . I . . . I forgot about the pain you've been through."

"Not been through Jack . . . living with. I still have to come to terms with an empty house." Sara closed her eyes and grew quiet.

"What about Luke, Sara?" asked Jack after a few minutes of silence.

"I still have hope, Jack. Until it's totally gone."

"And when is that going to be?" asked Jack. Sara pulled the collar of her sweatshirt jacket close around her face and turned toward the window. I blew it again, thought Jack. When she needs me the most, why do I push her away?

They drove the last few miles in silence, arriving at the RV at dusk. Luis's car was absent. Probably eating at one of the local dives, thought Jack. He carried Sara's small suitcase into the RV and watched as she went from room to room opening doors and peering into cabinets. "Thanks, Jack," said Sara. "I'll just change and go to bed early. You need not stay."

"I'll wait until someone returns. I don't want you to stay alone."

"Nonsense, Jack. Besides, I'm sleepy and I don't want to hear any more gossip about you and me." She looked at his ash-colored face. "Yes, I've heard it. I don't want Luke any madder than he is at me right now, so please go home," she said as she handed him a sealed letter.

Jack looked at her questionably, "What's this?"

"Just read it tonight. I'll see you in the morning."

"Wait, Sara!" She paused as Jack reached for his cell phone and called Luis.

"I'll come back right now," said Luis. "I'll have them box up the rest of meal."

"No," said Jack. "Just return to the station when you are finished."

After talking to Luis, Jack called O'Connell who was home nursing a splitting headache. "The meeting," he said, "was a complete nightmare. I'll tell you about it tomorrow. By the way, Jack, Brady just called in sick. I told him to go to bed. He's needs to feel better for tomorrow. I know you were counting on him tonight."

Jack reluctantly left Sara with her promise to lock the door and stay inside for the rest of the evening. Luis would be returning within a few minutes, he reassured her. Jack admitted he needed a good night's sleep before tomorrow. The vendors would be setting up on the lakeside parking lots and early arrivals would be pulling into the campsites and registering at the few hotels in the area.

Around six o'clock in the morning O'Connell would be placing the barricades around the lot where the regatta entries would be stationed. The boat ramp had been repaired and refinished, awaiting the first of the larger vessels to enter the waters of the lake. Deputy Brady, being an avid boater, would be overseeing the line of boat trailers and the excited participants.

Jack checked the RV's locked door, and glanced around the parking lot located behind the station. As he drove away, he remembered the letter in his hand. He pulled off the road under a large streetlight. His hands shook as he tore open the envelope. Jack held it close under the car's small interior light.

> *Dear Jack,*
>
> *I'm sorry to have caused so much anger in you the last couple of times we met. You're right. I am a hopelessly incurable optimist when it comes to love. But you're wrong when you think I have no feelings for you. I was raised by a solid family, who felt that love is a one - time shot that should be cherished and protected from anything or anyone who could harm it. I never counted on you entering my life. You offer me security, protection and care that I've never had with Luke. But, strong is my faith in reconciliation.*
>
> *Do you believe in hope, Jack? Or did you lose that along with your loss of Beth and your father? Hope is all I have right now. I plan on talking to Luke upon my return and patch up the differences we've had. After all, what good is life if you cannot live? I cannot live without knowing if he really loves me . . . it leaves a hole that cannot be filled. Pray for me, Jack, if you can.*
>
> *Hopefully, this letter will be a new beginning for us, Jack, and the tension between us will be over. Thank you, for everything you have done for me,*
>
> Your friend always, Sara.

Jack silently placed the letter on the seat and drove home.

Luke grabbed the same duffle bag that was rummaged through when he received the hit on the head at the old mansion. Must have been James, thought Luke. He walked around to the back entrance, entered the Reynolds' house, and went immediately upstairs to inform James of his presence. He didn't want to be knocked out again by the little man. The attic room was strangely quiet. Luke turned the flashlight toward the makeshift bed on the floor. Remains of last night's styrofoam dinner boxes lay in the corner. He kicked a pile of trash and pointed the flashlight at a flowered-covered notebook lying on top of an ivory colored file. He knelt on the floor and leafed through the small pad of paper. It was Sara's hospital diary. James must have taken it when he visited Sara. He read Sara's entries intently and stopped at the last page. "Someone's trying to kill me . . . please help me."

Luke tucked the book into his pocket and opened the file. It was the missing file Doc had talked about when he called frantically one afternoon. He tried to read the coded pages written in Doc's handwriting. What information did it contain? He stood up and brushed the dust and food crumbs from his pant legs. Where was James? He had promised to stay inside. Luke spent the rest of the evening searching the house for James and the hidden emerald. Neither was found.

Cramer was to arrive at seven. Luke waited for a half-hour. Maybe Cramer had convinced James to leave the house. When Cramer never showed up Luke closed the door of the old mansion, hopefully for the last time. By this time Monday, only a shell would remain.

"Can Jamesy go home now?" asked James, twisting his tie into a more comfortable position.

Cramer grunted. "Remember our deal James? I'm taking you to see Sara."

"Goody, goody!" said James excitedly. "Will Sara be happy to see me?"

"Yes. Especially in your new clothes. You'll get to see where Sara lives."

James plodded along, eager to see his friend. Late that afternoon, when Cramer arrived at the house after the visit from Jack and the sheriff, he found James dressed in his new clothes, admiring himself in the mirror. He looks great, thought Cramer, but to look exactly like the picture, James needed to have his hair trimmed and the short scraggly beard shaved off. Cramer grabbed the yellowed picture of Sara's father, and searched the house for a pair of scissors and a sharp razor. James looked frightened when he returned with the two instruments. "See?" he said, cutting a small lock of his own hair and shaving himself at the mirror in the lower floor bathroom.

James watched Cramer shave. When Cramer finished, James reached out his hand and touched Cramer's smooth skin. "Jamesy want." It took a while to turn James into the nicely groomed man that stared back from the mirror. "James?" he asked pointing to himself.

Cramer laughed. "Yes."

Cramer's informant had called to tell him that Sara had arrived early that evening, and was staying alone in an old RV behind the police station. Cramer led James down a trail that wound around the outskirts of town. When they arrived at the station, the ancient looking vehicle appeared dark and forlorn. Would Sara be in bed at this early hour?

"Go on, Jamesy," said Cramer. "Knock on the door. Don't forget your chocolates." James put his hand in his pocket and drew out a fistful of foil wrapped chocolates. He knocked once, then again a little harder.

"Jack?" asked a small voice from inside. "Is that you? Why did you come back?" Sara opened the door, slowly. "Oh, it's you," she said in a confident voice recognizing the little man from the hospital. She opened the door further, "Daddy?" She screamed. When Sara fell to the floor, James covered his eyes and screamed, too.

"I hurt her! I hurt her!" he repeated over and over.

Cramer grabbed his hand. "She was just surprised to see you, James. Just leave her the chocolates on the doorstep." Cramer pulled the door shut. "Come on, James, she wants to sleep a little bit more."

James asked with a quivering voice, "Not like my mommy went to sleep?"

"No. Not like your mommy, James. Let's let her rest." James followed him back to the trail. He walked quietly in front of Cramer. A short way down the trail Cramer grabbed the man's hand and redirected him to the parked car he had left at the office building that afternoon. "Let's get you home and change those clothes, James. You can have the rest of the chocolates."

When they arrived at the mansion, James replied, "I can't eat chocolates now. Jamesy been bad."

"You followed my rules just right, James. Now go inside and change your clothes. I'll put them away until next time." That ought to send Sara back to the hospital for awhile, he thought. Now, I need to get James to sign this final document giving the house and property to me. James changed his clothes, gave them to Cramer, and sat down on the dusty mattress.

"James hungry," he said to Cramer. "Other man didn't bring James food today."

"Was his name Luke?"

"Don't know name. He said he would bring food."

"Listen, James. See this paper and pen? Can you show me how you can write your name?"

James's face lit up. "I like to do school," he said excitedly.

"See this line? Can you write your name on the line?"

"It looks hard, but I'll try." First, he wrote James in a large scrawling flourish, taking up most of the blank space.

"That's great, James. Can you write your last name?"

"Reynolds," he said slowly. "That will be hard for James."

"Here," said Cramer, "do what I do." He took a scrap piece of paper and wrote a cursive R. "Now, you write this letter, right here." James did as he was told. "That looks great, James. If you do the rest of the letters, I'll go and get you some food."

"Pizza?" asked James.

"Sure," replied Cramer, "now, let's finish."

James followed, writing each letter carefully until he got to the letter "d". "James tired," he said.

"No food, James, until you finish." said Cramer. James continued to write his last name.

"All done," said James, happy to have finished the task.

Cramer sat down on the old mattress. "James, don't tell the mean man that you wrote your name for me. It's our secret."

"Okay," said James.

"If you tell," said Cramer, "no more pizza."

"James not tell. I keep secret with Jingles and not tell my mommy I can read and keep the garden pretty."

"Did Jingles keep the garden pretty, too?"

"Jingles grow beautiful flowers and let James keep some in his room. He was my friend."

"Well, James," said Cramer, "I want to be your friend, too!"

"You hit me, too, like you did your other friend?"

"What friend, James?"

"The man by the water. He was playing in the water. James like to play in water, too."

Cramer stood still. "What did you see at the water, James?"

"You were fighting together. James no like to fight. Poor man fell into the water."

"Did you tell anyone about this?"

"No. James scared. I saw other man come down the hill. I stopped to see the pretty orange hat then ran to the house.

"The hat that you took from the dumpster?"

James shook his head yes. "I like the color orange."

"James, I want you to take a drive with me in my car. We'll go and get that cheese pizza that you love so much!"

James clapped his hands, kneeled down on the mattress, and picked up his bear. "Goody, Goody! Bear come, too?"

"Yes," said Cramer, looking at the pathetic stuffed animal.

Cramer had James climb in the back seat. "Don't say a word! Understand?" James nodded. Cramer reached into the glove box, pulled out a bottle of aspirins, and rubbed his forehead. He couldn't stop thinking about the hat. Was it in the pictures taken by the camera that was pulled from the lake? He had only heard rumors that it was waterproof. He knew he would have to get those photos, somehow. His voice quivered as he ordered a large cheese pizza at the take-out window and climbed back into his car. He turned around to check on James and saw that the little man was sleeping.

Cramer rubbed his forehead for the second time. He had just leaned back in his seat when he saw Luke's car drive past. Cramer groaned. He had forgotten the seven o'clock meeting he was scheduled to have with Luke at the mansion. He and James must have been visiting Sara around the same time.

Cramer wiped the sweat off his forehead with the front of his shirt. It was a good thing that the two of them were gone when Luke arrived at the house. Did Luke notice the scissors and razor in James' room? Did he see the picture of Sara's dad, lying on the dusty floor? He shrugged his shoulders. He didn't need a meeting with Luke to discuss anything, anymore, he concluded. Now that the house and the property were his, there wouldn't be a casino. When the heavy construction machinery arrived on Monday morning, they would have nothing to demolish or build. They would be forced to leave and the machinery for the mining company would take their place. It seemed things were finally going his way. Except for James. What was he going to do with him?

CHAPTER 31

"Sara, wake up!" said Luis, shaking her violently. Sara finally opened her eyes. Luis sat her up and leaned her against the old sofa. "What happened?" asked Luis.

Sara shook her head, "I don't know." She jerked and sat up straight, "My father, my father, he's not dead!"

Luis shook his head. "Sara," said Luis, "Jack told me your father died a couple of years ago."

"No! No!" she screamed. "He was here!" She picked up the chocolates on the floor. "These were his favorite. His mother always had Nuville Chocolates in the house."

"Sara, a lot of people like Nuville Chocolates. They've been manufactured in this town for a long time. Jack and I used to buy them in the local corner store in Chicago when we were boys."

"My father's coat, my father's tie, the same hair cut. It was him!"

"You're tired and were probably just dreaming."

"Don't treat me like a child, Luis!" said Sara, pulling herself up from her sitting position on the floor. "Call Jack! Please!"

"Sara, let me get you a glass of water. Listen, I want you to stay in the station with me until morning. It's too dangerous for you to be alone." She reluctantly gathered her belongings, slipped on her robe, and followed Luis. Inside, he brought out a cot, set it up in a spare room, pulled a pillow and a blanket from the storage closet, and got her settled once again. He hesitated to call Jack. He knew his friend got very little sleep the past week.

"Jack," whispered Luis, "You need to come in. I think Sara's having a drug relapse or something. Anyway, I think she's seeing things."

"What kind of things?" asked Jack.

"Well for one, her father."

"Her father? He's dead!"

"Yep," said Luis, "That's exactly why I need you in here right away. And call the hospital. Talk with her new doc. Maybe he'll have an answer."

Jack hung up. He grabbed his handkerchief in case he had to take a trip to the hospital. He glanced at the hallway clock. What could have happened to Sara in the last two hours? She had seemed okay when he left her. Could she be having a breakdown? What drugs was she taking? He dialed the number of the hospital, told the receptionist what had happened and waited for a call. It came within ten minutes. "Doctor Price? Could I pick you up in ten minutes? Thanks sir. I'll be at the front desk." As Jack rushed out the front door, he glanced at the folded letter lying across his worn coat. He nervously pocketed the small paper. How would he respond to the letter now? Was Sara able to make judgments on her own?

Sara nestled in between the worn covers and soon fell asleep. The doctor insisted she have a sedative and a pain pill for the leg that had been held captive in the cast for a couple of weeks. "The leg must be weak. It must have given way, when the shock overtook her. I'll stop by around noon tomorrow." Jack called Sara's mother and told her about Sara. She was at the station within ten minutes.

"Jack, what now?" she asked in an anxious voice.

"I don't know, Mrs. Reynolds."

"Jack, remember, it's Peg to you."

He nodded. "I have to help with the regatta tomorrow. Could you stay with her? Luis will be here, too." Jack called the sheriff, awakening him from a troublesome dream.

"Thought my wife was returning for the RV, Son. What's up?" Jack told him about Sara's sighting of her father, and that she would be staying inside the station with Luis and her mother until tomorrow.

"Holy cow! What else can happen?"

"Are you awake enough to come in, Sheriff? I have some new information about Hudson's murder."

Fifteen minutes later, a disheveled and bleary-eyed sheriff wandered into the station and walked over to the coffee machine without a word. Jack let O'Connell empty his cup of black brew before he spoke.

"You, okay?" asked Jack.

"I will be in a couple of minutes."

"Sorry, I had to wake you, Sheriff, but I felt you needed to know what had happened before tomorrow morning." O'Connell nodded, poured another cup of coffee for himself and sat down. "Luis has confirmed that the boots in the lake were Richard Cramer's and the footprints at the scene of the Hudson murder were also his. He probably was the same person who conked me on the head. He must have been after that camera. The size of the feet in the pictures along with that orange hat makes Cramer the number one suspect. I'm requesting a warrant for his arrest."

"What else?" asked O'Connell, sleepily.

"The drugs from Luke's father's house don't match up with the ones in Sara's system. Two bottles of drugs were missing from the hospital pharmacy the day Sara went into the coma. The two medicines together with the drugs she was already taking could have produced coma-like symptoms."

"What about Locke?"

"Looks like it was just an accident. Although, we still don't know what Locke and Cramer were fighting about. The Reynolds' property is a valuable commodity. A casino. Limestone mining. And remember, Sheriff? The emerald? How many people in this town know about that rumor?"

"Seems things are getting crazier every day!" exclaimed O'Connell. "I'm worried about this weekend. Listen, Jack, I really need your help tomorrow. Do you think Luis can stay with Sara?"

"He's already given me his promise. Her mom will be there, too," replied Jack. "What's the weather looking like for this weekend?"

"Tomorrow is a little cloudy and cool, but Saturday looks great. Sunny, slightly breezy. Great for a regatta! Be ready at seven," he added.

"Sure, Sheriff. I'll bring the donuts."

O'Connell laughed, "But no sugar in my coffee, okay?"

"Fine," said Jack with a smile.

Jack took one last look at Sara, said a few things to her mother, and left. It would be hard to concentrate on the festival, thought Jack. Could one of Wakeegon's top citizens be in jail by next week? How would the crowd react to the casino exhibit that opened tomorrow?

"Cramer! Pick up and answer! Where are you!" shouted Luke into his phone. "Goodman is sick. Pierceton has no idea what he's doing, so I sent him home. Get over here, quick!" he finished as he threw the phone down on the table. Where was Cramer? He was already two hours late. No one had seen him since yesterday. Would he come up missing like Doc?

Cramer stretched and noticed that a voice mail from Luke was waiting for his reply. He shifted his position behind the steering wheel. Ignoring the call he dialed a number written on the back of a matchbox cover from Ray's Bait Shop, and asked for Andy. A woman answered, "You have the wrong number."

"Listen, Mrs. Stevens, I know your son is there. I saw him pull his car into your garage over an hour ago."

He heard a few muttered words. "What do you need Mr. C.?" asked a young man's voice.

"I have five hundred dollars in my pocket just for you. Just need a small job done."

"No way! I won't do any more jobs for you."

"Well, I hate to hear that. I guess now's a good time to let the police know about your short stint as a cable TV man."

Cramer heard soft breathing on the other end of the line. "Listen, Mr. C.! I'll be sent to prison for sure if the police find out it was me who cut those brake lines. I didn't know anyone would get killed."

"What did you think would happen, kid? I promise you, when I come into a lot of money, you'll get your fair share."

"When will that be?"

"Soon. Soon. If you're hard up now, I could make this job an even thousand."

There was silence for a few seconds. "Okay," he replied, "what this time?"

"I need a couple of pictures from the police station files."

"Police station? No way!"

"You could do it at night. Only one person on that shift. Meet me at the parking lot at ten. I'll be returning from the casino exhibit open house. No car. Okay?" Cramer hung up, satisfied that the evidence would be destroyed. By tonight, the Stevens boy would have the pictures. The house and property would be his as soon as he filed papers in the morning. Tomorrow evening, after the exhibit closed, he would tell Luke that the property belonged to the half-brother that it was promised to long ago. If Luke agreed to get rid of Jamesy, Cramer would share a portion of the wealth with him. He would not tell him that the casino would never be built.

"Over here!" yelled O'Connell. Where was Jack, he wondered.

"Back up! Back up!" Brady was busy helping an older couple move their camper out of the way of the regatta boats.

"Sheriff, where do you want me?" asked Jack, sleepily watching the activities.

"Jack! Glad you're here. Sorry you had such a bad night. Could you help me line up the boats? Mrs. Phillips has the contestants names and boat slip numbers. Looks great for tomorrow, doesn't it? It might be a little windy for practice this morning, though."

It seemed so long ago that the regatta plans were being discussed, thought Jack, stepping up to the water's edge and taking a big breath of air. He noticed that the traffic was beginning to appear from all directions, backing all the way up to Willie's restaurant and over the hill toward Hyattsville. People were arriving with their lawn chairs, tents, and campers, and were pulling their coolers on wheels to the best viewing areas. The area stores were already busy with customers who were purchasing charcoal, bottled water, and hotdogs. Locals would be planning a fry-up of fish and fries from the catch of the day. What was missing, thought Jack, was the serene atmosphere that had drawn the visitors to the previous regattas.

O'Connell was right. Jack had been at the lake only ten minutes when two separate groups of people stopped and asked him where the murder took place, and what pier did the man leave from who died in the explosion. He knew he had to watch his suspects closely today. Both Luke and Cramer would be busy showing the model of the new casino and answering questions. Sheriff O'Connell was worried that the crowd would burst into a ruckus when the locals found out the mansion would be stripped down to a shell, and local forests and hills razed for the parking lot and purposed golf course. After all, he had confided to Jack earlier, his premonitions had told him so.

Jack looked at his watch. Eight-fifteen. Just forty-five minutes until the exhibit opened this morning. He walked back to Brady's post, offered his assistance, and ended up helping one group of disgruntled boaters back their trailer into an open spot to change a flat tire. Jack wiped his brow and grabbed the set of tools from his car. This job would be easy compared to the calamity he could face later, he thought.

Cramer walked casually into the exhibit room, dressed in his finest. Luke was showing an out-of-town visitor the miniature model of the new resort and casino. He glanced up and frowned when he saw Cramer walk to the coffee counter and grab a fresh baked cookie. When the man left, Luke walked over to the counter. "Those are for our guests, Cramer. If you would have gotten out of bed on time and ate breakfast like the rest of us, you wouldn't need to eat that."

"My money paid for this cookie along with that," he said pointing to the model. "I'm late because I had a little business deal."

"This early in the morning?"

"Sure. Might be worthwhile for you, too, Jacobs, to rise up with the sun," said Cramer as he guided a middle-aged couple to the free coffee and cookies.

"Knew you two were in this crooked deal," said a loud voice belonging to Mr. Anderson.

"Mr. Anderson," said Luke smoothly. "How can we serve you?"

"You can start by telling the truth, Jacobs! Everyone knows the old mansion was left to Sara, the last remaining Reynolds. She's a sweet girl. How'd you get her," he asked waving his arms, "to give all of this to someone conniving as you?"

Luke laughed. "Mr. Anderson. How about I take you to dinner tomorrow night and discuss the whole thing?"

"Don't want to be seen with someone like you, Jacobs. What'd you do? Kill the old lady? By gosh, Sara's dad would be rising from his grave about now!"

"Come on, Mr. Anderson. Let's get you some coffee and talk about this right now," said Cramer.

"Well, I haven't had breakfast yet. Don't mind talking to you, being a fancy lawyer and all. Just don't want to talk to him," he said loudly, pointing to Luke.

Luke gave the man a dirty look and opened the door to let a large group of people into the small room. "Good day, everyone! I'm glad that you are here to see the proposed complex that will bring prosperity to our little town and put us on the map," he said proudly.

A man standing in the front of the crowd said, "We're here to protest your little scam, Jacobs. We're planning on stopping the excavation on Monday morning."

"Really? And how do you plan on doing that, Sir?"

"By sitting on the property and not moving until we have a chance to speak up."

Luke's face turned beet red. He picked up his phone and called the police station. "Someone will be right there, Mr. Jacobs," said a voice on the other end.

The crowd sat on the floor and chanted, "No casino! No casino!" Two minutes later, the door opened.

"They would have to send you, Wilder," said Cramer.

Jack nodded. "Folks, how can I help you?" They all began to talk at once. Jack held up his hand. "Let's grab some of these nice refreshments offered by these two men, then, we'll all go out under that big shade tree and talk." Luke glared at him, while the refreshments disappeared from the table.

"Thanks, Jacobs! Right nice of you," snickered Mr. Anderson holding up a handful of cookies.

When the crowd left and a subdued Mr. Anderson walked out the door, Luke said, "I'll get that man someday. I swear on my death bed."

"Which may come soon if you don't learn how to handle the old-towners," said Cramer. "They grew up here, just like you, Jacobs. Don't you have any appreciation of the town?"

"I'm trying to keep it alive."

"Is that your main reason for destroying the Reynolds' estate? This town has more to give than you can imagine," he said, as he thought of the vein of limestone waiting to be uncovered.

"Like you have any attachment for it, Cramer! You're the one who wants money and lots of it."

"I'm just saying, you better be thankful for what your old man left you and that beautiful wife of yours. Or, does she belong to someone else now?"

Luke walked across the room and shoved Cramer, knocking down the refreshment table and scattering its contents across the floor. Jack walked back in at the same moment. "Good thing we got our snack early," he said, eyeing the mess. "Just want to let you know you'll have a problem on your hands come Monday morning. Might plan on rising early, men." He smiled and left. Best to let them fight it out, thought Jack. By Monday, "Seven Men Investments" would have wished they had never thought of the casino.

CHAPTER 32

Jack walked to O'Connell's temporary festival office set up under a large sycamore tree. "How'd the little ruckus pan out over at the exhibit?" he asked Jack.

"Okay, I think, until Monday. They're planning a sit-in at the old mansion. Not enough of them to make a problem. I feel sorry for them, though. They want this little town to stay the way it was when they were growing up."

"I love this town, too," said O'Connell. "You were right, Jack. The town has changed. There's no way this place can survive staying the way it's always been, though. Something needs to be done. The only problem is that the planners for our community are just as crooked as Jacobs. It seems doomed from all sides." Both men stood by the water's edge to enjoy the fleet of boats gliding over the glassy water. "Let's just get through this regatta, Jack, before we decide to save the world," added O'Connell. Jack followed the sheriff to his makeshift office under the tree.

"Luis!" he said into his phone. "How's Sara doing?"

"She's not awake yet, Jack. Dr. Price was right about that medicine. Should do her good after the scare she had last night. What do you think happened?"

"This has been the second time she has claimed to have seen her dad. Had she mentioned it to her mother before?"

"No. Her mom thinks she just had a bad dream. It seems Sara started feeling guilty after her father's death. She married Luke without his blessing and on top of that, she had an argument with him the day he died. Though, I suppose you knew all of that, friend."

"I don't know what to think, Luis. She's been acting funny lately," said Jack.

"Jack, I think you mean she has been indifferent toward you. You know you need to back off. She's your client, first."

"I know, Luis. You don't have to remind me. We've come to an agreement," he said regrettably, "about the relationship between us." Jack had reread the letter several times before finally admitting that Sara would try to resolve the struggle between herself and her estranged husband no matter what.

"Jack? Jack?" shouted a voice over the phone.

"Sorry, Luis. Just thinking. How about over dinner tonight, I'll give you a recap of the big fight between Jacobs and Cramer today, and the protest group's devious plans for Monday?"

"Sounds like the weekend will be extended," sighed Luis.

"You're right, Luis. It looks like the regatta will be simplest thing that takes place this weekend. I'll be back at the station around five. Let's order Chinese for everyone."

"Sure thing, Jack. See you then."

Jack hung up, still wondering what Sara would say when she awoke. Was she dreaming? If so, where did all of those chocolates come from? Jack picked up the phone again, "Hey, Luis, just thought of something. Could you run a test on the footprints leading to the RV door?" He wondered if the same prints would appear again.

Cramer shut the screen door with a bang and started to cover the display of the casino model. He had spent part of the day cleaning up the mess on the floor and the rest of the day defending the benefits of having a casino in the small town. He had put on quite a show, all the while knowing that the construction would never take place.

"Since you didn't get rid of James, meet me back at the house tonight around eight, Cramer. We'll figure out what we are going to do with the little moocher," whispered Luke. "He has to be out of the house by six a.m., Monday."

"Maybe, he could stay with you. He is your relative," Cramer added with a laugh.

"Shut up, Cramer! I don't want any problems to delay construction, and I don't want someone's blood on my hands either," said Luke.

"You're so caring, Jacobs. But, you wouldn't mind paying someone else to have blood on their hands, would you?"

Cramer left, drove to Lolita's and ordered ham on rye. "Hi, Sweetie! I haven't seen you for awhile," Cramer said loudly, glancing around at the empty tables. "What did you do to the customers? Scare them away?"

"I told you that I didn't want to see your creepy face any more!"

"Lolita, what's the matter? Don't you want my money anymore?" he asked as he laid the dollar bills on the counter, "or do you want just Luke's?"

She slapped him across the face. "You will get your just rewards, Cramer! I told everything to the police!"

"Sure you did, honey, and I'm O'Connell's best friend."

"So don't believe me. Take the sandwiches for nothing. You won't be coming in here anymore. I hope you like prison food."

Cramer laughed. "Couldn't be any worse than yours, dear," he replied as she shoved them into a bag. He continued to laugh all the way to the car. He began to think about Lolita's words. Cramer began to wonder if he'd been set up by Jacobs. Did Luke think that he had something to do with Sara's accident? Is that why he wanted to see him alone at the mansion? Cramer's hands shook as he downed his sandwiches quickly. He had not felt this kind of fear since the day Luke's father appeared at his mother's doorstep.

Sara awoke, sat up on her bed, and rubbed her eyes until they fully opened. "Mom, what are you doing here? Where am I?"

"Sara, don't you remember anything from last night?" Sara shook her head then stopped suddenly.

"Daddy! He's still alive! I saw him, Mom, so clearly."

"Are you sure it wasn't a dream, Sara? You've been under a lot of stress."

"It could have been. Well, maybe. I don't know. It seemed so real. The chocolates, what about them?" asked Sara, looking around. "Where's Jack?"

"He's helping Sheriff O'Connell at the regatta. Sara, I think we need to talk about Jack. Don't you think you're becoming too attached to him?"

"My devotion is to my marriage." She hung her head, "But, I don't know how Luke feels about me anymore."

"I think he's getting himself into a lot of trouble with this casino project, Sara. I heard some interesting talk around town," Peg replied. Sara lay back down on the cot, and listened to her mother repeat the stories she had heard.

With tear-filled eyes, she covered her head with the scratchy blanket and fell back asleep. At exactly five o'clock Jack stepped in the room carrying bags of steaming Chinese food, the aroma filling the air.

"Sara! You're awake!" said Jack. "Hope you're hungry! I've brought enough food for a crowd," he laughed.

After everyone ate, Sara said, "Why am I here at the station, again?"

"Sara, we brought you into the station for your own safety. Do you remember being visited by two men last night?" Sara shrugged her shoulders. "There are two distinct pairs of footprints," continued Luis. "Whoever the men were came by the trail behind the station and left by car. We think we might have identified one of the set of prints."

"I saw my father, or a man that looked like him," said Sara. "He had the same clothes, the same haircut as dad, and brought me the Reynolds family's favorite chocolates. Though, now that I think about it, it could have been that little man that's been visiting me at the hospital. Though, why would he be wearing my father's clothes?" she paused. "What?" asked Sara, looking at Jack, "I'm not crazy!"

"Sara, listen . . . ."

"So, Luis, can I tag along with you tomorrow to the regatta?" Sara interrupted. "Mom will stay with me, right?" Peg looked at Jack. "Mom, I don't belong to Jack," Sara said, defensively. "I can leave when I want. The doc said if I had any more problems to call his cell phone. See?" she looked at Jack, "I'm covered from all sides."

"Sara, I don't mean to be controlling," said Jack. "Everyone in this room cares about you." They all nodded their heads. "I'm only asking you not to take any chances. You need to be on guard tonight. We're hoping by Monday we'll have someone under arrest and things can get back to normal."

"Things will never get back to normal, Jack! There is no more normal for me!" she said angrily. She stood and grabbed the clothes her mother had brought from the RV. "I'm getting dressed now. Anything else you want to say to me? No?" she asked then turned toward Luis. "Then, I'll see you tomorrow, Luis. What time?"

"We'll be here at the station around six a.m., and then head to the lake. You and your mom can ride over with us." Jack watched her leave. "She has it in for you, Jack," said Luis, "though I feel that maybe she's just frightened by everything. The uncertainties she has to face, and, her feelings about you."

"I just want her to be careful. If the suspect turns out to be who we think he is, she is in great danger until he is incarcerated." Jack walked to his makeshift office.

Luis sat down beside him. "I'll have someone keep an eye on her. Brady!" he yelled across the room, "How would you like a job other then handling fights over who gets what parking space? It involves a beautiful girl!"

"Thanks, Luis. I need to get over to the lake," said Jack. "O'Connell's going to be rounding up the deputies, having a final talk about the regatta tomorrow, and reviewing the problems from today."

"I'll let you know how things are going," said Luis.

Jack knew he was referring to Sara. "Just don't let her see you, Brady," said Jack. The young man nodded.

Jack found the sheriff standing under a tall tree surrounded by ten eager men. "Jack!" said O'Connell, "I want to introduce you to these fine men and then we'll go over tomorrow's agenda." After the men left, the sheriff said, "Guess what came in today? The search warrant for Willie's. We'll probably wait until after this weekend, although, by then, we should have some of these cases solved."

"How did the casino exhibit fare today, after that fiasco this morning?" asked Jack.

"All's calm. Though, we'll need to patrol that area heavily to keep an eye on that protesting group. You know, back in my day, Jack, we just sat down to talk."

"Well, like we said sheriff, things have changed."

"Yep," said O'Connell. "We used to know everyone in town and if you had a problem with someone, you just went to them and discussed it. No fighting, usually."

Jack looked at his tired friend. "I've already had dinner but I'd love a cup of coffee while you have a bite to eat. Then, I'm going home for an early bedtime."

"Me too, Son. Me, too," replied the sheriff, rubbing his eyes.

Sara and her mother packed up her remaining belongings from the old RV and drove to her mother's house. "Could you drive me to the scene of the accident, Mom? It's just a little further."

"Sara, the doctor . . . ."

"Said I could go home," Sara interrupted. "I need to see it, Mom. Now! Please?" Peg drove past her house, and rounded the corner on Old Creek Road. Two white crosses stood silently among the spring growth of grass and wildflowers. Sara began to sob. When her mother pulled over next to them, Sara began to cry uncontrollably.

CHAPTER 33

Cramer drove back to his condo. Would James tell Luke he had seen him kill Hudson? he wondered. He had told James he could keep the pretty orange hat if he kept his mouth shut. Maybe he could blame Hudson's death on Jamesy. He could say that the man was trying to destroy the beautiful gardens and stream around the mansion and James became enraged when Hudson wouldn't leave. He could also say that he had thrown away the orange hat in the condo dumpster and James had dug it out for his own use. Cramer already had the papers signed leaving him the house and property. He didn't owe the little man anything. Maybe he didn't need to steal the pictures at the station after all. Cramer opened the trunk of his car and placed a gun in his side jacket pocket. Monday seemed a long way off.

Luke pulled into the mansion drive and stopped in front of the house. He thought about Sara and her response to the casino. "I don't want anything to do with it, Luke," she had said. "I don't have any power to fight you or your business partners. I don't want my name tied to it in any way." He had not talked to her since she disappeared with Jack.

There was still plenty of light to search for missing treasure one more time, he laughed. Old Mrs. Reynolds had probably fooled everyone with her stories about the large stone. Maybe, she even told a few to Jamesy. He grabbed his flashlight, intent on questioning James and looking for the jewel one last time. He dialed Sara's number.

"Luke! Why haven't you called?"

"Well, Sara, two reasons. First, I heard you were with your boyfriend. And, second, I heard from someone that you had quite a little episode this weekend."

"He's not my boyfriend!" she yelled into the phone. "What do you mean by a 'little episode'? Exactly what did you hear?"

"They asked if my wife was as crazy as everyone has been saying. I defended you. I told them you were still recovering from your accident and our loss."

Sara was silent.

"Well?" asked Luke.

"I had my mother drive me to the scene of the accident today, Luke." There was a long period of silence. "Are you going to say anything?"

"I'm sorry, Sara. I miss the kids as much as you do."

"Luke, can we get together and talk?"

"Sara, I can't change anything."

"Maybe we can discuss my father's home and the casino, Luke. Where are you?"

He laughed. "I'm searching for the imaginary emerald, Sara. Your grandmother must have been nuts."

"Just like me, right?"

"I didn't say that, Sara."

"I'm coming to the house, right now!"

"Not tonight, Sara. I have business to discuss with my partners."

"Fine!" she said, hanging up and grabbing the car keys.

"Sara, where are you going?" asked her mother.

"Out!"

"Let me drive, dear. You haven't been behind the wheel since the accident," said her mother following Sara to the car.

"Leave me alone! I'm going to the mansion to talk some sense into Luke. He's meeting someone there to discuss business."

"Sara! Please stay away from him! Jack said that he is dangerous."

Sara stopped and looked at her mother. "So, Jack has charmed you, too, Mom? He's not going to stop me from reconciling with my husband." She slammed the door and drove the car down the driveway, the wheels skidding on the loose gravel.

Peg called Jack. "Jack! Sara's really upset. She's driving to the Reynolds mansion to meet Luke!"

Jack dialed Sara's phone. "Please pick up, Sara," he whispered.

"Hello, Jack. What do you want? Did my mother call you?"

"She said you're on your way to see Luke. Can you tell me why?"

"We've been over this before, Jack. There's always hope until it's gone."

"And when will that be, Sara? When he's dead or when he kills you?"

"He would never do that!" she cried. "I'm his wife!"

"He's unpredictable!"

"He's my husband, Jack!"

"By last name only! You haven't been husband and wife for years!" She became quiet. Jack could hear her faint sobs.

"I'm almost there, Jack," she said, her voice shallow and distressed. "I need to work this out alone."

"Sara!" he yelled into the phone. "Don't!" The dial tone blared loudly in the silence of the car. He pressed the gas pedal to the floor, the small pebbles of gravel hitting the underside of his car.

James was sitting in the corner of the little room, the last of the sunbeams shining on him and the glass-eyed bear. "Hello, James," said Luke, as the man crept further into the dark shadows. "I'm not going to hurt you, if you just listen to me. We're going to have a little discussion about where you're going to live after tonight."

"James live here," he said, crawling onto the dirty mattress.

"You can't live here anymore, James. Some men are coming to clear out the house."

"James be quiet, not tell mean man about orange hat and man hurt by water. James can stay in house if quiet."

"What man, James?"

"Man with stick hit friend hard. Man fall into water. James get orange hat to be quiet."

"Who was the man who had the stick, James?"

"He comes here and brings food. Now he be mad at me. James not quiet."

Luke stood very still. Did he hear a car approaching the drive? He walked over and looked out the oval window. "James," he said, pointing out the window. "Is that the man who had the stick?"

"He come now and hurt James!" he said, diving under the smelly covers. Cramer's footsteps could be heard on the wooden stairs.

"Jacobs! Are you in there?" asked Cramer. Luke stepped into the faint light. He turned on his flashlight, the soft glow lighting up the dim interior.

"So, James, we meet again," said Cramer to the figure huddled under the covers. He glanced at the orange hat beside the bed.

"What happened to his hair, Cramer?" asked Luke. "Some job of yours? Why?"

"Ask your wife, Jacobs. I got her believing that James is her deceased father. Looks just like him with the clothes and all," he said smugly.

"You're an idiot, Cramer! What if Wilder and his gang followed you back to the house? Everyone would find out that we're not the owners of this dump. Without the proper papers we're done!"

"James write name on paper," whispered a voice under the scraggly blanket.

"Paper? What paper, James?" asked Luke.

"He say write James on paper." The stout little man peeked out and pointed to Cramer. "It looked pretty," he added.

"Cramer . . . what's going on?"

"Nothing. I just drew up the proper papers as you suggested and had him sign over the property and house to me."

"You? Just you? Not the group?"

"It makes it more complicated. Anyway according to Locke, half of the assets belong to me."

"Locke! What's does he have to do with it?"

"Seems your father paid a visit to my mother one day and ta-da, here I am!"

Luke's look of shock brought out a loud laugh from Cramer. "You know about the birds and bees I assume? Anyway, that's why the old man paid for my school and took care of my mother until she died."

"You're, you're lying!"

"I have proof from the doctor who delivered me. I guess we'll be splitting the hush money our daddy left to Locke to keep his little secret, you know, since he's dead and all!"

Luke leaned forward and smashed his fist straight into Cramer's grinning face. "You've demeaned my family for the last time, Cramer!" he yelled as Cramer fell to his knees.

"Your family has always been crooked, dishonest, and," Cramer added, with his blood dripping onto the wooden floor, "filled with lust for one thing or another! You've finally come to the end, Jacobs!"

"Luke?" yelled Sara from the bottom floor. "Luke! Where are you?"

Luke turned sharply. "Go home, Sara!" he yelled in his loudest voice. "It's not safe for you here!" Luke grabbed Cramer and held him to the floor. Sara stepped into the room.

"What are you doing?" she screamed.

"Leave, Sara!" said Luke. "I'll handle my own problems."

"Seems like the biggest problem in this room is you, Jacobs," said Cramer standing up. "If only my plans for the accident didn't backfire you would be dead by now and the estate would be mine."

"Plans? Are you saying that the accident was meant for Luke, not me?" interrupted Sara. "How could you kill innocent children? My children died because of your greed!" she shouted sobbing loudly.

"I didn't mean for you to drive Luke's car that day, Sara. I felt terrible that they died."

"Terrible? You felt terrible?" screamed Sara, beating her fists on Cramer's chest.

"Stop it, Sara! Now, I'll have to kill you and your husband to get this stinking house."

"Luke, no!" said Sara, staring at the approaching figure. Cramer moaned and fell to the ground. Shaking, Luke stood over him, a bronze candlestick in his hand. Sara knelt down to touch the still body. "He's dead! He's dead!" Luke came closer to Sara.

"No! James won't let you hurt Sara!" said James, standing behind Luke with a sharp-edged shovel. He raised the garden tool high in the air, "No hurt! No more!" he shouted as he brought the shovel down on Luke's head. Sara screamed and fell to the floor.

"Jamesy take care of Sara now," he said, as he gently carried Sara's featherweight body outside to the garden and laid her among the flowers. James returned to the house to retrieve the shovel and his bear. "Sara pretty," said James as he ran his fingers across the metal shovel. "Have to have a sharp edge, James," Jingles, the gardener, had always reminded him. James smiled at the thought of the kind man. He walked outside, stuck the shovel in the ground, and pulled out the worn-looking bear, a present from Jingles, from the inside of his sweatshirt jacket. "Bear, Sara's friend now," he said as he laid the soft fur against her cheek.

James entered the house, walked through the pantry, reached for a matchbox, and closed the second door. Lighting the match he lay across the dust-covered floor. His adult sized body filled the tiny space that once felt enormous as a child. Reaching into his pocket he pulled out his last Nuville chocolate and placed it in his mouth. He pressed his face flat against the floor to look under the crack. Today, there was only darkness, except for the glow of the fire above him. A final tear fell to the floor that was once covered with the tears of a young, neglected boy. Closing his eyes, he relinquished himself to the curse that had held the family captive for decades.

CHAPTER 34

Jack's car slid to a stop as the fire consumed the old house. "Sara! Sara!" he screamed, as he jumped from his vehicle and started to run toward the house.

"Stop, Jack!" yelled Sara from the garden.

"Sara?" Jack turned around and yelled again, "Sara, where are you?" Sara, surrounded by flowers, stood up, and ran toward him.

"He's dead!" she cried, as he reached for her.

"Who's dead?" asked Jack.

"Luke. Cramer. My father's brother," she added, as the realization hit her. "They're all gone, Jack." He wrapped his arms around her as she buried her head in his chest, the tears dampening his shirt, as the fire trucks raced toward the house. When the flames finally diminished Sara walked to the garden, picked up the worn, dirty bear with one green eye, and handed him to Jack. "A gift from James, my uncle," she said, as the glass eye fell from the stitching.

"Sara, could this be the missing emerald?" asked Jack, as he held the stone up to the light. Sara reached for the stone, held it close to her chest, and began sobbing.

"That's why he wanted me to have it. The most precious thing he owned." She leaned over and rested her head against Jack. "Please take me home, Jack. I want to sleep in my own house tonight."

Jack called a frantic Peg. "She's safe. Could you stay with her tonight? She wants to go home. No. Not your house, Peg. Hers." Jack and Sara walked down the hill, where just a few weeks ago, her children had laughed and played. Now, there was nothing but memories.

O'Connell arrived and stood under the pines that grew at the end of the drive. "So much loss," he said sadly. "The boys and I will take care of this, Jack. You can go with Sara."

"Sheriff, I think she really just wants to go home and be with her mother."

"Sure, Son." O'Connell walked over to the growing crowd and asked them to please go back to their campsites and boats and wait for the news tomorrow. Most of the visitors left reluctantly. The townsfolk refused to leave.

"I guess it's alright," he said, looking at the group of familiar people. "The Reynolds and the Jacobs families were known to everyone in this town. The loss of the old mansion is felt by all," he added. "It's almost like the house refused to be turned into something it wasn't meant to be."

"The property and its beauty still remain, Sheriff," said Jack. "There will be no casino or mining to destroy it now."

Sara's mother pulled up behind O'Connell's car. "Sara!" yelled Peg, running toward her daughter. "Thank heavens, you're safe! You're safe!" The two embraced and cried for what seemed an eternity.

"Mom! Luke wasn't trying to hurt me or the children. It was Cramer. It wasn't Luke! It wasn't Luke!" she cried.

"Peg," said Jack, "Why don't you take Sara home and we'll call you in the morning. I'll need you to testify about what you heard in the house, Sara." She nodded and left with her mother.

Jack and O'Connell walked over to the fire chief. "Sheriff," said the chief, "I'm afraid anyone in there didn't have a chance. The house was old and built entirely of wood. A shame! Nothing but a shame!"

"There should be three bodies among the remains, Chief. Call me when it's safe to look for evidence around the outside of the house." The chief nodded.

"Well, Jack, I guess we can shut down the casino exhibit tomorrow. There are only two men left of the "Seven Men Investments" group. I'll round them up and keep them overnight," said O'Connell. Jack called Luis and informed him of the tragedy.

"I saw the huge red glow but didn't want to leave the station unmanned. Anyone hurt?"

"Luis," said Jack, "Put the coffee on. We'll explain everything when we get to the station."

Luis was ready with coffee and sandwiches when they returned. "The local women's club thought there would be a need for some refreshments," said Luis. O'Connell grabbed two sandwiches and pulled two comfortable chairs into his office. Jack spent the next few minutes describing to Luis what had happened at the mansion.

"Jack," interrupted the sheriff, yawning, "I know this is a hard time for all of us, but let's go over the things you can remember before the fire this evening."

Jack looked at Luis and O'Connell. "Well, this morning Luke and Cramer got into a big fight at the exhibit. The protestors were giving them a hard time. I guess they were more than a little edgy. Maybe Luke and Cramer were finalizing some business for the groundbreaking on Monday morning and met at the house. I don't know, Sheriff."

"Sara's testimony will be crucial, Jack. How did she end up outside?"

"A long story, Sheriff. You remember the talk about old lady Jacobs and the twin boys, one being Sara's dad? Well, it seems the brother that was disabled has been hidden in the house all of these years. He paid a visit to Sara recently, dressed just as her father would have looked when he passed away a few years ago. Even down to the haircut. Cramer must have black-mailed him into scaring Sara that night at the RV. Sara said her uncle must have paid several visits to her hospital room leaving behind the Nuville chocolates," Jack continued. "She said her grandmother used them as a reward for the boys when they were growing up. Do you remember that Sara's father was taken away from the old lady when he was a little boy? He was not allowed to visit his mother so he never knew what had become of his brother, James."

"Cramer let it slip that it was Luke that he wanted dead, not Sara. When Cramer came after Sara in the attic, Luke killed him with a candlestick from the old house. James thought that Luke was going to hurt Sara, so, he hit Luke over the head with a shovel. She said that's all she remembered before she blacked out."

"Unbelievable!" said O'Connell.

"By the way, I drove to the Stevens boy's house," interrupted Luis. "When I knocked on the door, his mother said he was out for the day. I waited around the corner in my car and sure enough he drove toward town a few minutes later. I brought him back to the station for questioning. He admitted to being the one who cut the brake cable in Luke's car. He was also the cable man who told Sara that her system was having trouble and that he needed to check her wires to the house. He was paid by Cramer to do the job," added Luis.

"I knew that jerk was involved somehow!" blurted out O'Connell.

"Stevens didn't know Sara would be driving the car with her children," Luis continued. "He seemed morose over the whole deal and wanted to come clean. Then one morning, he saw Cramer throw something into the lake. Cramer said that if he ever told anyone about the accident or what he saw, he would kill him. It was Cramer who started the fire with his cigarette down by the pier, not Stevens. And get this! The boy said Cramer was in his stocking feet. The boots had to have been Cramer's! He's probably the one who conked you over the head, Jack, and took your camera. He must have thought that your scenic pictures of the property and squirrels also showed a man in an orange hat hiding in the background."

"And now for the final clincher," exclaimed Luis, "I got a phone call from the rest home over in Hyattsville. Seems a doctor who was a resident there demanded to talk to the authorities about something he did over thirty years ago. He admitted that Richard Cramer and Luke Jacobs are half-brothers. The doctor falsified the birth certificate and was paid well to keep quiet. When Cramer's mother passed away, and Samuel died, Locke was the only other person who knew the boys' past."

"Old Samuel must have been around in his younger days," commented Jack. "That's probably the reason Cramer and Locke got into the big fight at the pier."

"Holy cow!" said O'Connell, placing his hands on his head. "My brain is bursting from all this information!" Jack yawned and looked out the window facing the lake. The old mansion atop the hill could no longer be seen above the treetops. "Let's call it a day. I've got the best men around taking care of the regatta, and it seems our biggest problems are over. This should be the first time that any of us will get a good night's sleep in weeks," said O'Connell. Luis nodded and the two men left Brady in charge.

Jack climbed into his car and put on his favorite jazz CD. He called Peg to ask about Sara, and was told that she was sleeping like a baby, the first time without any medication. "I'll bring her to the station first thing in the morning, Jack," she offered. Jack drove to his house and placed his hankie on the chest by the front door. He walked straight to his room and fell asleep across the bed without undressing.

The next morning three tired men sat at the desk, ate powdered donuts and drank the Sheriff's thick coffee when Sara and her mother walked in. Both women looked rested and wide awake. "I'll see she gets home, Peg," said Jack.

Sara sat close to Jack. "I don't know where to start. Yesterday was the first day Luke and I spoke to each other, since I can remember," she said honestly. "The last time I talked to him, he was still looking for my grandmother's emerald. Of course, you know it was in the stuffed bear given to me by James. It was probably put there by his mother to keep it safe from treasure hunters like Luke." She looked at Jack. "The jewel expert has it locked in his safe. I'll know by Monday what it's worth."

"Sara," asked O'Connell, "Tell me, what exactly happened on the third floor of the old house?"

Sara looked at Jack. "Go ahead, Sara. I'll stay right here," replied Jack, closing the office door. Sara spent the next few minutes rehashing the events that lead up to the deaths of the three men.

"That's all I can remember, Sheriff. I passed out, and woke up with Jack shouting my name. I was lying among the flowers with the bear in my arms." Her eyes became misty.

The sheriff closed his notebook and turned off the tape recorder. "We'll contact you in a couple of days, Sara."

"Come on Sara, I promised your mother I would bring you home."

"Jack, could we stop by to see the regatta for a few minutes," asked Sara. They drove toward the lake. Jack pulled over into the parking lot beside Ray's Bait Shop. They sat quietly on a bench, watching the boats. "They seem to be floating in the wind," said Sara interrupting the silence. Jack nodded.

"My mother's coming down to see you, Sara," said Jack. "She sends her regrets."

"Thanks, Jack," said Sara, her voice quivering. "There will be a memorial ceremony for Luke. His remains will be buried by his father," she added softly.

"What about Cramer?"

"Samuel already had a plot for him with the family. I can't help feeling sad over the fact that the two boys never knew they were related until right before they died. There are no Jacobs left now. Not even my children," she said sadly.

"So, what will you do now, Sara?"

"Try to find a purpose for my life. I've no marriage to mend, no family to care for. My mother wants to start some business or other with me. Seems I've been ignoring her, too, and she's been feeling as lonely as me. We'll see."

"Sara, about the letter. I'm sorry if I caused you sorrow. You've had enough of that without me making things worse. I really do care about you, but I also understand you have a lot of things to struggle through in your life right now. If I can help in any way, just ask."

"Thanks, Jack. Let's walk by the remains of the old mansion. I need to begin my healing. Someday, I want to see where my children are buried. Will you go with me, Jack?" They walked slowly to the house, Jack taking Sara's hand in his. She held it tight.

CHAPTER 35

O'Connell called Jack, "It's going to be a long day, Jack. We'll go over everything, and then plan our strategy for the news conference in the morning."

Jack drove by Lolita's, saw that it was boarded up and drove to "The Barbecue Pit" to purchase two pork sandwiches dripping with sauce. Several years ago he had felt the need to be a vegetarian as part of his mission to save the environment. He had planted a garden each year, and became a spokesman for recycling, especially at the police station. His fellow workers felt he went overboard with disposal bins for soda cans and plastic bottles but obliged him because of his cheerful attitude. He gulped the sandwiches down, wiped his mouth and smiled to himself. The vegetarian lifestyle was not for him.

Luis and the sheriff were waiting for Jack at the station. The interrogation table was covered with papers and folders. "How's Sara, Jack?" asked Luis.

"As good as she can be right now. We walked by the old mansion and stood under the pines. It will take time. I used to think that she was frail and fragile. Even though she's been through more pain then we can ever imagine, Sara's become stronger, more confidant. She's already talking about starting a business with her mother. Finances won't be a problem for her since the family emerald has been found. I'm not sure if Luke left her anything, except misery," added Jack as he leaned over the piles of paper. "Is there any organization to this, Sheriff?"

"That's what we're going to do this afternoon, Jack. Luis has a system, or so he says."

Jack looked at his friend with wonderment. "Don't look at me that way," laughed Luis. "It's pretty simple," he said as he sat down in the chair on the far right. "Jack, please take notes of the information you want the public to have tomorrow. See," he pointed to the stacks of papers and files, "it goes right around a circle from case to case, starting with Sara's accident." Luis lifted an old newspaper clipping with a picture of the smashed car on the front page. "Local family suffers tragic loss," were the black headlines scrawled across the top.

Luis continued, "We now know that the Stevens boy who worked for "Rays' Bait Shop" was paid by Cramer to cut the cables of Luke's car. Stevens did this posing as a TV cable man. Luke had taken Sara's car that day to get new tires, so she drove Luke's car instead. Remember, he was crashed out on the bed from a drinking spree that day. Sara's two children died from the cruelty of this crime," he added sullenly.

"Sara, bedridden, suffered a loss of memory from the crash. At that time, Doc Thorton was a trusted family physician and psychiatrist who had cared for the Reynolds family for years. From what I could read from the file that was found in Cramer's car, Sara had sought counsel and help for her depression long before the accident. She returned to Doc a few weeks ago with a note that was found in her husband's laundry that read, 'get rid of the last remaining obstacle,' followed by a penciled letter 's.'"

"Doc Thorton changed his status from healer to killer when he first placed Sara in the cast and gave her drugs to fog her memory at the request of her husband, Luke Jacobs," continued Luis. "Jacobs wanted the old Reynolds' place for his own and thought a good way to do it was to make Sara incompetent and to take over the estate. Doc apparently owed a huge debt from his gambling. He thought Luke would reward him for placing Sara into a coma, but Doc didn't plan on disappearing that night."

"Has there been any word on Thorton?" asked Jack.

"None," answered Luis. "That's still a mystery. Once we have the other cases solved, we'll have more time to pursue his disappearance. His sister is still calling the station every day."

"Go on, Son," said Sheriff O'Connell pointing to the table. "You're doing a great job."

"I'm turning it over to Jack, now," he said smiling at his friend.

Jack reached for his father's camera still wrapped in plastic. He smiled as he read the name Elijah James Wilder stamped on the side. "It seems," said Jack, "that the 'Casino Seven,' excuse me, 'Seven Men Investments,' was involved in more than just the plans for the new Six Pines Casino. They were in jeopardy of losing their license. Unpaid bills and under-the-table permits were handed out over a period of years. Hudson's phony concerns over the protection of the environment surrounding the project were causing the group a lot of lost time and future financial losses. When I finally got to question Willard, he admitted the group wanted to get rid of Hudson," Jack added. "No one knew that Cramer and Hudson were planning to sabotage the permits by planting Indian artifacts in the hills on the old mansion's estate, and that a mining permit to uncover a vein of limestone in those same hills had been issued under Hudson's name. It was Cramer who filled a pollution report. Whether it was his concern or another ploy to slow down the permits we don't know. At least it explains the water test kit located at the site of Hudson's death."

"Something must have gone wrong with the deal, you know, for Cramer to have killed Hudson," said O'Connell.

"That we do not know," said Luis. "Maybe Cramer just wanted all the money from the mining for himself."

"The Stevens boy admitted he saw Cramer throw something into the lake," said Jack, pointing to the picture of the pier nestled in the blackened grass. "It was probably the boots and camera. When Cramer left, he also threw his cigarette out the window, starting the small fire down by the pier. Cramer knew Stevens saw him that morning, but Stevens was in debt to Cramer big time so he kept his mouth shut."

"But, what I don't get is how was Cramer planning to get the estate from Luke?" asked Luis.

"Luke and Cramer have been fighting each other for possessions and status since they were boys," said O'Connell. "I don't know who sent Luke that note Sara found in his laundry that day. Every one of those men was out for his own neck, and each of them wanted as much of the casino wealth as possible."

"We now know that Cramer and Jacobs were half-brothers," said Jack. "The doctor from the nursing home said that the only other person who knew of the deeds of Samuel Jacobs was Grayson Locke. Then, James made his appearance. That threw another rock into the wheel. A file was found lying on the ground next to the pier where Cramer chased Locke that night, and a rusty black metal box that washed up along the shoreline contained more information. It was the evidence that Cramer had been looking for. Locke had probably told Cramer the secret that he shared with the old man, and that he had planned on destroying all records relating to it. He never knew what was coming when he stepped into that boat that night. No one would have known the truth until the doctor who assisted Cramer's birth called me this weekend. Seems Cramer found out about him and visited him a few days before. The old man's conscience got to him, I guess."

"What about this guy called James? Was he the real brother of Sara's father?" asked Luis.

"Seems he was living in the house the whole time," replied Jack. "As he grew older, the old lady kept him locked in the upper floors until she died. When she didn't appear one day, James went looking for her. He climbed out the window at night and roamed the town searching for food. He must have found out about Sara and his relationship to her. James started to visit her regularly in the hospital. He was the one who left her the chocolates. The little guy must have been surprised one day when Luke showed up at the mansion. Both Cramer and Luke could have been bribing him to keep quiet and out of sight."

"One of them must have brought James dressed as Sara's father to the RV that night," stated Luis. "What happened after that, I really don't know. Did Luke and Cramer get into a fight over the casino or the birthrights? No one knows what they were fighting over on the third floor of the house that day."

"Sara said she could hear them when she entered the front door. Luke told her not to enter, that it wasn't safe for her to be there," added Jack.

"And James?" asked O'Connell.

"James felt Sara was in danger. He must have felt the curse of the old house to set it on fire."

"Curse?" asked O'Connell.

"The family always felt there was a curse that was passed down from generation to generation. Looks like they were right," Jack concluded.

"There," said Luis, pointing to the newspaper clipping. "We've come full circle."

Luis walked over to the window and looked out over the lake. "Unbelievable," said O'Connell, once again.

Jack walked around the table one more time. "All of this loss and sorrow. And add to that the unnecessary deaths of five people, just for power and greed."

"Seven," said O'Connell. "Don't forget Sara's children. And Doc? Who knows what on earth has happened to him."

The men nodded their heads and finalized the note cards for the morning's press conference. Jack drove slowly home. Instead of taking the shortest route, he drove around, glancing at the houses and businesses that made up the little town of Wakeegon. He had become fond of the people over the past few weeks and, like them, mourned the loss of innocence that once covered the town. Entering his house, he placed his familiar hankie on the chest by the door and grabbed a handful of writing paper. He had planned on writing his own letter to Sara. The next morning, Sara called.

"Jack!" said Sara excitedly. "My mom and I have just been talking about what we want to do with our lives and have come up with the greatest plan!"

Jack laughed. "Slow down Sara. Take a breath then go on."

"Well," said Sara, "Mom figures that the emerald will be worth quite a lot of money. We plan on rebuilding the old estate house."

"But, I thought you hated that house, Sara."

"I did. But it won't be used for evil this time, Jack. We plan on honoring James and my children by making it a home and learning center for the physically and mentally disabled." She paused and asked, "Well, what do you think?"

"I think it sounds great, Sara. Maybe we could toss around a few ideas at breakfast. Are we still on for tomorrow?"

"Yes," said Sara. "I'll drive over to the station early. Around seven?" she asked.

"Great!" said Jack. "See you at seven," he added as he hung up the phone. He read the letter that he had written to Sara, once again. Should he have poured out his heart to Sara? Would she be ready for a relationship with him?

Sara arrived at exactly seven the next morning. She was dressed in a blue-green skirt with a light blue sweater and the excitement she felt made her cheeks and lips appear pinker than normal. "Morning, Sara," said O'Connell, smiling at Jack as he said it.

Jack reached for his jacket as Sara held onto his arm. The two walked toward the back door. "Nice morning isn't it, Sheriff," said Sara. O'Connell winked at Jack as he passed.

"Sara," asked Jack, "Are you sure you're ready for this?"

"We're not going to the gravesite today, Jack. I decided I wanted to do it alone."

"Well then, where are we going?"

"I want to ask your opinion about a few things."

"What things?"

"Well, I told you about the plans for mother and me to open a school for the disabled in honor of my children and James. The jewelry expert called this morning. And guess what, Jack? The emerald is worth more than I ever imagined. He said he'll give me a solid price at the end of this week, after he does a little research. Add to that the insurance policy Luke left to the children and me, plus his father's estate. We'll have a facility that will bring Wakeegon prosperity and the honor it always deserved. We'll be able to hire many people from the area and give the town new life and hope."

Jack looked at her contented face. "Sara, I'm so glad for you, your mother, and the town." They both walked in silence until they reached the hill where the remains of the burnt house stood. Sara let go of Jack and ran down the hill, her arms in the air and her hair flying around her face. When she reached the bottom, she lay on the green grass and yelled to Jack to come and sit beside her.

"Run, Jack! Don't walk!" When Jack reached her side, he was laughing and gasping for breath.

"The most fun I've had for a while, Sara." Jack sat down beside her. She leaned her head against his shoulder.

"Jack, do you remember me telling you about how my children would run down this very hill? They would ask me why the wind blew away their dandelion crowns, and I told them it was the angel's wings," she paused and wiped her eyes. "That's what I want to name the school, Jack, 'Angel Wings.'"

"I'm sure the angels are watching over them right now, Sara," said Jack. "I think the name is perfect."

Sara got up, put her arms around Jack, and gave him a kiss on the cheek. He returned the kiss but on the lips. They remained there at the bottom of the hill for a few more minutes before walking back to the station.

CHAPTER 36

Sara left Jack at the door with a promise to dine with him the following evening. Jack walked into the station and greeted an excited sheriff. "Jack, we've just received a phone call from guess where? Key West! Seems a man fitting Doc's description was found washed up on the shore of one of those marine research centers down there. But get this . . . he went under the name of Luke Jacobs. Now, why would Doc Thorton want to be known as Jacobs? He hated the man. Anyway, they want us to send someone down there so I suggested you and maybe Luis, if he wants to go." Jack looked at Luis. He nodded. "They want you to leave for the Keys in the morning," added O'Connell.

Jack walked into his house, phoned his mother about the news, and went about packing the necessary clothing, and plenty of handkerchiefs dampened with cinnamon oil for the trip. He reached into his jacket pocket and pulled out the letter he had written to Sara.

> *Dear Sara,*
>
> *As you will hear in the morning, I am leaving town to investigate the death of Doc Thorton. I didn't want to awaken you, so Sheriff O'Connell will give you the information where you can reach me. He promised to look after you. I hope the plans for the school go well and that you and your mother renew the relationship you once had. You have given me a new hope in my life. I pray when I return, that we too, can have a new beginning with each other.*

You were right. I was blaming God for everything and had shut Him and everyone else out of my life. Not only do I plan on becoming the leader in my family, I also want to emphasize the role of the environment and the care of the world God left to us, just like my father. I want to further my studies and make it my life's goal. Maybe you could help me look at the different programs offered and give me some advice.

I want to apologize and acknowledge that you were right about Luke. Maybe giving him a second chance would have made a difference. In the end, he wanted to protect you from danger. He must have still cared for you when he asked you to stay away from the house that day.

I will miss you, Sara. I left a present by the gravesite to give you hope for the future and your new life. I regret that I can't see you before I go. I'll look forward to talking to you soon.

P.S. Remember that "Somehow good always prevails,"

Love, Jack.

Jack packed his car late that night and mapped out the directions to the precinct in Key West, close to the famous Hemingway House on the corner of Whitehead and Olivia Street. He looked forward to seeing the sights of the Keys, and planned on visiting several marine research centers during his stay.

The sun was just coming up as he backed the car out of his driveway. Jack drove by the remains of the old mansion, and pulled into the parking lot of Ray's, hoping to watch the sun rise above the east side of pines. He stopped by the small café selling donuts and coffee, and looked back over his shoulder one more time. He wished that things would be different when he returned and that the town would become renewed with hope and a chance for the future. Jack turned on his favorite jazz tunes and pulled onto the highway.

Sara was still in her bathrobe when O'Connell knocked on the door. "Morning, Sara," he said. "Jack wanted me to tell you he is going out of town for few days and not to be unhappy with him about tonight's dinner date. We received a phone call at the station from Key West, of all places, identifying a man's body that fit the description of Doc Thorton." He looked at her surprised face and then went on, "Jack will be working on the case, and Luis will join him in a few days." O'Connell paused, "Jack wants me to check on you every day if that's okay?"

"Thanks, Sheriff," said Sara. "I appreciate your concern."

He handed Sara a sealed envelope. "Jack wanted you to read this."

Sara nodded. "Sheriff O'Connell?" she asked softly, "Would you like to dine with me tonight?"

He stopped and turned around. "I'd love to."

"Good," said Sara, "I'll be at the station at six." O'Connell smiled and got into his car. Sara watched him leave, then, sat down on the bench outside her front door and read the letter from Jack. Later, she dressed warmly, and headed toward the town's cemetery. She walked past the remains of the old mansion and thought how ironic it was that Luke died in a fire, the very thing he feared the most. Sitting under the pines, she shed tears once more for the family she had lost. When the retreat and hospital for the disabled were built, Sara would make a statue of two children running, their hair tangled up in the wind. A small worn bear would be carried in the crook of the little girl's arms, whose face would be carved with a smile that would last a century.

Sara wiped her eyes and walked to the top of the highest hill. The peak provided a panoramic view of the country below. Her eyes settled on the tiny cemetery surrounded by a picket fence and honeysuckle bushes down below. She grabbed a bunch of new daffodil blooms. A white cross stood out against the colorful sunrise. Sara walked slowly, trying to keep her balance on the gravel walkway. At the bottom of the incline, the walk stopped directly in front of a large grave marker. She raised her eyes and read the inscription, "Jedidiah Reynolds, a man of integrity and love." Turning her head left, then right, she drew closer and began to weep over the two smaller headstones engraved with pictures of flying angels. My little angels, she thought.

She cried for a while. Raising her head she noticed the beaded rosaries. They must be a gift from Jack and his mother, she thought. The gift of hope he had talked about in his letter. Sara removed the three strings of beads from the gravestones, each one different and ending with a small cross on the end. Jack's presence had given her strength and courage. Now, his absence would give her hope for the new life she must lead. She rose and followed the gravel trail into town. A gust of wind tore the flowers from her hand. She gave a soft laugh and said quietly, "Angel Wings."

ABOUT THE AUTHOR

Victoria Rachel Clifton presides in the Indiana countryside close to many small towns resembling Wakeegon, minus the murders.

An avid gardener, she lives with her husband and a multitude of animals amidst prairie grass and flowers.

A Taylor University psychology honors graduate, she is convinced she inherited her intelligence from her three sons and six grandchildren.

Victoria (Vicki) strives to want for little and to love God much.

CPSIA information can be obtained at www.ICGtesting.com
Printed in the USA
LVOW12s2343171214

419301LV00002B/3/P